Night of the Demons

Christopher Artinian

CHRISTOPHER ARTINIAN

NIGHT OF THE DEMONS

Copyright © 2023 Christopher Artinian

All rights reserved.

ISBN: 9798378424382

CHRISTOPHER ARTINIAN

DEDICATION

To Hilda. This one's for you.

CHRISTOPHER ARTINIAN

ACKNOWLEDGEMENTS

Thanks to my amazing wife, Tina. Her endless support is something I will never take for granted. This book has been a long, long time in the making, and its release is a testament to her belief.

Thank you to my dear friends, Annella and Monika, for their help with pronunciations of words I had no right even attempting to say.

Thank you to the gang across in the fan club on Facebook. You're all awesome.

Thanks to my dear friend, Christian Bentulan, for another fantastic cover. Also, many thanks to my editor, Ken. A fantastic editor and a lovely chap too.

And finally, a huge thank you to you for buying this book.

PROLOGUE

THEN

Murdo Macleod plonked himself down in his favourite armchair. It was a stinky, threadbare old thing, but it was also the chair where he had received the final kiss from Mary, his wife. Hence, it was his favourite.

He stared into the flickering flames of the fire as the peat and wood burned fiercely and he remembered back to all the good times. They had come to an abrupt halt the previous year when Mary had gone to the woodshed to collect a few logs before dinner. It was winter and late afternoon, so darkness had already fallen and a biting cold hung in the air.

After a few minutes, Mary still hadn't returned and he had wandered out expecting her to be jabbering away to Donalina Stewart, the postwoman. It was not uncommon for her to be so late as she spent much of her day catching up on island gossip rather than delivering letters. Instead, he had found no one, not even Mary. A pile of logs was strewn over the ground, and one, in particular, had caught his eye in the torchlight. The bark had been gouged by what could only have been a claw. That image had etched itself into his memory, a single freeze-frame reminder of the heartbreak and horror that he'd felt at that moment.

It was not uncommon for the odd sheep to go missing at that time of year. The disappearances were usually explained away by them becoming trapped in peat bogs or getting too close to the cliffs in rough weather. Those were the explanations anyway. Any losses were reimbursed by a community fund set up by the island council. But people.… It did happen, but not to an islander for the longest time.

Every place has its own stories, its own legends. The Isle of Cora was no different in this respect, but to most of the inhabitants, the stories were more than just stories.

In his sixty-four years as a resident of Cora, he had heard of dozens of tourists vanishing mysteriously in the winter months. The police had come across from the mainland to investigate each one, and each one had remained a missing person case with no official explanation as to what had happened. It wasn't deemed particularly suspicious. Five minutes trekking across a waterlogged moor was all it would take for an outsider to appreciate how dangerous the terrain was. Climb into a kayak on the wrong day and the Atlantic currents would wash you out to sea in a heartbeat and reduce your vessel to broken pieces on the rocks. If you hit a patch of black ice on one of the hill peaks, it would be the easiest thing in the world to fall to your death, disappearing into scrub never to be found again.

The Inner Hebrides were beautiful but deadly if you didn't respect them. That was the story the islanders pushed. Many thousands of tourists came and went with no incident. Island hopping was what they called it. Hop off the ferry. Spend the day sampling the local culture in the village. Have a wee dram in MacDougal's pub. Take photos of Donald Wallace playing his bagpipes in the square and get back on the ferry or spend the night at MacDougal's, White's guesthouse or the small campground behind it. That was enough for most.

The adventurous ones trekked further afield. Some camped, some rented cottages. They all had their own ideas of what Cora was, of what they'd find on the island and within themselves. An unlucky few found more secrets than they bargained for.

Murdo reached for the bottle of twelve-year-old single malt whisky from the Cora distillery. He wasn't a big drinker, but his fireside reminiscences had taken him back to that fateful afternoon. Maybe it was because the first winter chill had arrived. Maybe it was the way the sun had seemed to linger on the horizon painting the sky so many shades of pink and orange, just like it had done the day of Mary's disappearance. Or maybe it was that he was just missing her more today and he wanted something to ease the pain a little.

They had never had children, and unlike so many islanders who married so they would not spend their lives alone, Murdo and Mary had found love of sorts. It wasn't the burning love one read about in romance novels, but it was a comfortable, caring love. A single tear ran down his cheek. *I'm sorry, Mary. I'm sorry.* He'd said the same thing a thousand times before and there was only so much he could be sorry for given the circumstances, but he was, with every fibre of his being.

He unscrewed the top and poured a healthy measure into the waiting tumbler. *Even the sheep have seemed quieter, more melancholic today. Or is that just my imagination?*

He was filled with a thousand regrets. Mary had said the night before that she was sure she'd seen a figure on the edge of the property. A black outline, somehow darker than the night behind it. Murdo had dismissed her words, but how he wished he had listened to her. How he wished he had not let her go to the wood shed. If they had gone cold that night, then he would still have someone to talk to, to share with. He would have his lifetime companion, his best friend. Instead, he only had his thoughts and regrets. *I'm sorry, Mary.* Further tears accompanied those that had already painted silver streaks down his face.

The thick amber fluid sloshed in the glass as he grabbed the whisky and inhaled deeply before taking a sip, then a gulp, then several more, draining the glass and pouring another.

"Aahhh!" He leaned back in his chair and continued to watch the flames as they danced in front of him. *Maybe I'll do my rounds early tonight. I'll check on the sheep, put my feet up and drift off listening to a late-night talk show.*

He took another drink and smiled to himself as Rebecca let out a loud and grumpy bleat. He and Mary had named her after Mary's mother simply because she rarely shut up. They had hand-reared her after she'd been rejected by her mother, and now she was part of the family. If ever Murdo went to market again, she would be safe. It was a big if, however. Crofting had been in his family for generations, but since Mary passed, there was little about it he enjoyed.

The few sheep he kept meant that he didn't have to live in silence. When he set foot outside the door, Rebecca and a few of the others would always give him a little vocal reminder that they were there, that he wasn't completely alone.

He was about to take another drink when he stopped dead as Rebecca suddenly let out a sound more like a scream than a bleat. The tumbler clattered on the table as he slammed it down and rose in one single movement.

The chilling sound came once more, and Murdo ran to the door, grabbing the handle and flinging it open. The frigid evening air rushed in to greet him, as did a symphony of frightened cries from his animals. He stepped out into the night and in that instant, he knew what this was.

The same spasm of unease that jolted through him when he had seen that strewn pile of logs stabbed him again now. The moon shone brightly, but a low, thick fog from the moor hung over the croft and the surrounding area like an eerie blanket.

Another childlike cry of fear rose from Rebecca and most of the other sheep, pleading with him, warning him.

Terror gripped Murdo. Could this really be happening again, almost a year to the day? He felt goosebumps spread up and down his arms as he stared into the haunting white soup that spread over his property providing safe haven to who knew what horrors. He exhaled a shuddering breath feeling more like a frightened lost child than a man in his later years as the fear of what lurked nearby gripped him.

His stomach began to churn, and despite the cold, he could feel beads of sweat begin to form on his brow. He remained there for several more seconds until, finally, he came to his senses a little.

He marched back into the house, leaving the door open. A waist-high metal cabinet sat in the pantry with a tower of old newspapers on top. He fumbled in his pocket for the key and struggled a little with the lock before he opened it, revealing the Classic Doubles shotgun that he hadn't touched since the night Mary disappeared. He loaded two shells and grabbed another handful, shoving them in his pocket before leaving the warmth and security of his home a final time and charging out into the darkness.

More goosebumps rippled up and down his arms. *Is this really happening? Am I really going to see the thing that took my Mary? Is this what the legends say it is? Is this the Deamhan Oidhche—the Night Demon?*

The chorus of torment continued for a moment, but then, almost as if he had gone deaf, it cut out in an instant. He stood there, a few metres away from his open door as it beckoned him to return to the womb-like warmth and safety within. A loud, hollow pop sounded from the fire, and it was only then that he realised that he hadn't gone deaf and the sinister quiet surrounding him was the calm before the storm.

His heart was racing faster than ever. Fear, hatred and self-loathing swelled within him. *This is it. I'm going to see it, the demon that took my Mary.* This was the thing that had meant, rather than laying her body to rest, they had filled her coffin with stones. This was the thing that had made him lie to the world. The truth could never get out. The truth would turn Cora into some godless tourist attraction destroying its history and traditions, destroying everything sacred about the island. The head of the council, the minister of the church, and the elders had all spoken to him, all convinced him that his sacrifice was for the greater good. That one day, he questioned why he was being asked to do this. *I understand now.*

If the truth had come out, so would the chances of him coming face-to-face with this hell-sent aberration.

The fog was almost luminescent in the glow of the cold moon. It seemed to hang in the air, and Murdo's eyes travelled out and over it, searching for anything that didn't belong. His head turned slowly from side to side and, suddenly, Rebecca's terrified voice began to sing again as other members of the ovine choir joined in.

It wasn't just the sound that made the hairs on the back of his neck stand up. It was the feeling—the feeling that he was being watched. The feeling that somewhere in that misty lake was a centuries old creature that was coming to reap his soul as it had done to so many before. He feared it, of that there was no doubt. His shaking hands, raised hackles and streaming sweat were a testament to it, but there was another part of him that wanted justice for what it had done to Mary, and that was worth the terror ... at least he hoped it was.

He continued his vigil for several moments, and that's when he knew that he had come up against this thing before, long before the night he had stepped out into the cold to discover his beloved wife was gone.

There's something about country living that town and city dwellers will never comprehend until they've experienced it. It's not just the lack of streetlights on a night. It's not the vast openness that stretches into the seemingly never-ending darkness, unpunctuated by walls and buildings and a thousand parked vehicles. It's a sense that there is something beyond the blackness, beyond what the eye is able to see. Most of the time, it's a vague insinuation of a presence, but sometimes it's more. Sometimes, it's a figure in the long swaying grass or a silhouette where a silhouette shouldn't be. It's only fleeting and often forgotten the second one walks back into the artificial glow of electric light, but nonetheless, it's something everyone who has lived in the country has experienced. It's something that gave birth to a thousand stories, a thousand legends, a thousand superstitions.

But as Murdo stood there now, he knew that it was real. It was as real as the shoes on his feet or the gun in his hands. He had come up against this thing before, not once, but many times.

"W-Was it me you came for?" he called out, rendering Rebecca and the rest of the sheep silent. The words tangled a little as they came out of his mouth, as he realised the glass of whisky had gone to his head a little. "Was it me you came for that night?"

There was no response, and he cast a longing look over his shoulder to the open door behind him. The flickering glow of the fire continued to beckon him to return to the warmth and safety within. But he'd waited for this moment for so long, and despite his abject fear, he returned his gaze to the murky cloud settled over his yard and beyond.

A noise unlike any that had gone before rolled towards him. It was a loud, high-pitched rasp like some tortured, amplified inhalation sucking everything good and pure out of the night air. It was most certainly nothing born of man or any beast he had seen up until this point.

"Was it you, y'bastard?" He called out again as a fresh tear rolled down his cheek. Murdo rarely swore. He had been brought up in a devout family, and although he wasn't as religious as his mother and father, he still had a Bible on the fireplace; he still went to church every Sunday, even though he remained silent for the duration. He still led a decent life. "Well, was it?"

He wasn't quite sure what he expected. He was no more likely to get an answer from whatever was out there than he was from Rebecca or one of the other sheep. But suddenly, there was a response, and his blood ran cold.

The drum of pounding feet shattered the quiet and rumbled towards him, seemingly making the ground where he stood shake. "Oh, my dear God."

Still, he saw nothing, but the sheep began to cry and wail once more as the impending threat grew. He raised the shotgun, aiming it one way then another. The drumming became louder, but still, he couldn't get a fix on where it was coming from.

BOOM! The shot seemed to make his entire universe quake, but as the final echoes subsided, he was greeted by silence. *Did I get it? Was that it?*

Then the chilling, grating, ungodly rasp shrieked through the darkness again before the pounding feet started to race once more. Fear consumed Murdo, but he wanted to confront this creature. He wanted to kill it and to bring the legend of the Deamhan Oidhche to an end once and for all. *Can it even die?*

He fired another shot, but this time, before the report of the shotgun had quieted, he turned and ran. He leapt over the threshold, slamming the heavy panelled oak door behind him and sliding the bolt across. The sound of his shivering breath rose above the crackle of the fire as he stayed there with one hand pressed against the wood as if somehow that would help keep out whatever lurked in the darkness.

Seconds passed, then a minute, then two. Still, his heart galloped as his eyes bored holes in the wood and his imagination tried to picture what monster had stormed towards him.

Finally, he removed his hand and took a step back. *Did I get it?* A thud behind him charged his body, causing every hair to bristle. "Oh, dear God." It had been a long time since he had mentioned the Lord's name, but tonight he had said it twice, and now he wondered if he would ever get the chance to say it again as he slowly turned.

Murdo looked across to the sideboard and let out a breathless laugh as his tabby cat, which had been absent all day, now looked down at a pile of letters and bills it had pushed onto the floor. She lifted her head towards him and let out a belligerent meow.

"You certainly pick your times to make an appearance, don't you, Porridge?" Murdo said, turning back to the door. He broke the shotgun, loaded two more shells and backed away from the entrance a little farther. *Am I safe? Has it given up? Is it lying dead out there?*

He listened carefully for the sounds of Rebecca and the others, but there was nothing to hear. Then a throaty hiss rose from behind him and he turned to look at Porridge. The old cat was on her haunches, her hackles were raised and her eyes were wide staring towards the door like Death himself was standing behind it.

There was a loud and sudden bang against the wood, making the frame rattle, and Murdo took another stride back. He raised his shotgun and pointed it towards the oak panels. Porridge continued to hiss, but no further sound came from outside for a few seconds. Then scratching began. At first, it didn't sound dissimilar to the noise Porridge herself made in the middle of the night when the mood took her to wake the house up. Then it got louder and louder, sounding not like a cat but a tiger ... ten tigers. The door shimmied as the deafening scraping sound continued.

Murdo was frozen, his eyes glued to the bolt as it gradually began to rattle loose. His imagination ran wild as he tried to envisage what kind of unholy monster was on the other side of the wood. His eyes widened further as the door splintered. *That was over an inch thick. Please, God. Help me.*

More tears rolled down his face, but these weren't for Mary. It took a lot for a man of Murdo's years and upbringing to admit he was consumed by fear and even more to admit the tears he was crying were for himself, but at that moment, he couldn't deny the truth. He was more scared than he had ever been, even on that fateful night when Mary had vanished.

Suddenly, the scratching stopped, and Murdo backed away a little more, sure that any second the door would explode and some monster of unfathomable horror would burst in to take him. The shotgun wavered as his hands, and indeed his whole body, trembled with fear. *What is this thing?*

Porridge let out a fearful yowl behind him, and Murdo quickly glanced over his shoulder to see the tabby jump from the sideboard and disappear down the hallway. There was a part of him that desperately wanted to follow, but the rational part told him that, one way or another, this was ending tonight.

The scratching recommenced, even louder now as more wood split and shattered. Murdo felt his chest constricting; he felt more sweat begin to bead on his forehead as the splintering, scraping concerto rose even higher in volume.

BOOM!

An ear-splitting animalistic shriek sliced through the night. He'd witnessed beasts suffer. He'd listened to them cry out in pain, but this was something new. This was something that didn't just chill his blood but the very marrow in his bones.

The demon let out another haunting yowl, not just reverberating around the yard outside but somehow squeezing through the jagged gaps in the door and filling the kitchen with Hell's torment.

Murdo continued to shake as he stood there staring towards the entrance waiting for the next wave of the attack.

Whatever it was beyond the oaken barrier let out another tortured screech and then ... silence.

A minute passed, then two, then three. It was a full ten minutes before Murdo finally lowered his shotgun. Sweat was streaming down his back as well, and he knew better than anyone that it wasn't just down to the licking flames of the fire behind him.

He took a single tentative step towards the entrance, then another before pausing and staring towards the ruptured hole in the door. His imagination ran wild trying to conjure an image of what kind of beast could shred solid oak in such a way. He took another step, then another, before finally reaching out and sliding the bolt across.

He waited again for a moment then pulled on the handle and allowed the door to swing inwards, half expecting something to come hurtling at him from the foggy darkness beyond the entrance, but nothing did.

His eyes immediately focused on a patch of black on the ground. He retraced his steps into the house to grab his torch and when he returned and focused the beam, he saw it wasn't black at all but red. It was blood. The same colour blood as that of any beast he had ever encountered. *Oh, my God.*

He stepped out of the house, avoiding the crimson puddle, and walked further into the farmyard, panning the torch from side to side and clutching the shotgun as firmly as ever. Rebecca and the others were quiet but not silent. The anguish in their voices seemed to have dissipated. The dense mist still hung over the yard and surrounding land, but further splotches and streaks of red cut a path towards the forest.

Murdo's heart slowed a little and he took in a deep lungful of air, countering any effects of the whisky that may still have lingered in his system. One by one, his senses began to return to him, and despite the evidence suggesting the threat was over he felt uneasy being out in the open and headed back to the house.

He leaned the shotgun up against the wall, locked the door and slid the bolt across before marching over to the telephone. He picked up the receiver, and it was only when he tried to dial that he noticed his hands were still trembling. He took another breath and tried his hardest to focus, slowly keying one digit after another.

"William?" he blurted as his call was answered. "It's Murdo. It came back."

"What came back?" asked William Munro, the leader of the island council and elder of the church.

"What do you think?" There was a long silence on the other end of the phone before Murdo continued. "I got it though. I got a shot off and it ran. It ran towards the forest."

"You shot it? Have you been drinking, Murdo?"

Murdo looked towards the whisky. "No."

"You shot it? You definitely shot it?"

"I shot it, and it bled a path right into the forest."

There was another long pause. "Are you okay?"

"I'm alright. My door's seen better days, but I'm alright."

"I'll call Thomas and I'll be over soon. You fix that door now."

The line went dead and Murdo looked at the receiver for a few seconds before returning it to the cradle. A scratching sound suddenly began behind him and a fresh fear coursed through his veins. He ran to the door to grab his shotgun, but before he reached it, a loud meow from the kitchen raced to catch up with him. He stopped in mid-stride and let out a small chuckle as Porridge continued to claw her cat tree with gay abandon.

"I swear you'll be the death of me, girl."

*

Few residents of Cora slept that night. A posse of armed crofters with dogs followed the blood trail into the forest. They nearly lost it when it reached the river, but they split up and scoured the opposite bank in both directions, eventually picking it up once more. The dogs finally led them to an expansive growth of tall, spiny bushes set some way back from the nearest thing to a footpath.

It was obvious something had drilled a not-so-subtle path through the undergrowth. Blood reflected in the beams as they shone their torches through the burrowed tunnel. It still dripped from the thorns, branches and leaves. Angus MacNeil began to hack a way through with his sickle. The fear that had accompanied them their entire lives had eroded during the course of the night. The Deamhan Oidhche had been a thing of myth, legend and nightmare—an unkillable monster that would plague the island through the ages. But now they knew it bled; they had begun to realise it could be stopped, and tonight, they were going to stop it. Stories would be told about them for generations—the croft men who tracked and killed the Night Demon.

"Y'wee shite," Angus hissed as a thorny branch sprang back in his face.

"Here, you've done enough, Angus. Take a break for a while," Innes said, taking the sickle from his cousin. He continued the work, hacking his way through the barbed bushes while more than a dozen torches shone beyond him, lighting his path.

They all knew what was at stake, and not a single man let down his guard. "There's nothing more dangerous than a cornered and wounded beast, lads. Keep your eyes open," Angus said as he bent over, resting his hands on his knees in order to catch his breath. He did hard physical work every day, but cutting a route through such thick growth had nearly rendered him breathless.

The dogs had lain down, not sure if their work was done or not but grateful for the respite, while all their owners stood watching Innes. Expletives and curses filled the air as he continued. "It's like cutting through barbed wire with a butter knife trying to hack through some of this stuff," he growled.

"Here. I'll take over for a while," Calum offered.

"Nah. I'm okay for the moment. I'll just be glad when we're—" He cut off in mid-sentence as something caught his eye. "Wait a minute. I see something."

"See what?" Angus asked.

"Rock."

"What?"

"There's something behind these bushes." He continued scything and hacking until he had uncovered exactly what it was. Others had now followed him, using the beaten path to snap and force back more of the thorny shrubbery, widening the route.

"It's a cave."

At first, what they all set eyes on in the torchlight appeared to be little more than a large, wide, chest-high boulder, half buried in the ground, but on closer inspection, a narrow tube-like opening, carpeted by the bloody streaks of the beast led down into a subterranean blackness none of them even wanted to contemplate.

"Wh-what do we do?" Calum asked. "Do we go in?"

"No," Angus replied.

"What then?"

"John, Joseph, you come with me. Thomas, Doug, the rest of you, stay here. Anything pokes its head out of there, you finish it off. We'll be back before daylight." Angus immediately retraced his steps out of the thicket. John, Joseph and the others cast one another uncertain glances in the beams of artificial light; then the two named men reluctantly followed, racing to catch up with the seemingly self-appointed leader.

"What have you got in mind?" John asked as he and the other man caught up with Angus.

"We're going to end this once and for all, and we're not going to risk anybody's life doing it."

*

Morning had broken by the time William returned to Murdo's place. A thick piece of board had been nailed over the damaged panels on the door and it was clear to anyone that Murdo hadn't slept a wink. The low sun bled through the net curtains, finally laying the darkness to rest, and a pot of piping hot tea sat in the middle of the kitchen table while Murdo tried to pluck up the desire to eat the toast he'd been nudging around his plate for the last few minutes.

Porridge sat on top of her cat tree, her tail periodically swiping from side to side for no reason. Her head pricked up as William walked in, but she did not dismount, she merely observed.

"They tracked it down, Murdo," William said with a smile as if it was he who had been out there.

"They did?"

William nodded. "Aye, they tracked it down, and they're going to put an end to this once and for all." He looked at his watch.

"Going to? They haven't done it yet?"

William ignored the question. "They trailed it through the forest and finally found its lair. If you hadn't shot it, this day might never have come."

"Lair?"

"A cave of some kind, so Angus said."

"And they're going in after it now?"

William shook his head. "No."

A distant rumble rose into the air and Murdo jumped up from the table, knocking his chair over. "What the hell was that?" he asked, rushing to the door.

The same question would be on the lips of most residents of the island, and as he stepped out into the cool morning air, he turned towards the forest where the last echoes of the explosion still shook.

"Angus used explosives from the quarry. Aye, that thing just got its own tomb. Today, Murdo, the stories end. The legend of the Deamhan Oidhche has reached a fitting conclusion."

Murdo looked at him for a moment. "But—"

"No buts. No what-ifs. No doubts. It's over. It's over." He cast one final smile towards the other man before heading back across to his car. "You'll come around to ours tonight. Eight o'clock. Don't be late. We'll have ourselves a wee ceilidh." William climbed into the car, started the engine and drove away, giving one final wave as he navigated out of the yard and onto the track.

There'd be others there, probably the whole village. They'd all be celebrating, but surely it was too soon. There was so much that didn't make sense. This legend was born long before Murdo had taken his first breath. It had gone back generations, centuries even. *How can it just be a thing of flesh and blood? How can a shotgun shell and a few explosives be enough to bring this terror to an end?*

Murdo went to the ceilidh, and the villagers and more besides were present. People told stories and drank and danced and it all went on until the early hours. Uneasiness blanketed Murdo as he walked home with just the moon to light his way. Goosebumps rippled up and down his arms as they had done the previous night, and when he finally got to his house, he lit a fire and fell asleep in front of it with his shotgun by his side.

The next morning, he fed Porridge and ate his own breakfast before going out to check on Rebecca and the other sheep. The days passed, then the seasons. The following winter came and went, and not a single tourist went missing. No reparations were paid to crofters for missing livestock either. It was only on the anniversary of that night that Murdo finally accepted the facts. It was over, just as William had said on that fateful morning twelve months before. As Murdo looked towards the photo of his beloved Mary on the mantelpiece, there was a part of him that knew the beast of Cora was gone, but he was certain its story would live forever.

1

NOW

Seb stood back from the bathroom cabinet and shook his head as he looked at himself in the mirror. He placed the drill down on the toilet seat and folded his arms.

The sound of thundering feet came to a sudden stop, and a moment later, two heads peeked around the door. "What do you want?" he asked in a surly manner.

"Nice way to greet your children, Dad," the girl replied. "You could at least pretend to like us."

"We've been over this. There's no law that demands it. I'll keep you fed and put a roof over your head, but there my obligations come to an end." The two twelve-year-olds laughed. When his wife had told him she was pregnant, he had never even considered the possibility of twins, but here they were, a boy and a girl, scarily similar and in tune in every respect. Neither Charlie nor Luna had been keen on the idea of uprooting and moving to a remote Scottish island, but they were gradually warming to the idea … very gradually.

They would find something they liked about the place only to discover something else they didn't like, which would send them into a sulky rut, reminding their parents how close they were to becoming teens.

This house was about five times bigger than their old place in London. There were a lot of outbuildings and even some stables, as well as more land than they could ever have imagined owning. They were going to have a swimming pool built, and vague promises of horses and dogs hung in the air in order to keep the pair sweet, but they would come later. First, the family had to make the place their own.

"That cabinet doesn't look very safe," Charlie said.

"No. I don't want either of you touching it. It's not safe," Seb replied.

"Why have you put it up then?"

"Because your mother asked me to put it up."

"But it looks like it might fall apart at any minute."

"I know."

"Then why did you put it up? It doesn't make sense."

"You'll understand when you're older."

"What will I understand?"

Seb exhaled a deep breath. "You'll understand that, sometimes, when you're married, no matter how much you warn someone that they're making a mistake. No matter how much you tell them that something won't last two minutes when they see it in an antique shop window. No matter how much you plead with them not to go ahead because it will only end in disaster. You just have to accept that the only way they'll understand is when they see it fall apart in front of their eyes."

"But that's stupid."

"For your sake, for your sister's sake and for my sake, don't say that to your mother, Charlie."

"But—"

"No buts, Charlie. Sometimes, you just have to do things, no matter how ridiculous, pointless and cretinous they seem to any normal person. You just have to do them because if you don't, you know that your life will be made totally and utterly miserable."

The two youngsters laughed. "I think I'm going to stay single," Charlie replied.

"Very wise, Son. Very wise." Seb dragged his eyes away from the cabinet and looked towards the twins. "Did you two want something or were you just coming in here to poke fun at my DIY skills?"

"Mum will be on in five minutes," Luna said.

It took Seb a few seconds to comprehend what she was talking about; then it dawned. "Shit! I'd nearly forgotten. Good save, Luna," he replied, opening the door fully and walking past them. "And don't tell your mum I swore either; otherwise, that'll be another black mark against my name."

"You're the man of the house," Charlie replied. "You should be able to say what you like."

"You really have no concept of how a marriage works, have you, Son? We have an equitable division of labour, responsibility and decision-making in this house."

"What does that mean?" Luna asked.

"It means your mum's responsible for making the decisions about what work I should do and when. She also sets the house rules, and number one on that charter is no swearing in front of you two."

"Mum swore the other day."

"It's not good to tell tales either." Seb paused for a second. "What did she say?"

"Fuck."

Seb's eyebrows arched upwards. "For future reference, and so that I never have to hear that coming out of your mouth, we refer to that as the F word."

"Okay."

"What were the circumstances?"

"I thought I wasn't supposed to tell tales."

"You're not telling tales. You're helping me improve your mother's behaviour around you."

"Are you sure you're not just wanting information so you can use it against her the next time she blames you for something?"

Seb stopped and looked at his daughter. "That is paranoid, slanderous and downright hurtful. Possibly. Depends how much trouble I get into."

The twins laughed again. "She broke an egg on the floor."

"And she dropped the F-bomb for that?"

Luna shrugged. "It went over her Louis Vuittons."

"You've done well to bring this to my attention. It's important we help your mum improve herself."

"More important than giving you the grounds for a counter suit?" Charlie asked. Seb cast his son a puzzled look. "I've been watching *Damages*. I think I want to be a lawyer when I grow up."

"I thought you wanted to be a fireman."

"I did until I found out how much they earned and how much lawyers earned."

"You'll go far, Son."

He turned to Luna. "Do you still want to be a vet?"

"It depends."

"On what?"

"Well, having some animals like a dog or a cat or a pony around here would really help me make my decision."

Seb's eyes narrowed. "You're a hustler, do you know that?"

"What's a hustler?"

"Ask your mother. On second thoughts, don't. Come on, we'll miss her."

The living room, much like the rest of the house, was in a state of flux. Several cardboard boxes sat in the middle of the floor, waiting to be unpacked. Wallpaper had been stripped from three of the walls and a start had been made on the fourth. The TV, however, had already been mounted. In order to keep the twins happy, that had been one of the first jobs on Seb's list.

The three of them slumped down onto the sofa as the newsreader finished up. "There'll be more from me in an hour, but for viewers of BBC One, we're going back to Lisa and Paul in the studio."

"This is it. There's Mum. There's Mum," Luna said excitedly.

The camera held the two presenters in focus for a moment before their guest was introduced. The studio was festooned with tinsel and other decorations while a large, sparkly Christmas tree stood behind one of the sofas. "This morning, we're delighted to welcome Summer Richards, the author of the best-selling book *One Last Secret*. Hello."

The camera closed in on a woman with flowing black hair and dark features. She was wearing a white dress cut just above the knee, and whether it was out of a tube or not, she had a tan that suggested she'd spent the last few months in the Med. When she smiled, she revealed a set of snow-white teeth.

Oh my God. She's so beautiful. Seb's heart skipped a beat. This wasn't unusual. Still, after so many years of marriage, she could take his breath away; she could turn him into a weak-kneed teenager. It was her superpower.

"Hello," Summer said, her face lighting up.

The phone started to ring in the hallway. "We're recording this, aren't we?" Seb asked.

"Duh!" Luna replied.

"I knew it was a mistake not to beat you more when you were younger," Seb said, climbing to his feet and heading out to get the phone.

"Hello."

"Hi, handsome," Summer replied.

"Who is this?"

"Comedy gold."

"We're just watching you on telly. How are you calling me?"

"I knew it was a mistake to marry someone older. It's so easy for you to get confused, isn't it?"

"I'm six months older than you, you cheeky cow."

"The interview segments aren't all done live. There's so much to pack into the Christmas week shows that sometimes the live feeds run over, so it's much easier to have the interviews on tape."

"Tape? Now who's a dinosaur?"

Summer giggled. "Alright. I'll give you that one."

"From the few seconds I saw before someone decided to phone me, you looked amazing."

"Aww. You're sweet."

"Love you."

"Love you too. Listen, I'm just heading to the airport. It says the flights are all running on time. What's the weather like up there?"

"Sunny. Calm. Crisp."

"And have you checked the forecast?"

"I'm not a fucking weatherman." This was another thing they'd had to get used to. Listening to the weather forecast had become something they needed to do every day, especially if travel was involved.

Summer giggled again. "Have you?"

"Yeah. It's going to be like this until tonight. They reckon there's a winter storm heading for Scotland tomorrow though. At least there's no rain forecast like the other night. That was mental. I've never seen anything like that before."

"Will the storm reach us?"

"Looks like the mainland gets the brunt of it."

"But there are no problems with the ferries today?"

"No problems at all. I checked the CalMac site and all services are running normally."

"That's a relief. I can't wait to see you."

"And the kids, of course."

"Oh yeah. I forgot about them. I thought they might have left home and started lives of their own now."

Seb smiled and popped his head around the corner. "Your mum says hi." Neither of them looked up or acknowledged Seb, they just carried on watching. He stepped back out into the hallway. "It seems they prefer TV mum to phone mum."

"Ungrateful little bastards."

"Tell me about it. It's your fault. You spoilt them from day one. I told you we should have sold one of them off for organ harvesting so the other would always be on their best behaviour."

Summer laughed again. "Did they fight like they usually do when they put up the tree?"

The permasmile that had been etched on Seb's face ever since picking up the phone vanished in a heartbeat. "Err, oh yeah. You know what they're like. Little bastards."

There was a short pause. "You haven't got the tree up, have you?"

"What kind of a man do you take me for?"

"One who's a terrible liar and hasn't put the tree up."

"Crrrcrrrckk. Crrrcccckkk. This is a terrible connection. You're breaking up. Crrrcccckkk!"

"I'm on a fucking landline, Seb, and so are you."

"Ah!"

"That tree better be up by the time I get back."

"It will."

"And the bathroom cabinet—"

"The bathroom cabinet's already on the wall."

"Oh. Okay. Cool. How are the builders getting on?"

Seb shrugged. "I don't know. Okay, I'm guessing; otherwise they'd be letting me know, I'm sure."

"Haven't you been checking on them?"

"Jezyk is a more than capable project manager. If he needs to consult me for anything, he knows where I am."

"And they're okay?"

"What do you mean?"

"I mean in the caravans. They're okay?"

"They've got top-end-of-the-range mobile homes. I'd hardly call them caravans. I don't even want to think about how much all this is costing us."

"You don't need to think about how much this is costing. That's one of the reasons I'm calling. Carla Forest from Universal spoke to Buddy before I went on air."

"And?"

"It's a go. They want me to fly over after New Year's to talk about the treatment."

"You're getting treatment? That's such a relief. Do you think they'll be able to do anything about your ego or is that a lost cause?"

"Again. Comedy gold. Did you hear what I said? This is huge for us."

"I'm teasing. You'll be able to tell me all about it when you're back here."

"I was thinking maybe I could get Mum and Dad to house sit and child sit for us, and you and I could go over there together."

"What, seriously?"

"We've talked about going to LA like a hundred times. And Buddy said they'll be giving us the red carpet treatment."

"Would Buddy be going?"

"Of course. He's my agent, but he'll probably be spending most of his time in meetings. It would be a nice little break for us."

"Won't you have work to do?"

"Sure. Some. But I'm pretty certain we could find some quality us time too."

"Tell me you really want me there and I'm not just going to be a piece of eye candy that you roll out at every available opportunity."

Summer laughed again. "Damn. You can always see right through my schemes."

It was Seb's turn to laugh now. "I like this idea. Your schedule's been crazy for the last few months. A little break might be just what the doctor ordered."

"I can't wait to see you tonight. I've got you an early Christmas present."

"Oh? Any clues?"

"You'll like it."

"You're crap at clues. Is it something to eat?"

"Always with the eating."

"It's Christmas. It's not my fault all the good stuff appears in the shops at Christmastime. Is it that panettone you got from that little place off Regent Street last year?"

"It's not food."

"Oh. Okay. Is it something for me to wear then?"

Summer giggled. "Err. You could, but I don't think you'd do it justice."

"Hmm. So, it's something for you to wear?"

"Might be."

"Are there any airlines that can get you here faster? Can Buddy pull some strings and get you airlifted across by Search and Rescue rather than having to take the ferry?"

Summer giggled again. "There are limits to what he can do."

"Evidently." Charlie and Luna appeared in the hall at the same time. "Hang on a second. The beasts are stirring."

"Is that Mum?" Luna asked. "Tell her she was brilliant."

"Did you hear that? Your daughter said you were dire. Something about googly, popping eyes. Didn't you get much sleep last night?"

"I didn't say that," Luna said, snatching the phone from Seb. "You were great, Mum." The young girl angled the receiver so her brother could talk too.

"Yeah, Mum. You looked amazing." There was a pause. "The Christmas tree?"

Seb snatched the phone away from the children. "Y'know, the most important element of a relationship is trust. If you want to continue in your role as my wife, you're going to have to—"

"Please. I'm begging you, please have it all done for when I get back. I don't want to have to think about putting all the decorations up. I just want to chill for the next few days. I want to enjoy Christmas in our new house with my family. I don't want to think about work, I don't want to think about anything but having fun, and I definitely don't want to think about smashed baubles, tinsel and garland littering the floor for the next two days. Please, Seb. Please."

Seb let out a long sigh. "You two, go find the Christmas tree and find the box with all the decorations."

"But—"

"No buts, Charlie. Go do it, now."

He watched as they disappeared down the hall before bringing the phone up to his ear again. "I promise you. This place will look like Santa's grotto by the time you get here."

"Thanks, babe."

"Hey."

"What?"

"You looked amazing. I can't even begin to tell you how proud I am."

"That's so sweet. You always make me go warm and fuzzy, y'know that? I love you."

"Yeah. Love you too. Now, fuck off, I've got work to do." Seb hit the end call button and laughed to himself. He could picture Summer still with the phone in her hand, laughing as she looked at it, only half disbelieving that her husband had told her to fuck off then hung up.

He placed the receiver back in the cradle and went to join the children as they began their epic search to try to find the decorations.

*

This is such a sweet gig. Jezyk stepped out of the caravan and into the crisp morning air. He had been up long before the others, safety-checking all the equipment for the day's work, but he had enjoyed a longer-than-usual breakfast break and a leisurely chat with his wife and children on the phone.

This was the last day before the Christmas break. By tomorrow evening, he would be back in Glasgow and in the warm embrace of his family. He was used to dealing with rich people. Most of them were total arseholes, but not the Richardses. They had come from not very much, and yes, she earned figures that Jezyk couldn't even imagine, but neither of them had forgotten how to treat people, especially those who worked for them.

They had hired new top-end-of-the-range mobile homes for him and his crew to live in while they worked. They had hired an extra Portakabin, which had a pool table, a dart board, a brand-new PlayStation and a sixty-five-inch TV. First, his team worked on the house. There had been much to do. It had needed a new roof. Two ceilings had needed replacing where rainwater had leaked through. They had rewired it and put in a new central heating system. Mr Richards had suggested they knock it down and start again, but Mrs Richards had fallen in love with the place and justifiably so. The bones of it were good, and it possessed charm and character that you never saw in modern houses, no matter how expensive.

Jezyk looked across to the main building and a smile lit his face. He had done much to be proud of, but restoring life to such a property made him feel good inside. The final touch had been painting it white, as per Mrs Richards' wishes. She had always wanted a little white cottage by the sea, and although this was hardly little, painting it had been a perfect finishing touch.

His team was six-strong. He had worked with them all many times before, and there were still a few weeks left to do before this job came to an end. Two of the outbuildings needed work, as did the stables. New fences needed putting up, and today, they were breaking ground on the pool. Mrs Richards wanted a pool house. A pool house on a Scottish island. The thought of it made him smile again. It was a crazy extravagance, and for the amount that they were spending on restoring and adding to this place, they could have probably found something with far less work and expense needed elsewhere. But then again, they'd struggle to find something with this view.

He unscrewed the top of his travel mug and took a sip of piping hot coffee then turned a full circle. *She is right. This place is magical.* To the north of the property was a sweeping forest that rose up into the hills. There were more hills and woodland to the east beyond the moor, and it was only a short walk down to the bay; when the autumn weather had allowed, he and his team had gone down there in the evenings and had barbecues and a few beers. It was really like no other place he had worked or been, for that matter. He would be sad when the contract came to an end, but one day he would come back here with his family.

"Jez, JEZ!"

The call from Bazyli, his right-hand man, suddenly jarred him from his thoughts. "Yeah?" he said, taking one last look towards the forest and turning towards his friend.

"We've got a problem."

"We're heading home tomorrow. I'm not accepting any problems today. Save them until we get back."

"Yeah. I would if I could, but you're going to need to see this."

"Don't make me hate you, Baz. I like you too much to hate you."

"There's something wrong with Emil."

"You interrupted my quiet morning to tell me that?" Jez felt bad about the comment as soon as it had left his lips. Emil had a troubled past. His youngest child had died two years before and he had hit the bottle hard. It had nearly cost him everything, including the rest of his family and marriage. But he had found the church, abandoned the booze and, other than being a little too pious on occasion, had become a model employee once again. "What is it?"

"I ... I think he's drunk."

"What?" Jez immediately forgot all thoughts of Christmas and returning home. He almost ran past Bazyli as he put his hard hat on and headed towards the digger. "You let him operate machinery while he was drunk, for Christ's sake?" he asked as his friend caught up with him.

"I didn't know he was drunk. I mean why would I?"

It was a good point. Even at the height of Emil's alcoholism, he was very adept at hiding it from even those closest to him. They arrived on the scene to see the other men standing in a loose semicircle around the digger as it scooped up a large pile of earth, deposited it, then picked it up again and placed it back in the hole. They all watched now as he did this over and over again with the same mound and the same hole.

"Has anybody spoken to him this morning?"

"No," replied Alex, one of the other men. "He was already out here when we arrived."

"Shit."

"What are you going to do?" Bazyli asked.

"I'm still trying to figure that out." Jez looked back towards the house. "A boozed-up builder in charge of heavy machinery is good grounds for us being shown the door, so whatever we do, we'd better do it quickly."

"Hey! HEY, EMIL!" Bazyli shouted, waving his hands and marching into the digger's view.

"What the hell are you doing, you idiot?"

It worked for a moment, and the arm and bucket paused in mid-air as Emil watched his friend frantically wave his arms to attract his attention. A few seconds passed, and before he knew what was happening, the door to the cab swung open. Alex and Bazyli grabbed Emil roughly, yanking him out before Alex cut the engine and jumped back down.

Emil struggled and pulled, desperate to climb back in. He took a swing at Bazyli, but his coordination was all off and, instead, he spun around, falling in a heap on the ground.

The other men surrounded him, ready to jump in if things spiralled out of control, but Bazyli put his hand up. "It's okay. It's okay."

Emil started to cry, which scared everyone a lot more than seeing him so belligerent. He was six feet three and built like a castle keep. He could deadlift twice as much as any of the others, which was why the feat of dragging him out of the cab was as impressive as it was.

"What the hell's going on here, Bazyli?" All the men turned to see Seb standing there.

"Err … it's okay, Mr Richards. We've just got a little issue that we're sorting out."

"I saw the digger going haywire. Is there a problem with it?"

"Err...."

"You can't escape your demons. You just can't escape them." Emil slurred his words while continuing to cry, and Seb stepped forward, breaking through the loose semicircle of bodies.

"Please tell me you didn't have someone pissed out of their skull operating a fucking mechanical digger, Jezyk." Seb had spent the early part of his turbulent life in the foster care system. His first jobs had been on building sites, and he could swear with the best of them. He could fight with the best of them too, and as much as he'd changed, if someone put the welfare of his family at risk, he reverted to his hard-as-nails old self.

"It won't happen again, Mr Richards."

"You're damn right it won't happen again." Seb looked around at the other men. They were good workers, and this was the first time there'd been any kind of issue, but someone drunk and in control of a mechanical digger while his children were around was something he wasn't going to tolerate. "Get him some coffee, and I don't want him using anything bigger than a drill from now on."

"You've got it, Mr Richards. Again, I'm sorry. I don't know—"

"I'm sorry," Emil blurted, curling into a foetal position on the ground and beginning to sob loudly.

"Oh, God."

"I tried. I tried, and I tried, but they follow you. They follow you everywhere, even when you think you've got rid of them. When you think you've seen the last of them, they follow you."

"Dad?" Luna called.

"Go back inside, sweetheart," Seb replied, putting his hand up to stop her from approaching any nearer. "I'll be in in a few minutes." He watched her retrace her steps and then turned to Jezyk and Bazyli. "Let's get him into the caravan and start sobering him up." He looked to the other men. "The rest of you, get back to work. My wife is arriving this afternoon and I want her to be pleasantly surprised by how things are going here. I also want no mention of this incident … ever. Do we understand one another?" The other men all nodded respectfully while Jezyk and Bazyli heaved Emil up and guided him back to one of the caravans.

The Richardses had provided the workers with coffee machines for each of the caravans too, and thankfully, a half-full pot was waiting as they manhandled Emil into one of the waiting chairs. Seb poured him a large cup and spooned in three sugars. It seemed almost treacly in consistency as he stirred it. He went over to where the three men were sitting and plonked it down in front of Emil. "Drink that," Jezyk ordered.

The big man's eyes were still red and swollen, but he nodded and did as his friend said. He winced a little at the strength, heat and sweetness of the coffee, but the jolt helped him calm a little and he relaxed back into his chair. "You're all good workers," Seb said. "I'm happy with what you've done to date. I don't care what you do on a night. If you fancy a drink to wind down after the day, that's all well and good, but what happened out there is unacceptable."

Jezyk put his hands up. "I know, Mr Richards, sir. I'm sorry. There is no way I will let this happen again. We'll straighten this out and—"

"What happened, Emil?" Seb interrupted.

Emil stared at him for a moment. His pupils were dilated, and fresh tears hung in the corners of his eyes, but he took another drink. "I'm sorry," he said, sniffing loudly.

"Okay, you're sorry, that's good. But someone could have been hurt, and that's not good. What happened?"

The big man started to cry again. "I'd got rid of him. Don't you understand? I'd got rid of him."

"What are you talking about?"

"I hadn't had a drink for the longest time." He touched his mouth. "Not a drop passed these lips. Not a drop."

"Okay, but here we are, so I'll ask you again, what happened?"

Emil looked at Bazyli then Jezyk. They had both been good to him. They had helped him through his darkest times. But now he wondered if there would ever be an end to the dark times and, more to the point, if anyone would be able to help him. He took another sip of coffee and reached under his shirt, grabbing the crucifix around his neck and kissing it. "It took me a long time to get sober. It was hard."

The other men hung on his every word. "Go on," Seb replied.

He took several more gulps of coffee, finishing the mug and handing it to Bazyli for a refill. The foreman walked across to the machine and got him a top-up before Emil continued. "During the worst moments, I felt I had truly lost my mind. Sometimes when I was not even drunk, I saw things."

"Saw things?" Seb asked. "What kind of things?"

"All kinds of things. Sometimes it would be people who weren't there. Sometimes it would be figures in the darkness or in the distance. It would be things that sent chills and shivers through me, things that could not be. And seeing these things just made everything worse."

"But you came out the other side though."

Emil was still slurring his words a little, but he'd sobered dramatically in the last few minutes. He looked at his two friends and then towards Seb. "Yes. So I thought."

"What do you mean?"

"Last night, everyone had gone to bed. I stepped outside for a last cigarette before I turned in. It was calm, considering the weather we'd had the night before. I sat on the steps and lit up. I was there maybe three or four minutes just looking up at the moon and the stars and thinking about going home to see my family when suddenly I felt uneasy … like I wasn't alone … like I was being watched."

"Okay. And it wasn't one of the other men having a quick fag before bed too?"

"I thought this at first. I looked around and called out, but no one replied. I stood up and looked towards the house. I wondered if it was you or one of the children."

"Yeah. My kids aren't really big smokers."

Emil forced a smile. "No. I thought it was just my imagination, but then that familiar feeling came over me. You know that feeling like electricity that runs through your body before something happens like a storm?" He looked at the other men, but there was a lack of comprehension on their faces.

"Go on, Emil. What happened next?" Jezyk asked.

"Then I saw it. I saw the Czernobog."

"What? What the fuck's a Czernobog?" Seb asked.

Jezyk's entire team were of Polish descent. He and Bazyli had moved to Britain in their early teens, but the rest of them had been born and raised in the UK. However, their parents and grandparents had regaled them with stories from the old country, and Jezyk looked to Bazyli before turning to Seb. He was more than a little embarrassed as he spoke. "It is from Polish folklore. It is the king of monsters, the ultimate evil. But, as I say, it is folklore. Just make-believe."

"Yes," Emil replied, taking another drink of coffee. "It is make-believe, but I saw it. I saw it standing by the fence post over there. Taller than me, much taller. A thin, black figure in the darkness just staring."

"No offence, Emil, but judging by the amount you drank I'm surprised you didn't see a pink elephant in a tutu."

"No, Mr Richards. All this happened before I even touched a drop. This is what made me drink again. I realised that there is no escape. It didn't matter that I had stopped. My demons will follow me until the day I die. There is no escape from them. I will never escape." Tears flooded his eyes again as the other men glanced towards one another.

"Look. It is obvious you got little sleep last night. I think getting a couple of hours will help," Jezyk said.

"That sounds like a good idea," Seb replied.

"I know you think I'm just a mad drunk. I know what I saw. I know that figure in the darkness was not just a figment of my imagination. I know it," Emil protested, looking at both men with pleading eyes.

"Whatever it was, rest will do you good," Jezyk said. "You need to thank Mr Richards. Most other bosses would have given you your marching orders."

Emil looked towards the steaming coffee and thought about arguing and pleading for them to believe him, but he knew it was a lost cause. "I'm sorry. I'm sorry that I let you down."

"Look," Seb began. "You've got two weeks off from tomorrow. Spend it with your family. Get your head sorted out. There'll be a job waiting for you when you get back here, but I can't have anything like this happening around my children again. Do you understand me?"

Emil nodded. "Yes, sir," he replied quietly.

Bazyli helped the big man up. "Come on. Let's get you a couple of ibuprofen to help you sleep this off."

Seb and Jezyk watched them go. "I will dock him a day's pay for this. I will make sure—"

"No need for that," Seb replied. "Has he ever freaked out like this before?"

Jezyk sat back in his chair and stared at the other man. "Things got very bad when he was drinking before. He nearly lost everything. Then he quit and got better, stronger. Up until today, he was my most reliable worker. Whatever spooked him last night spooked him good."

Seb looked out towards the wide, rounded corner fence post that Emil had pointed to. "He sounded confused. And it does get really dark out here. It might have been an owl sitting on the post or something. I mean those things can get really big, and perspective at night is always hard to judge."

"It may have been, Mr Richards. Or it may have been what he said."

Seb let out a laugh. "That devil thing?"

"I don't mean literally. I mean his mind may have conjured it. Maybe he hasn't fully recovered from the problems he suffered a few years ago. Maybe his mind was playing tricks."

Seb shrugged. "Maybe. Anyway, I trust you've got this in hand now," he said, rising from the table. "'Cause I've got a Christmas tree to put up before Mrs Richards gets here, and if I don't, that thing that Emil reckons he saw will seem like the fucking queen of the fairies compared to what my wife will turn into."

Jezyk let out a laugh. "Yes, Mr Richards. And again, I am sorry."

"It's over with now. We'll just forget about it."

"Thank you, sir."

*

Emil sniffed deeply and fresh tears ran down his face as he slipped off his boots and peeled off his shirt. "Get some sleep," Bazyli said. "You'll feel better when you wake up."

Emil climbed into bed. "I didn't make it up."

"Nobody thinks you made anything up, my friend."

"They didn't say it, but you could tell they were thinking it."

"Like I said, get some sleep. You'll feel better when you wake." Bazyli started walking away from the bed, but Emil's powerful hand reached out and grabbed his arm.

"It was real. It was as real as you or me and it stood there watching me. It was blacker than night. I had seen it before, Bazyli. When I was at my lowest, at my worst, it came to me, and it comes to me again now. I cannot let it take me. Promise you'll help. Promise you'll help me."

Bazyli looked at the big man's arm and noticed all the hairs standing on end. Almost as if it was a chain reaction, suddenly, the hairs on his own arms stood to attention as well, and the hackles pricked up on the back of his neck. Even though Bazyli could not bring himself to believe in the Czernobog or any part of the tale that Emil had related, he felt his fear as if it was his own and his heart began to beat a little faster in his chest. He looked into the other man's pleading eyes.

"You, me, Jez and the others are brothers. We will always be here for one another in good times and bad."

Emil released his grip a little. "Thank you. Thank you, brother. Because I can feel the bad times are coming. They're coming, and only a miracle will stop them."

2

It had been a long but rewarding day for Summer. When she had been trying to finish work on her first trilogy, Seb had held down three jobs to make sure the family didn't go under. He got up at four a.m. and worked as a cleaner from four thirty to six thirty. Then his teaching job ate up the rest of his day out of the house. On Saturdays, he helped his friend who ran a painting and decorating business. She had protested, but such was his faith in her that he had insisted. His commitment and belief were the things that meant failure wasn't an option.

Even when she was trying to hawk the books to every agent and publishing house in the country to no avail, he maintained his unswerving conviction that she would one day make it big as an author. Then Buddy had taken her on as a client, and first, she started earning a part-time income from writing, then a decent full-time one, and then she was making so much money that Seb quit all three of his jobs and started work as her personal assistant and general dogsbody. Her last book had blown away all expectations the pair had when she had first put pen to paper.

A UK production company had serialised her first trilogy, her fifth book had been adapted for the stage and was currently on tour around the country, and now her latest book was going to get the Hollywood treatment. She had become a household name, and Summer was the first to appreciate how crazy that was. Most authors, even those lucky enough to do it full-time, never had this kind of stuff happening. It was all a bit surreal. It was not unusual for her to be stopped in the street for an autograph, and a few people had come up to her in the airport asking her to sign newly purchased copies of *One Last Secret*.

It would be easy for it all to go to her head. *This right here, right now is reality. This is what I do it all for, and this is what I'll always do it for.* Charlie and Luna clung to her like limpets for the first five minutes after walking through the door. This was the first time they'd all been together in this house as a family since buying it.

It was already dark outside, but that didn't matter. The glow of the Christmas tree lights and the roaring fire made sure that it was warm and welcoming inside.

"You guys have done an awesome job with the tree," she said.

"Did you expect any less?" Seb asked.

"Err...."

"Don't answer that."

Eventually, the children let go of their mother. Eventually, they all had dinner and spent the evening hearing about all the exciting things that had happened to Summer while she had been on her trip. They heard about the famous people she'd met while she was doing the talk show rounds. They heard about the lines of fans forming outside Waterstones and Foyles. And eventually, Luna and Charlie made their way to bed, content that their family was back under one roof.

"They're quite something, our little tykes, aren't they?" Summer said, putting her feet up on the pouffe and taking another sip of wine.

"Ha, you can say that again. But they're not so little anymore," Seb replied, slouching back into his chair.

"Thank you for putting the tree up. I was dreading getting back here and having to face it." There was a loud thud from one of the other rooms and both of them looked at each other and laughed. "You'd think Luna would be the graceful one, wouldn't you?"

Seb smiled. "So, do you have any plans for what you'd like to do tomorrow?"

"I thought we could go explore. We could go for a hike, and I know you stocked up from the supermarket, but it's a ferry ride away, and it's not like we can just hop across whenever we need a loaf of bread, so maybe we could check out the general store and the rest of the village."

"We don't need to. We've got our own bread maker now."

"You know what I mean. It would be nice to meet some more of the locals too. They're going to be our neighbours now."

"So, that's it? Your first full day in our new home and you want to go to the local shop and meet some of the locals. I was right. I knew you'd want to start living the high life and leave me behind when you became successful."

"Get lost," she replied, laughing and flinging a cushion. It landed about a metre away from him.

"What the hell was that?"

"It was a warning shot."

"Oh yeah. Like you weren't aiming for my head."

"I can go off people y'know."

"You can't possibly go off me."

"True," she said, climbing to her feet and walking across to him. She plonked herself down in his lap and swung her legs over one arm of the chair before leaning in and kissing him.

He closed his eyes as he tasted her warm, wine-flavoured lips. "I don't know what you've heard about me, but I don't go all the way on a first date."

"That's too bad. I guess I'll just have to take your present back to the store next time I'm in London."

"On second thoughts...."

Summer took a sip of wine. "How are Jezyk's boys getting on?"

Seb flashed back to that morning and the incident with Emil. "Good. It's all going well. They're finishing off the old equipment shed and they've broken ground on the pool house."

"And the polytunnel?"

"I phoned the supplier this morning to make sure it would be here for the fifteenth, and they confirmed."

"You did say the fifteenth of January, didn't you? I've got absolutely no faith in that man after the run-around he's given us. It wouldn't surprise me if he meant the fifteenth of never."

"Trust me. They won't let us down. It will be here on the fifteenth. You've just got to know how to finesse these people to get the best out of them."

Summer let out a small giggle. "Oh, I see. You're the finesser, are you?"

"Yep. I'm thinking about having some cards made. Seb Richards, professional finesser."

She leaned in and kissed him again. "Well, Mister Richards, how about you grab us another bottle of wine, we go to bed, put some music on low, and we can both see what else you can finesse."

Seb did his best Beavis and Butt-Head laugh. "We're going to do it."

Summer giggled again and slapped him playfully. "I'm trying to be sexy and romantic, and you're spoiling it."

"You don't have to try. You can't be anything else."

"Ooh. Good save."

"So, are we then? Are we going to do it?"

Summer laughed and climbed to her feet. "You get the wine; I'll turn everything off in here and I'll meet you in the bedroom."

It would take some time for the recently plastered walls to dry enough to be painted, and as Seb lay in bed waiting for Summer to emerge out of the en suite bathroom, he began to think about the mountain of work that was still ahead of him. It would be worth it in the long run though. They had both felt that same special something when they had set eyes on this place for the first time.

Although the house was just on a single floor, it was built in a large L-shape and was well-soundproofed. The children's rooms were positioned opposite one another next to the communal bathroom at the toe of the L. There were several more rooms in between them and the master bedroom, and as music played from a large Bluetooth speaker on the bedside cabinet, Seb knew that no matter how high he turned the volume, the twins would not be disturbed.

He picked up his phone and made a selection. The gentle introduction to Portishead's *Glory Box* began to play, and right on cue, Summer appeared in the doorway and leaned back against the frame. She wore a strapped black lace chemise and combed her fingers through her hair seductively as she moved in rhythm to the music.

"Holy shit," Seb said, and Summer laughed. "Remind me to write to Ann Summers and thank her."

"Well, you can if you like, but this is Marks and Spencer all the way."

"Ha. Yeah, right."

"I'll show you the receipt when we're done."

"When we're done? It sounds like we're about to have a wrestling match." Summer continued over to the bed and sat down, grabbing the phone from the bedside cabinet and scrolling through the music. "I was enjoying watching you dance to Portishead."

"I'm just finding something more appropriate."

"I thought that was."

"Listen. I've not been with my man in over two weeks, and a girl has needs."

"This wouldn't have anything to do with meeting all those hunky actors on the talk shows, would it?"

"They're just boys. I want a real man."

"That reminds me, I need to order some more strawberry lip balm. This central heating is really making me chap something terrible."

Summer settled on a song and placed the phone back on the bedside cabinet. The unmistakable guitar intro to Heart's *Crazy On You* began to play, and Summer stood once more, grabbing her glass of wine and taking several gulps while swaying to the music. She placed the glass back down and paused for a moment; then, as the guitar segued into the fast, rhythmical strumming, she leapt on top of Seb like a jaguar. They both fell into a bout of uncontrollable and childish laughter. This was their world. They were the only two people who truly got each other. They could be as silly or as playful, or as sensual, as they wanted to be here.

They held each other tightly and laughed and nuzzled and kissed, then kissed some more before they fell into the magical excitement and sensuality that belonged to them and only them.

The next morning, it was the sound of a knock on the front door that woke them. Seb raised his head, a little confused. He looked at the clock. "Shit!" he said, scrambling to put his clothes on as the knock came again.

"There's somebody at the door," Luna shouted.

"Well, for fuck's sake, don't get it, will you?" Seb said under his breath, causing Summer to giggle as she slipped on her underwear and put on her thick robe, tying the sash tightly.

Seb stepped out into the hallway as the knock came again. He walked to the thick wooden door and opened it up to reveal Jezyk standing there with a smile on his face. Behind him, his minibus idled and the crew waved politely as Seb looked over to them. "This is us heading to the ferry, Mr Richards."

"Oh ... right. I'm sorry; I'm usually up before now."

Summer appeared in the doorway next to him. "Hi, Jezyk. I love what you've done with the place."

Jezyk smiled. "It is a special house and, with you back, a special home. I just wanted to say goodbye, and I hope you have a nice Christmas and New Year."

"Wait a minute," Seb said, disappearing for a moment. He reappeared with an envelope and handed it to Jezyk. "Here's a Christmas bonus for you to share out amongst the lads."

"What, seriously? You pay us well, Mr Richards. There is no need for this."

"It's just a small token to thank you for all the hard work you've put in," Summer replied.

"Yeah. What she said," Seb added.

"Thank you so much. Have a good Christmas."

"You too." They both watched as he walked back to the waiting vehicle; then they waved in unison as the minibus departed. "It's going to be weird waking up each day and not having them around."

Summer rubbed Seb's arm. "Aww. You're missing them already. That's so sweet."

"I suppose I've got you and the beasts to keep me company."

"Please don't call them that."

"You know I'm only joking," he said, closing the door and blocking out the cold morning air.

"I know that. But what happens when they get to school and they slip into a conversation somewhere that their dad calls them beasts?"

"People will find it funny ... endearing even."

"Yeah. I've explained this to you before. How you perceive yourself and how others perceive you are two completely different things."

"Some people are just devoid of a sense of humour."

"And some aren't. Let's just try to have a few months without getting called in to see the headmaster or alienating our neighbours in the first full week of living here."

"If I knew you were going to put all these stipulations on our relationship, I think I'd have thought twice before allowing you to drag me down the aisle."

She paused in the hallway and turned him around to look at her. "Please," she said, tiptoeing up and kissing him.

"Okay. I promise. I'll wean myself off calling them beasts."

"And?"

"And I'll try not to upset any neighbours."

"It shouldn't be difficult. I mean the nearest one is like a mile away or something."

"Is this why you wanted a place out in the sticks like this? So I wouldn't have any neighbours to piss off."

"It was one of the considerations." She kissed him again. "Now, come on. Let's get the kids fed and we can begin our day of adventure."

"Leave it with me." He turned and shouted down the hallway. "Wednesday! Cousin Itt! Breakfast."

"Nice. Much better. We are so going to fit in here."

*

Munro's General Store had been in the family since the early 1900s. In addition to having a petrol and diesel pump on the side court, it included the post office, sorting office, and Thomas Munro, son of the retired William, was also the island's nearest thing to law enforcement. On paper, he was nothing but a special constable who still hadn't completed his training, but in the eyes of the islanders, he was the local bobby.

Although having hung his shopkeeper's apron up some years before and handed over the mantle to his son, William still filled in now and again. He continued his role as the head of the island council and church elder, and as the store was the hub of the community, he spent many an hour reading the newspaper in the attached café.

There was little to do on an island of this size with a population of less than five hundred but gossip, and William had turned it into an art form.

It would still be an hour or so before the day's papers arrived, so he sat at his favourite table with a mug of hot tea and the previous day's *Daily Record*. The window looked out across the main square of the village, and he raised his eyes after each paragraph to see if there was anything worthy of his attention.

There was a hair salon-cum-barber's shop, which opened just three days a week in the winter. Today was not one of those days. The Cora guest house was a place where one could get a nice evening meal on special occasions. This and MacDougal's pub sat at opposite ends of the square like duellers at a gunfight. At this time of day, there was rarely any activity, and the only other place of commerce was the tourist information stroke gift shop, stroke charity shop, stroke whatever else the council deemed it needed to be on any particular day. This opened from eleven 'til three in the winter months.

Most patrons of the general store made a point of passing William's table to get updated on the latest news, but rarely was the news newsworthy because rarely did anything happen on Cora since that fateful night.

But today, William's brow creased and he lowered his newspaper as he saw Mairi McBride running across the road in the direction of the store. Mairi's husband worked offshore, and her coping mechanism was comfort eating. She'd gained a good four stones in the past few years, and she'd hardly had a gymnast's physique to begin with, so to see her running was most unusual.

William took a sip of his tea, folded his paper and placed it down on the table before climbing to his feet in anticipation of her entry. The bell above the door rang loudly as she burst inside. Mairi did not miss a step as she hurtled up the main aisle to the counter at the end.

She stood there for a few seconds, leaning forward, gripping the confectionery rack for balance while she caught her breath. Her cheeks and face were flushed as she tried to regain control of her breathing.

Thomas and his wife, Isobel, waited behind the counter with bated breath while William trod the path Mairi had blazed up the centre aisle. "What is it? What on earth is going on for you to come in here like some mad woman?" he asked, finally joining her at the counter.

She looked across at him, still unable to speak for a moment. When she had finally calmed, she looked from William to Isobel to Thomas. "I … I need to report a missing person."

Thomas shot a look towards his father, and both men raised an eyebrow. Mairi was prone to drama, and that was exactly what this sounded like. "Okay, Mairi. Take it easy. Now, who do you think is missing exactly?" Thomas asked.

"I don't think she's missing. I know she's missing. Ellie. I went to wake her up this morning and her bed hadn't been slept in."

Thomas glanced towards his father again, and both shared a knowing look. Ellie liked boys … a lot. Mairi's coping mechanism was food and Ellie's was boys. She was sixteen, and while most island girls of that age tended to be quiet and reserved by mainland standards, that was not the case with her.

"Okay. When did you last see her?"

"It was after dinner last night. She said she was going around to Caitlyn's for a while."

"And you didn't see her when she came back?"

"She often stays late at Caitlyn's, but she's never stayed out all night without telling me."

"And have you checked with Caitlyn?"

"Yes."

"And what did she say?"

"She said she left there last night at about eleven."

"And have you phoned around any other friends?"

"Yes, yes, yes. I've done all that. Why do you think I'm here?"

"Okay. Just take a breath." Thomas turned to his wife. "Get Mairi a cup of tea while I start making enquiries."

He walked into the back, and a few seconds later, William followed him.

"Who's she been seeing of late?" William asked as he joined his son.

"Spin the wheel and pick a number."

William let out a raucous laugh. "Och Son, you're a bad 'un," he said, laughing again.

"Hello. Hello, is that Cath? It's Thomas. Let me speak to Caitlyn, will you?" There was a pause, and he looked towards his father, shaking his head irritably as if this was a huge waste of his time. "Caitlyn, I've got Mairi here in pieces. When Ellie left your place last night, did she say she was going straight home?" There was a longer pause this time.

"She wasn't around at ours last night."

"What do you mean she wasn't round at yours last night?"

"Err ... she asked me to say she was in case Mairi called."

"For the love of.... I'm a busy man, y'know Caitlyn. I don't have time for children's games."

"I'm sorry."

"Right. Where was she?"

"She was seeing Duncan Macintosh."

Thomas let out a long, exasperated breath and scrawled the name on the pad in front of him. "Right. I dare say Mairi will be having some words with your mum in the not-too-distant future, but that's all for now."

"Yes, Mr Munro. Sorry."

Thomas hit the end call button and scrolled down to the Macintoshes' number on his mobile. "David, it's Thomas. Can I speak to Duncan, please?"

"About what?"

"Apparently, he and Ellie McBride met up last night and Ellie never made it home."

"Oh, Jesus. He hasn't woken up yet, but I'll give you good odds on who'll be next to him when I open his door.

What the hell's wrong with these youngsters? We were never like this."

"It's a different world, David. They're all in a race to grow up now."

"You've got that right."

"Aye." Thomas's daughter, Tara, seemed older than her years, but she was a good girl, nothing like Ellie, and he hoped she never would be. He pulled the phone away from his ear while David banged loudly on a door.

"Duncan. If you've got anyone in there with you, make sure they're covered up, I'm coming in." There was a pause of a few seconds before he spoke again. "Thomas, nobody's here. Duncan's bed hasn't been slept in."

"What? When did you last see him?"

"About eight last night."

"Right. Leave it with me. As soon as I've got any news for you, I'll be in touch." He hung up and looked at his father. "This gets curiouser and curiouser. He didn't make it home either."

If this had happened a few years before, the warning bells would have been ringing, but that particular nightmare had come to an end. "What are you thinking?"

"I'm thinking they're both probably passed out drunk somewhere."

"They're little more than bairns."

"They're sixteen years old, Dad, and let me tell you. Sixteen-year-olds now are different to sixteen-year-olds when you were growing up." He picked up the phone once more and hit the speed dial. "Caitlyn, it's me again. Where do you lot go these days?"

"What do you mean, Mr Munro?"

"Look. I'm not playing games. I'm not wanting to get you or anyone else into trouble. I'm not wanting to do anything but find Ellie and Duncan right now."

"Duncan's missing too?"

"Yes. Now tell me. Where do you go if you want to spend some time together these days?"

"I … err … I…."

"Listen to me, Caitlyn. You might think you're protecting your friend, but you're not. Something could have happened. They could have gone for a late-night walk and slipped into a bog or off a cliff into the sea. Now, is that really worth your precious secrets?"

Caitlyn took a sharp intake of breath as these terrifying scenarios flooded her head. "The Norse mill," she said.

"What?"

"That's where we go, sometimes. The Norse mill."

"Right." He hung up the phone, too irritable to say goodbye.

"The Norse mill," he said, looking at his father.

"Ach, it's nice to know that lottery money was put to good use." The Norse mill was a tourist attraction on the island. It had been little more than two big piles of stones before they'd received the grant to restore it. Now the pair of buildings had been fully renovated, thatched roofs and all.

"Fancy a ride out?" Thomas regretted asking the question as soon as it had left his lips. He loved his father, but there was a part of him he hated too. He hated the secrets. He hated the way he put the island and their supposedly godly way of life before everything. William and the other elders stopped this place from moving with the times. They had made it so all the young people couldn't wait to escape when they were old enough. They were the reason his Tara would go across to the mainland at eighteen and probably never set foot back on Cora again. The old ways were dead, but William and the other elders still held enough influence and power to keep them on life support and make sure others had to live to their will. Thomas was trapped between being a good man and a good son, and it was a battle that constantly raged within him.

"May as well. If both of us go, it'll certainly put a scare up them if nothing else."

"Wasting my time like this, I fully intend to give them a good scare."

3

Charlie and Luna ran ahead as they reached the boundary of their property, where it joined the forest. It was the first time any of them had ventured this far, and they were all eager to discover what bordered their new home. The twins were in all the advanced groups at school and their minds were like sponges.

They had been to the bay a couple of times and both were fascinated by the wide array of unusual birds down there. Up until two days ago, they had never seen an oyster catcher, or an Arctic tern, but now they had seen dozens.

They had bombed their Instagram feeds with pictures, and although their former school friends had enthusiastically liked the first few photos, by the time they reached double digits, interest had waned somewhat.

"They get that nerd thing from you, y'know," Seb said as he looked across at his wife.

Summer wore a bobble hat and scarf, and all that he could see of her face was from the bridge of her nose up to her forehead, but he could tell she was smiling. "I'll gladly take responsibility for their intelligence and inquisitive nature. They definitely got those things from me."

He took hold of her hand as they walked along. "What did they get from me then?"

Summer shrugged. "Sporting ability, probably."

"Neither of them can so much as kick or catch a ball without falling over or injuring themselves."

"There we go then."

"And we laughed and laughed and laughed."

"Hey. Don't go too far ahead, you two. They don't have a Search and Rescue chopper based on the island." The twins looked back but then forged ahead regardless, disappearing into the trees.

"They get that from you as well."

"What?"

"Pig-headedness. Impulsiveness. Refusal to obey figures of authority."

"I don't refuse to obey figures of authority."

"You refuse to obey me."

"You're hardly a figure of authority."

"I'm your husband."

"Exactly."

They continued for fifteen minutes or so, heading deeper and deeper into the woods. With each step Summer took the smile broadened on her face. Her life was normally like a whirlwind, but this was the opposite of that. This was calm. This was peace. This was perfect.

"MUM! DAD! LOOK AT THIS!" Charlie shouted at the top of his voice, breaking her quiet reverie.

Summer and Seb finally reached their children and looked down into the vast, steep crater that lay in front of them. "Let's all move back from here," Seb said.

"Do you think it was a meteor or something?" Luna asked.

"Yep. They definitely got their intelligence from you," Seb muttered before turning to his children. "No,

Luna. This is a sinkhole, which is why I want you to move back from the edge."

"It looks like it's just happened," Summer said.

"I told you the rain was mental the other night."

They all looked down into the pit. There was a murky pool at the bottom, and a few trees had collapsed into the large crater. At the base of one of the banks was a wide-open hole measuring about two by three metres and a small ledge in front of it. Darkness lay beyond. "Do you think that's a cave or something?" Charlie asked.

"I have no idea and even less interest in finding out," Seb replied.

"We could get down there easy."

"I told you we should have let the doctors put them on a brain damage watch list. And now look. It's too late."

"What's that smell?" Luna asked.

Up until that moment, none of the others had noticed it, but now, as they breathed in, it was impossible to ignore. "Phwoar. Have you let off?" Charlie asked, and Luna took a swipe at him jokingly.

"That's gross. It's coming from down there. Do you think it could be a sewer or something?" She looked towards her parents.

"Yes, Luna. They built a sewer in the middle of a forest where nobody lives," Seb replied.

"Well, what is it then? It honks."

"I don't know."

Summer already had her scarf over her mouth and nose, but now she put her hand up as well. "I don't care what it is. Something that smells that bad can't be good for us, so how about we just carry on with our hike?"

"Good idea," Seb replied, placing a hand on the shoulders of his children and guiding them away.

It wasn't long before they were running ahead again. "Be careful," Summer shouted after them. "If there are any more holes like that, your dad and I aren't going to fish you out."

Seb reached out and took his wife's hand. "This is nice."

"You have no idea how long I've been looking forward to this. When I was doing those interviews and photo shoots, all I was thinking about was being here with you guys."

"Love you."

"Love you too."

They carried on walking for a while before Summer spoke again. "Did we do the right thing? Should we have uprooted them and dragged them so far away from all their family and friends?"

"Let's face it. They didn't really have any friends, and our family couldn't wait to see the back of them."

Summer laughed. "Seriously."

"Look. In London, you couldn't breathe in a lungful of air without coughing your guts up. The classrooms were overcrowded and crime was going through the roof. I mean, Jesus, there was a stabbing in their school, for Christ's sake, and after what happened with…." His words trailed off. They had vowed not to talk about what had happened with Luna in case they tempted fate.

"I know, but—"

"You can't feel guilty for this. It's the best thing. A few years and they'll be sodding off to uni or prison or something. Whatever they choose, they won't be our responsibility anymore. But right now, I like the idea of them being in a small school with small class numbers. I like the idea that they can stay out after dark and you don't have to worry about some sicko waiting to pounce. I like the idea that they can be kids."

They carried on walking for a few more seconds. "They're a whisker from not being kids anymore, but I suppose you're right."

"Of course I'm right. Listen," he said, squeezing her hand a little tighter. "I know I joke around a lot, but I was always worried down there. I don't feel like that up here.

Those two are among my top fifty people in this world, and I'd be quite upset if anything happened to them. Remember when I lost my favourite pair of gloves last year? Well, multiply that by two. Up here, we'll never need to worry about the kinds of things we did down there."

Summer smiled and nodded. "And I suppose it will do them a lot of good being around nature like this."

"Course it will. They barely got any exercise down there. We could make these walks a regular family thing." Summer suddenly beamed. "What?"

"I like the idea of us having a regular family thing."

"We can have lots of regular family things up here. And we can have lots of regular you and me things up here too." He brought her gloved hand up to his mouth and kissed it.

"MUM! DAD!" Luna shouted.

Seb let out a long sigh. "Or, alternatively, we could just abandon them both in the woods and let them live wild."

"Let's put a pin in that idea." The pair of them caught up to their children and were about to ask why Luna had shouted for them when they both stopped dead. "Whoa."

"Err…. Whoa!" Seb echoed.

"What are they, Dad?" Charlie asked.

Dozens of identical stick sculptures hung from the trees. "I've got no idea," Seb replied. Summer grabbed her phone and started taking photos. "What are you doing?"

"What does it look like? I'm taking photos."

"Course you are. What else would you do when you run into a load of weird symbols scattered around a forest?"

"Hey Mum, there are more over here," Charlie cried, also taking snaps now.

"What are these things?" Summer mumbled, not expecting to get a response.

"They're Celtic symbols to ward off evil spirits," Luna replied.

"How do you know that?"

"Harry Pine's blog."

"Who the hell is Harry Pine?" Seb asked.

"He's a blogger."

"I'm not averse to beating children. Let me just make that clear."

Luna giggled. "He's a travel blogger. I follow his blog and watch a lot of his videos. He's so fit," she said, showing Summer her phone.

"Whoa," Summer said again.

"Err ... hello," Seb said.

"He came to Cora last year and he wrote about these." She scanned through the text before Summer took the phone from her daughter and started reading for herself.

"It says that they encircle an entire area. It says there was a witch burnt here in the late seventeen hundreds and these protective symbols are to make sure her vengeful spirit never escapes."

"Uh-huh," Seb replied, reaching up and plucking one of the symbols from a low-hanging branch.

"Dad, don't touch it," Luna pleaded.

"I'm telling you now. No way has this been here since the eighteenth century." He walked across to where Summer was standing and pointed to the modern-looking string.

"Maybe they replace them every so often. Keep it fresh for tourists," Summer said.

Seb shrugged. "Possible. It is a pretty good story, I suppose."

"It's a great story."

"Harry Pine says—" Seb placed a hand on his daughter's shoulder.

"Harry Pine is a grown man and twelve-year-old girls ... no, scratch that. My twelve-year-old girl should not be talking about how hot he or anyone is."

"Are you my dad or my grandad?" Luna asked, and Summer burst out laughing.

"What?" Seb replied disbelievingly. "What did you just say?" Luna grabbed her phone from her mother and walked away while Summer continued to chuckle. "I'm glad you find all this funny. Today, she's drooling over grown men; tomorrow, she'll be pregnant."

"Oh, my God. You do sound like a grandad."

"Hey. She's my little girl."

"Kids grow up much faster these days." Summer reached out and grabbed his hand again. "If you thought bringing her up here would stop her from being interested in boys until she was eighteen, I think you're going to be disappointed."

"I suppose I could put bars on her windows and lock the doors."

"That's the spirit. Never give up." She leaned across and gave him a kiss. "Come on. This hike is really starting to get interesting."

*

Thomas brought the car to a stop in the small car park. "I'm telling you now," William began. "If they've caused any damage, their parents are paying for it. Five years we waited for that funding to come through. Then it took another year to put the team together who could actually build the thing."

"No arguments here, Dad," Thomas replied, climbing out of the car. They both walked over to the swing gate and passed through, making sure it was firmly closed behind them. The area beyond was common grazing ground, and although neither of them had knowledge of it being in use at the moment, it didn't mean that someone hadn't moved a few sheep there in the last few days.

They followed the gravel footpath up the hill, and Thomas slowed a little to make sure his father could keep up. William was a proud and stubborn man, and although there was no way he could avoid ageing, he did everything he could to keep any difficulties a secret, even from his own family. He never let his guard down, not even with his son.

They finally reached the peak and looked down the slope towards the two thatched buildings and the small river that ran into the bay below.

"Well. From a distance, it all looks fine."

They carried on, heading through another swing gate. "Ellie? Duncan? I hope you're both decent," Thomas called out, and William chuckled a little. There was no response as they approached the mill. "Ellie? Duncan?"

Both men flicked on their torches and stepped inside the first small stone building. Their hearts sank a little to see graffiti spray-painted on the walls. "The little bastards," William hissed. "They've got no idea what work went into this." They headed back out and across to the other hut. "Have you any idea what was involved in getting these build—" He stopped as he stepped inside and shone his torch around. He had felt sure that they would find both youngsters there, but, instead, they found nothing.

Thomas panned the beam up and down and from side to side, looking for any clues. He headed back out and into the other hut. William followed him and watched his son as he circumnavigated the large stone pit in the middle of the floor and reached out, tentatively touching the paint. First, he gently pressed at it with his fingers; then he mashed his palm against the wall and brought it away again, angling the beam towards his hand. "It's bone dry." He examined the graffiti a little harder and noticed it was duller in places. "This could have been done a while back for all we know. When was the last time you were here?"

"Early summer, probably." The locals had rarely visited the place after the opening ceremony, and although William was sure the wall art hadn't been there when he was last here, there was no accurate way to date it.

Thomas scratched his chin for a few seconds then headed back outside. He flicked off his torch and turned slowly, looking for any signs of life beyond the swaying grass. "I wonder how serious the two of them are," Thomas mused.

"Why?"

He shook his head. "Just thinking out loud, Dad."

"You don't suppose they've skipped, do you?"

It wasn't unheard of. Six years before, two teenagers had left the island in search of adventure in Glasgow. They were found by the police two weeks later. Apparently, one of the reasons they'd gone was because the girl was pregnant and they were both too scared to tell their parents. They and their families only remained on the island briefly after that before moving to the mainland.

"I mean she does have a bit of a reputation does Ellie."

"That's putting it politely."

"And David isn't the most understanding of people. If his son came to him and said that he was about to become a grandad, I'm not sure he'd take it too well."

"So, what now?"

"Now I put a call in to Feathers," Thomas replied.

Even though most tickets were bought online rather than at the ticket desk these days, no person or vehicle could get on board the small island ferry without Feathers knowing about it.

"You do realise, if you ask him about this, it will be around the island before you've hung up the phone."

"There is that, I suppose." He plucked out his mobile and hit the call button.

"Hello?" It was Caitlyn again.

"Tell me. Other than the mill, where else might they have gone?"

"Err … in summer, a few people would go to the bothy on the ridge."

"Can you think of anywhere else?"

"Err … no."

"Tell me, Caitlyn, how serious were Ellie and Duncan?"

There was a pause before she answered. "They'd seen each other a few times."

Thomas breathed out a heavy sigh. "Okay," he said before hanging up.

"We've got one place left to try. The bothy on the ridge."

"People still go there?"

"Teenagers, apparently."

Cora was a small island with a small population, and although bothies were commonplace in many parts of the highlands and islands, there was just one still standing on Cora. It had fallen into a state of disrepair some time back, and it was never high on the council's list of priorities, but there were repeated suggestions over the years to restore it.

"It's worth a punt, I suppose."

"If there's no sign of them there, though, I'm really going to have to call Feathers."

4

Seb looked across at Summer and his heart warmed a little as he saw the broad smile engrained on her face. They had been walking in the woods for just over three-quarters of an hour, and even at this time of year, there was much to see. It didn't matter that many of the trees had lost their leaves or that the ground was still waterlogged in places thanks to the torrential rain from a couple of nights before. What mattered was they were together as a family. They were out of the city, away from the hubbub, away from traffic jams and honking horns and road rage. They were exploring their new home.

A shriek of laughter rang through the woods from up ahead. They'd lost sight of Charlie and Luna again, but it didn't matter. In London, if they weren't able to lay eyes on them for more than ten seconds, they would both start panicking, but up here, there was nothing to worry about.

Yes, some of the locals would probably take a little getting used to, but Seb had met a small handful, and they had been fine. Different but fine.

"We did the right thing, didn't we?" Summer said less as a question and more as a statement this time.

"Yeah."

"The world's a lot smaller. Ever since COVID, most people prefer to do stuff over Zoom now anyway. It's easier to live and work in a place like this."

"Are you trying to convince yourself or me?"

"Both, I suppose."

"You don't need to convince me. You're a writer, Summer. That's your job and that's what you do. As long as you've got a laptop, you can do your job. I know I'm oversimplifying, and there's a lot more to it, but it's not like you're a builder or a shop worker or a bus conductor. What you do isn't dependent on showing up to a certain place every day. You can literally do it from anywhere in the world. We've got a phone line at home; you've got a mobile; there's email, messenger and a thousand ways to keep in touch with anyone you want. Occasionally, you might have to travel, but most of the time, you'll be here with us. I mean you had to travel even when we lived down in London, so the only difference is that it will take you a bit longer to get home."

"Yeah. You're right. And what a home, huh?"

"When it's finished, it's going to be amazing."

"I can't believe you're letting me build the pool house," she said, chuckling.

"Letting you? Summer, you're the one earning all the money. You can have whatever you want."

She let out a long sigh. "I'm not getting into this argument again."

"You know what I mean."

"No. I'm not having it, Seb. Every penny I earn is as much down to you as it is to me. More so, even."

"That's not—"

"You kept us all clothed and fed while I was writing *Forest in the Sky*. That trilogy took nearly four years, and you held it together doing jobs you detested. Every day you'd come home from work exhausted, and I could tell you hated every minute. I could tell you were working for dickheads, and you wanted to tell them what you really thought, but you stuck it out for me … for the kids."

"That's not true. It was just for you. I'd quite happily have sold the kids. I've been very clear on this matter."

Summer laughed. "You always try to make me laugh to change the subject. But you know I'm right. Everything we have is down to us, not me. And y'know, this place is spectacular. When the kids go back to school in January, and the house is done, then maybe it's time for you to pick up your camera again."

Seb had scratched out a small income as a freelance photo journalist many years before. He had sacrificed any ambitions of taking it further when his responsibilities as a husband and then a father took hold, but he couldn't deny that holding a camera in his hands gave him a buzz. "Maybe," he said distantly.

"Maybe nothing. We came here for a better quality of life, and that means for all of us."

"I've seen some amazing shots of the Northern Lights that have been taken from here."

Summer squeezed his hand. "There you go then. That's reason enough to pick up your camera right there. We can have a family campout at the beach. It'll be fun."

"Again, with the kids. Can't we just tie them up in the garden with a bowl of water or something and just you and I go instead?"

"Sure. Why not?"

"Seriously, though. It'll be cool."

For the first time in a long time, Summer saw happiness on her husband's face that wasn't governed by their relationship or the family. He was thinking about himself, of something he could do, of a future where he could achieve his own goals and ambitions. "I love this. I love that you're starting to think about this. You could have one of the bedrooms as your darkroom or whatever."

"Darkroom? It's all digital these days, Grandma."

"Okay, smart arse. Your studio then. You know what I mean."

"MUM! DAD!" Charlie shouted excitedly from up ahead somewhere.

Seb and Summer rolled their eyes but nonetheless sped up a little to see what this fresh commotion was all about. "What is it, Charlie?" Summer asked as they reached him.

"What do you think this is?" He held out his hand and both adults just stared at the object in his palm.

"Err … I don't know," Seb replied, reaching out and taking it. He held it up between him and Summer, and both of them looked at it carefully.

"Is it a bear claw?" Luna asked.

"Yes, Luna, it's a bear claw because all the forests in the Inner Hebrides are just swarming with bears."

"What is it then?"

Seb and Summer cast each other a confused look. It did look like a claw. It was black and hollow inside, almost as if it had been shed. Seb slid his middle finger into it, but the curled, razor-sharp tip still extended another three centimetres beyond his own nail.

"Do deer have claws?" Charlie asked.

"I'm begging you, never come out with anything that stupid in school. We'll have the social services at the house in no time. They'll think we're making you sniff glue or drink lead paint or something."

"Seb. Behave," Summer said, placing a hand on Charlie's shoulder.

"Whatever it is, it looks old and weathered, like it's been here for a long time. Where did you find it?"

"By the base of that tree," he replied, pointing to a magnificent oak standing in the middle of a clearing.

"So, what is it, Dad?" Luna asked again.

Seb continued to turn it from side to side, examining it. "I know," Summer said, snatching it from her husband.

"Okay, Professor. We're waiting," Seb replied.

"It's a horn."

"A horn?"

"Yeah. Like the end of a goat horn or something."

It really, really looks like a claw. "I suppose it could be," Seb replied.

"Granted, it's seen better days, but I bet you that's what it is."

"Weird colouring for a horn, isn't it?"

"I don't know. How many goat horns have you seen up close?"

"You make a fair point. Do they have goats on the island?"

"This has been a crofting community for generations. I dare say they've had lots of things on this island, and I think whatever this belonged to is probably long gone now, poor little thing."

Seb looked at it again then looked at his children. "I think your mum's probably right. Ockham's razor and all that."

"What's that?" Luna asked.

"It means that the simplest explanation is usually the right one. We should have known your mum would have come up with the simplest explanation." The two children laughed, and Summer pushed Seb.

"Yeah, well. At least I came up with a reason. You didn't come up with anything, so what does that say about you?"

"Better to remain silent and be thought a fool than speak and remove all doubt."

"What does that mean?" Charlie asked.

"Don't worry about it, Son, but thanks for illustrating the point."

Summer pushed Seb again. "Stop being horrible to our children," she said, laughing, then leaned forward and kissed them both on the head. "Don't listen to your father. He's only like this because you prefer me to him."

"It's true," Luna said, looking towards Seb. "We do."

They all laughed this time before Charlie and Luna ran off again. "Little bastards," Seb muttered under his breath.

"Aww. Don't worry, darling, it's not just our kids. Everybody prefers me to you."

"Funny girl," he replied, pulling her close and kissing her before the pair continued hand in hand.

*

Thomas pulled the handbrake on and turned off the engine. They were parked in a passing place, which was a definite no as far as the island code went, but he was on official business or as official as an unpaid trainee special constable's business could be.

"They'll have had to walk some to get here," William said.

"Aye." Thomas looked at his watch. "It's twenty to eleven. I'd have thought they'd have shown up by now." He opened the door, and his father climbed out from the other side.

"We've got weather coming," William said, looking towards the dark grey clouds."

"Aye. Who knows, we might be having ourselves a white Christmas after all."

"Let's just hope it holds off long enough for us to be back in the warmth."

Thomas opened the boot and pulled out a pair of hiking sticks. "Here you go, Dad." He handed them to his father.

A proud smile crept onto William's face. His son always thought of others before himself. "Thank you."

The bothy was in view, but it would take them a while to make the walk. They would have to cross an expansive and boggy moor, hence the hiking poles. "I used to make this journey all the time when I was younger," William said as they began on the ill-defined footpath leading onto the moor.

"I dare say. I also dare say that was back when the ferry just ran once a week and catching a salmon in the river meant you could have something on the menu other than mince, tatties and neeps."

A fond smile crept onto William's face as he reminisced. "Aye. We spent many a morning and afternoon in that bothy warming ourselves up or sheltering from the rain until the clouds passed." The smile vanished as he remembered back to why they were there now. "I dread to think what condition we're going to find it in now."

"Times change, Dad. Kids aren't interested in fishing or hiking anymore. They're interested in their Instagram accounts and YouTube and their Snapchats."

William shook his head sadly. "I don't know what's wrong with the world these days."

Thomas pulled his mobile from his pocket. This was a notoriously bad area for getting a phone signal, and it didn't disappoint now. "Dammit. Have you got a signal?" he asked, looking at his father.

William pulled his phone out of his pocket. "No."

"I just wanted to tell Isobel that she'd be by herself for another half hour or so."

"We'll be back before then," William replied, suddenly forcing himself to take bigger strides.

"I don't want you overdoing it."

"You don't worry about me. I was making this journey long before you were born."

"You're a stubborn old so-and-so. Y'know that?"

A wry smile crept onto William's face. "If I wasn't, you wouldn't be here now, and your mother would be married to Angus MacMillan and living in Toronto."

"Well, it's a good job you are then, isn't it?"

The pair travelled side by side where the footpath allowed. In some places, it disintegrated away to nothing and William used the hiking poles to feel out a way through. Every local understood what this terrain was like. One wrong step and they could be swallowed by the moor. The thick, sludgy peat would absorb them, and they would endure the most torturous of deaths as the black soupy runoff filled their mouths, then their lungs.

By the time the pair of them had reached the bothy, a thin sheen of sweat sparkled on William's head despite the chill in the air. The paint on the blue, slatted door had chipped away to nothing in places. There was a triangle missing from the small, cruddy window, and it had been stuffed with wood, dried grass and mud. It was a patch-up that would have brought shame on any man on Cora, which immediately led the pair of them to believe that it was youngsters who had done it.

It was not pretty, and it was not that efficient, but it would block out more wind and rain than not. "Even at sixteen, I'd have been embarrassed to do something like that," William said, and his son laughed.

"Duncan! Ellie!" he called out as they came to a stop outside the door. There was no response. "Duncan! Ellie!"

At that moment, the first fluttering of snow began, and both men instinctively turned up their collars. The moor was not a good place to be in a snowstorm, and although the clouds above them seemed light enough, the ones coming their way looked full. Thomas opened the door and stepped inside. For a moment, he couldn't believe what he was seeing, and a chill far colder than that of the morning air ran down his spine.

He was joined a second later by William, and the normally stoic head councilman let out a gasp of horror. "Oh, dear God."

*

After that fateful night, things started to get a little better for Murdo. He had managed to lay some of the ghosts that had haunted him since the disappearance of his wife to rest.

It had taken him more time than most to accept that the reign of the thing they had referred to as the Night Demon had come to an end. Even after he had visited the site of the explosion and Thomas and the others had talked him through step by step everything that had happened, he had not fully come to terms with it.

But gradually, time played a role in convincing him. Days became weeks, and weeks became months, and there were no reports of any animals or people going missing. There were no strange bumps in the night. Rebecca and the rest of the sheep didn't let out any more warning cries. It was over. The dark cloud that had hung over the residents of Cora for so long had finally given way to the sun and better times.

Murdo was jarred from his thoughts as the kettle suddenly started whistling. He grabbed a tea towel and removed it from the range, pouring the boiling water into a waiting cup. He stood there for a moment as the teabag steeped, then finally removed it before heaping in two sugars and adding a drop of milk.

He took a sip and winced a little. He always had his tea strong and sweet, and this cup didn't disappoint. He walked across to the window by the door and looked out. Snow was just beginning to fall, and a thin smile cracked on his face. Two years before, he'd sold off his tractor and most of his equipment, and now the barn where they were once stored was where Rebecca and the rest of his flock holed up in bad weather. He had lured them all in there with a bucket of feed earlier on, feeling in his bones that the snow was on its way. After sixty-seven years as an islander, he could read the seasons and the days as well as anyone.

He had put plenty of hay down for them, and even though Murdo knew Hebridean sheep were one of the hardiest creatures in existence, the soft part of him still associated Rebecca closely with his wife, and so he had a drive to take care of them as well as he could. It was mad, really, and he knew a lot of the locals thought he'd gone off his rocker, but he didn't care.

Rebecca was an old lady now, and although a few of her friends had succumbed to age in the past couple of years, she was still going strong and keeping him strong too. He would often find himself talking to her.

Mary wouldn't have liked this weather too much, would she, old girl? Did I tell you about the time Mary and I went to Aberdeen? He would strike up one-sided conversations with the sheep just so he could talk about his late wife out loud, just so he could hear himself say her name without feeling like he was going mad.

It wasn't as if there was anyone else to talk to. If he didn't go into the village, he could sometimes go a whole week or even two without seeing another soul. He sipped his tea and was about to return to the roaring fire when he stopped dead.

In the few minutes he'd been standing there, the snow had got heavier and was already settling in the yard out front. But that's not what had caught his eye. He squinted a little as he focused on the trees beyond the field where Rebecca and the others spent much of their time. A single figure had emerged from the woods and now stood there staring towards the house. A shiver ran down Murdo's back. *Oh, Mary, Mary, Mary. I'm seeing things now.*

5

Thomas and William could do nothing but just stand there for a moment. The snow was already drifting into the small bothy, and good sense would have deemed that they shut the door, but good sense, or indeed any sense, escaped them as their eyes tried to process what they were seeing.

"It's alright, Ellie," Thomas said, eventually guiding his father through the entrance and finally shutting the door behind them. "It's alright," he said again but not believing the words any more the second time around either.

The teenager was huddled in a corner. Her arms were wrapped around her knees, and she swayed back and forth slowly like an old woman in an off-kilter rocking chair who had lost her mind. Her eyes were wide and staring. The mascara that had once adorned her lashes now lined her cheeks in black streams. Her shirt had been torn, revealing a ripped bra too, and fiery red welts on her upper arm told the men everything they needed to know about what had happened.

"Ellie. Ellie!" William said, but still there was no response. The breeze whistled in through the makeshift repair in the window, and the gentle tap of the snowflakes began to drum an irregular but more frequent beat.

"Ellie!" Thomas said again, taking a step towards her. He would have asked where Duncan was, but that could have made things even worse. It was as plain as day to anyone to see what had gone on here. Duncan had wanted more than Ellie was willing to offer and…. Two men were probably not the best people to press the girl for an explanation, so they would get her back. They would get her back to her mother and the warmth, and then they would find out. Thomas slipped off his coat and stepped a little closer. He eased it over her shoulders, but still, she just rocked back and forth. "Ellie, there's snow coming in. We're going to have to get out of here. Do you understand me?"

There was no look of comprehension on the girl's face. There was only a distant madness. "Thomas, come here a second, will you?" William stepped outside and his son followed him. "You need to be careful. If she's been out here all night, she could be suffering from hypothermia. Any sudden shocks to the system could trigger a heart attack."

Thomas lifted his face as the snow continued. "If we don't get her out of here, how do you think that's going to work out? If she doesn't have hypothermia now, she soon will."

William's face contorted a little as he cast his eyes across the moor. Visibility was already reducing, and he knew only too well that his son was right. Delaying their exit any further wouldn't just be bad for Ellie but for all of them. They returned inside. "Ellie! Ellie!" No matter who spoke, no matter how loud or how quiet they were or what they said, it made no difference. She just continued to rock and stare. William let out a long sigh then reached out and gently took hold of her arm.

Ellie immediately recoiled, releasing a nightmarish, deafening nasal howl. She shuffled back into the corner as fresh tears appeared in her eyes. The unnerving sound continued, and William stood looking to his son for guidance.

Thomas just shrugged. He'd not dealt with anything like this before. In fact, he was pretty certain that nothing like this had ever happened on the island before. *That little bastard Duncan's going to pay for this. This isn't Glasgow or Birmingham or London, it's the Isle of Cora. It's one of the safest places to live in the UK.* He looked again at the screaming girl in the corner. She had always been a force of nature and, in actual fact, a real troublemaker too, but now she had been reduced to little more than a terrified child. *What the hell did you do, Duncan?*

*

Porridge let out a grumpy meow as Murdo opened the kitchen door letting in a waft of frozen air. He'd put his thick coat, gloves and hat on. There was a time when he'd have gone out in this weather with just a jersey, but now the cold would stick to him like treacle if he didn't wrap up warm.

Since leaving the house, three more figures had joined the first. *It's a family, but what the bloody hell are they doing on my land and in this weather too?* The snow was getting heavier by the second. He opened the gate and started across the field.

*

"I think we might have ventured onto someone's property," Summer said as they all watched the approaching figure.

"Here we go," Seb replied. "Don't make eye contact, kids, and if he says you've got purty lips, make a run for it. Your mother and I will meet you back at home. The one who makes it gets all the others' stuff."

Both children laughed as Summer slapped her husband on the arm. "Behave. This is the closest thing we've got to a neighbour … probably. And since you got us lost, we're probably going to ask him for directions."

"We do not need to ask anyone for directions."

"Says the man who can lose his way walking in a straight line."

"I know exactly where we are."

"Where are we then?"

"On the other side of the forest."

"Uh-huh. And where's our house in relation to here exactly?"

"Over there, somewhere," he replied, waving his hand in a vague direction to their left.

"Through the blizzard, you mean?"

"It's hardly a blizzard. It's just a fluttering."

"Hi," Summer said, waving and breaking away from her family on a full-scale charm offensive.

"Err ... hello," Murdo replied, taken aback a little.

"I think we got all turned around in the forest," she said, walking up to the fence.

"Oh." The snow was coming down harder now. "You've picked a heck of a time to take a holiday up here."

Summer smiled. "We're not on holiday. I think we might be your new neighbours."

Murdo looked confused for a moment. "You're the ones who bought Smith's old place?"

"That's right."

"Och, you've got your work cut out over there." He'd heard mutterings from the folks in the village about the team of builders, joiners, plumbers and electricians they'd brought in to get the place ready for the arrival of the big shot author and her family.

"Well, it's all coming together slowly. Starting to feel like a home though."

Murdo looked towards the two children. "And what are you doing out here on a day like today?"

Summer looked up at the sky. "We kind of got caught in it. We thought the snow was coming later."

Murdo smiled. "You'll get used to it up here. One minute it can be bright sunshine, the next, it can be howling gales." He looked at the clouds. "It's heavy, but it won't last."

"Um … this is a little embarrassing, but we've kind of lost our way a little bit. You couldn't point us in the right direction for home, could you?"

Murdo chuckled. "Ach, you'll get used to the forest too." He nodded. "Come back to the house and I'll give you a ride. You don't want to be out in this."

"Oh, we don't want to put you to any trouble."

"It's no trouble."

They followed the fence along to a gate, which Murdo opened up, and the Richards family filed through one by one. They trekked across the field as the snow continued to fall. An Audi A3 was parked at the side of the house, and Murdo told them to get in while he retrieved his keys.

"Well. This is very nice of him, isn't it?" Summer said, turning around to look at her family in the back seat.

"I suppose. We could have been home in no time though. I knew exactly where we were."

"Uh-huh. You keep telling yourself that, Magellan."

Murdo joined them, and by the time he started the engine the snow had got heavier still. "I hope you've got candles and a real fire," he said.

"Why?"

"You'll find we get a lot of power cuts on the island in winter. Doesn't take much. Wind, snow, rain, they all take a toll."

"The power was off for about an hour the other evening. I thought it was our workmen who'd messed something up; then it came back on again."

Murdo nodded as he waited for the windscreen to clear. "The night of the downpour? Yes, mine was off too. You'll get used to it."

"I'm not sure that's something I want to get used to."

Murdo chuckled. "Don't have much of a choice. The entire network needs modernising, but it's hard to justify with so few people on the island. Two years ago, during a snowstorm, we were without power for three days."

"That's something to look forward to."

"Like I say, make sure you've got plenty of candles. You'll get used to the way things work up here."

"Reason four hundred and six for staying in London," Charlie said.

Murdo leaned up and looked into the rearview mirror to see him. He let out a warm laugh. "Forgive me. I've not actually introduced myself. My name's Murdo. And who might you be?"

"I'm Charlie, and this is my twin sister, Luna."

"Twins, eh?"

"Yeah," Seb replied. "We haven't actually figured out which is the evil one yet. It seems to alternate on a daily basis. I'm Seb and this is—"

"Summer," Murdo interrupted. "You're quite the hot topic on the island. We once had Tom Jones visit a few years ago, but we've never had a celebrity living on the island."

"I'm hardly a celebrity," Summer said, more than a little embarrassed.

Murdo chuckled again. "Well, you're more of a celebrity than anyone else we've got living here, so enjoy it." He checked the rearview mirror again to make sure the back screen was clearing before ramping up the heater a little further. "Another minute and we'll be able to set off. You always want to make sure you've got full visibility in these conditions."

"So, how long have you lived here?" Summer asked, looking towards the old croft house.

"All my life."

"Wow! I can't even imagine that. I bet the island's seen some changes in that time."

"Not many." Summer turned to look at him to see he was smiling. "Island life is very different to what you've been used to. There's less of a hurry. Things are a lot simpler."

"Simpler's good. Simpler's what we want."

"Yeah," Seb replied. "But ideally, simpler with electricity rather than not."

Murdo looked in the rearview mirror again, this time at Seb. "Who knows, we might get lucky this year. Right then," he said, turning back to the front. "Let's get you home."

*

"It's bloody freezing," Thomas said through gritted teeth as they forged their way back across the moor.

After some screaming and fighting, the two men managed to force Ellie to her feet and get her out of the bothy. They both felt terrible. The girl needed help and probably counselling and possibly even a rape test. She needed all the things they couldn't provide, but at the same time, they knew that her skin already felt icy to the touch, and if she spent any longer out there, she might very well freeze to death. It was like pulling a band-aid off. They had to do it quickly.

Now, though, they were in step. William walked ahead, feeling out the way with his hiking sticks. The snow was settling fast, and it wouldn't be long before their return to the road would be far more hazardous as drifts gathered on the uneven track and covered some of the more treacherous sections.

"WAAHH!" William cried out, disappearing from view.

"DAD!" Thomas had been forcing Ellie forward one pace at a time, and after their initial fracas, she was allowing him to in the main. She occasionally stopped and just stood there for a moment staring into the distance. Her eyes looked like they could erupt with fresh tears at any moment, but on the whole, they had been making progress. Now, though, she froze, glaring towards the empty space that had been occupied by William just a second before. A terrifying animalistic cry began in the back of her throat. She shrieked, and it echoed across the wide-open moor.

Thomas was more than a little concerned about Ellie, but he couldn't afford to think about her now as he ran down the embankment where his father had vanished just a second before.

His heart raced. *Where the hell are you, Dad?* It seemed impossible, but he knew on this island, on these moors, the impossible was always possible.

"Huuuaaahh!" A loud intake of breath followed by an equally loud, sloshing sound helped Thomas zero in. His father had rolled into a gulley, completely submerging in the sludgy, peaty runoff from the moor.

"Dad," he cried again while Ellie's scream behind him fell silent. "Are you okay?" he asked, jumping down into the ditch and helping his father up. The water was knee-high and icy cold. As he dragged William to his feet, he started to feel sick in the pit of his stomach. The older man was coated in a concoction that looked like dark brown paint. Thomas reached out, wiping it from his father's eyes and face. It was frigid to the touch. The hiking poles were still strapped around the older man's wrists, and Thomas heaved his father out of the gulley, taking hold of the sharpened sticks and digging them into the ground to give them both a little purchase. "Come on, Dad."

William coughed and spluttered for a moment. "I … I lost my footing."

The snow was still falling heavily, and there was yet some distance to cover before they reached the car and, more importantly, the heater. "It's easy to do with this snow on the ground."

"No. I was meant to be finding a safe path for us." Thomas suddenly felt guilty for all the bad thoughts he'd ever had about his father. At that moment, he seemed to be nothing more than a frail old man.

"Look. Let's not worry about that now, okay? Let's just get you back onto the—OH SHIT!" He glanced in Ellie's direction only to see she was no longer there. "She's heading back to the bloody bothy." Thomas took a tighter hold of his father and both of them scrambled the few feet up the embankment and onto level ground.

"Go. Go," William ordered, leaning forward onto the poles and allowing himself to catch his breath while his son set off at a sprint after Ellie.

This is crazy. This is absolutely crazy. Thomas was even colder now. He could barely feel his feet as he followed the prints in the snow. "Ellie! Ellie, please, we need to get back to the car. Ellie!" *What the hell happened to this girl?*

Suddenly, she disappeared from view as his father had done a moment before. He continued to sprint until he was standing over her. Unlike his father, she hadn't fallen into a ditch; she had merely stumbled and fallen flat on the ground. She was still trying to struggle to her feet when Thomas reached her. He grabbed her as gently as he could, but, like she had before, she struck and swiped and clawed, trying her hardest to get away. She let out another high-pitched nasal scream.

"Ellie. Ellie, stop. We need to get back to the car." Still, her eyes did not focus on him, but eventually the scream abated and he was able to guide her into a rhythm as they began to walk.

"Are you okay, Son?" William asked through chattering teeth.

"I'm okay. What about you?"

"I-I think I need to g-get somewhere warm."

"Okay, Dad. Come on."

The three of them continued, as did the snow. By the time they reached the car, Thomas's hands were shaking as much as his father's. He opened the back door and bundled Ellie in before running around to the passenger side and helping William. "I-I'm sorry, S-Son. Y-your c-car's going to b-be filthy."

"B-bloody hell, Dad. Do you really th-think that matters right n-now?" He closed the door and rushed to the driver's side, skidding and nearly landing on his back before grasping the wing mirror for support. He finally climbed in and turned the key in the ignition. The engine had cooled down in the time it had taken them to recover Ellie. Thomas sat there for a moment, willing the fan to start blowing warm air. He reached out and hit the demister button and flicked on the front and rear wipers before placing both hands under his armpits. He could still hear his father's chattering teeth.

He looked in the mirror to see Ellie staring dead ahead. *It's like she's completely lost her grip on reality.* He leaned forward, pulling a rag from the door pocket and wiping the interior of the windscreen. Beads of condensation trickled down as he moved the cloth from side to side. Even though he didn't like driving with restricted visibility, he liked what was happening in the car far less. At the very least, his father and Ellie could get a bad chill, and he didn't even want to think about the worst-case scenario.

He eased off the handbrake and they pulled away. It was already late morning, and something told Thomas that this was going to be a long, long day.

6

Seb knelt down in front of the fireplace. Almost as if Murdo had prophesied it, when they entered the house, they found that the power had indeed gone out. Despite the warmth from the heater of the car, all four of them had been chilled to the bone on their forest trek, and although the radiators were on low, a real fire would heat them up quicker than anything.

"Here," Summer said, handing Charlie and Luna blankets while her husband got the fire going.

"There's no Wi-Fi," Luna whined.

"Well, there won't be, sweetheart. The power's down, so the hub won't work."

"And there's no signal on the phone."

"It's probably the weather. It's really coming down out there. Maybe the power to the mast has gone down too."

"I can't believe we moved here. This never happened in London."

"Yeah, well. We need to learn to appreciate the things we have got up here, not dwell on the things we haven't."

"This is shit."

"I beg your pardon?"

"It is."

"You have no idea how lucky you are."

"Ha."

"Let me tell you something. Your Dad and I—"

"I know, I know. You lived in rented houses and you didn't have two pennies to rub together," Charlie said, flinging off his blanket and marching out of the room.

"Get back here," Summer growled as her son disappeared down the hallway.

"He's right," Luna said, climbing to her feet too. "I mean what kind of place is it if you can't even get online? It's like living in the Dark Ages or something." She headed to the door, too, and dodged her mother's reaching hand.

"The pair of you—"

"Leave it, Summer," Seb said gently as the flames began to consume the knotted paper.

"I'm not having my children speak to me like that." She started to head for the doorway, and he grabbed her, taking hold of her hand.

"They'll come back soon enough."

"They're given absolutely everything they ask for, Seb."

"I know. You don't have to tell me. You spoil them."

Summer walked over to the sofa and slumped down. "Was this a mistake?"

"Was what a mistake?"

"Coming up here. Taking them away from all their friends, from … civilisation."

Seb went to join her on the sofa and eased his arm around, pulling her closer. "Don't start all this again. Yes, it will be a culture shock to start off with, but they'll get used to it. It's not like we're asking them to live on a desert island and never head back to the mainland. We'll be going over a few times a year. And as far as the leccy goes, we'll get a couple of generators."

"A couple?"

"Yeah. A diesel one and one of those new-fangled solar things."

"New-fangled solar things? You sound like my dad," Summer said, giggling.

"It's bad enough that I've got two smart-mouthed kids. Don't you start too."

They both relaxed back a little on the sofa and stared into the flames as the kindling caught. Summer reached across for the blankets that the children had discarded when they'd stormed out of the room. She pulled one over her and the other over Seb. "They seemed to be enjoying themselves when we were in the forest."

"They were enjoying themselves. They're kids. They've got the attention spans of guppies. They're out of the forest now, and virtually everything they do hinges on them being online. It's not like it'll kill them to be without their phones for a few hours."

"I was really looking forward to coming back home, too. I was really looking forward to going on that walk. I had it all planned in my head. I was really looking forward to just being with my family and I was hoping they were looking forward to being with me."

"Well, I was looking forward to being with you."

Summer leaned her head onto his shoulder. "I meant the kids."

"Thanks."

"You know what I mean. You and I will always look forward to being with each other. We're soulmates. But I was wanting this to be a nice family time where we could all connect in our new home. I wanted to create some special memories and—"

"Whoa, whoa, whoa." He kissed her on top of the head. "Just slow down. It's the first full day you've been back. This is just one hiccup. So, the little bastards kicked the toys out of their pram because the power's down. So what? They'll get over it. And you keep wondering about whether we've done the right thing. There were over a hundred and forty murders in London last year, eighteen thousand reported rapes, over fifty-four thousand burglaries. You know how many there were up here? None. That's how many."

Summer shook her head. "Is that a good enough reason though?"

"That wasn't the only reason, Summer, and you know it. Don't let the little bastards make you start second-guessing all the decisions we made. We went into everything. We did the research." There had been a plethora of reasons they had chosen to move besides the crime rate. COVID had been a big wake-up call, and the threat of something even more virulent taking hold had seized them both in their most paranoid moments.

Summer let out a deep sigh. "You're right. I know you're right."

He kissed her on top of the head again, and as he did, a beep sounded in the hallway as the power came back on. "See. It was just a little outage. We're living in the sticks now. We'll get used to the way things work up here."

"I suppose," she replied, starting to get up.

He pulled her back towards him. "Where do you think you're going? This is cosy, and the fire's just starting to take hold."

"I need to—"

"No. You don't need to do anything. We're taking a break for the next few days. There's nothing we *need* to do. It's been a busy year, and by the sound of it, next year is going to be busier still. Let's just enjoy the little things. Let's just enjoy holding each other and staring into a real fire while the snow continues to fall outside. We moved up here to help us appreciate the simpler things. Let's start appreciating them."

*

When Thomas had pulled up in front of the shop, Mairi had burst out of the door and skidded on the path, nearly falling into the road. Her eyes were red and swollen; it was obvious she had been doing little other than crying since they had left her. A look of joy swept over her face as she peered into the back and saw her daughter. It was only temporary though. As she opened the rear door and saw the lack of response from the traumatised teenager, a thousand horror stories flashed into her mind of what could have happened to her.

"Ellie? Ellie?" Panic was already rising in her voice. "What happened? What happened to my daughter?" she asked as Thomas climbed out of the car. William got out of the passenger side, and when she saw that he was covered in a sludgy peat solution, her tone became even more frantic. "Oh, my God. What happened? What happened?"

"You need to calm down, Mairi," Thomas replied.

"Calm down? Don't tell me to calm down. I need to know what happened to my daughter."

"I-I need to g-go get sorted out," William said.

"Okay, Dad," Thomas said. The snow was still falling, and there was a part of him that felt guilty for not helping his father, not sticking with him and making sure he was alright to get home, but he had other things on his mind. He looked down at his trousers to see that they were almost black up to his knees too.

"Oh, my God. What happened?" Isobel asked as she stepped out of the store and first looked in the direction of her father-in-law as he walked away then at her husband.

"It's a long story."

"Ellie? Ellie," Mairi said again, almost crying. "What's wrong with her? What's wrong with my girl?"

"She's been unresponsive ever since we found her." Thomas turned to his wife. "I need to get changed and put some warm clothes on," he said, looking up towards the grey sky. "Do you think you can help get Ellie out of the car and into the back?"

"I need to get her home," Mairi said, starting to climb into the car.

Thomas grabbed her arm. "Listen to me. We found her at the bothy. We don't know what the hell happened. There was no sign of anyone else. I at least need to try to talk to her. Do you understand me?"

"She's my daughter and—"

"Yes, she's your daughter, but right now, I don't know if I need to get the police across here or what."

Mairi's eyes widened as the implication of what Thomas was talking about finally registered. "Oh, my poor girl."

He eased his grip on Mairi's arm. "Listen. Just help Isobel get her inside while I get out of these soaking clothes. Okay?"

She finally nodded and Thomas left them to go get changed. He took his mobile phone out and scrolled through his contacts as he headed behind the counter and into the back.

"Cora Ferry Terminal," came the voice on the other end of the phone.

"Feathers, it's Thomas."

"Well then. This is an honour. What can I do for you today, Mr Munro?"

"Listen, Thomas. I don't want to hear any of your data protection crap. I need to know if someone got on that ferry this morning. This is serious. Do you understand me?"

If it was that serious, Feathers knew that Thomas would end up calling the police on the mainland and they'd get the information from him anyway. Getting the mainland police involved in island affairs was always the last thing any of them wanted. "Who?" he asked eventually.

"Duncan Macintosh."

There was an even longer pause this time. "What's he done?"

"As far as I know, he hasn't done anything. He's just missing and I need to cover all my bases before I put a call in." Part of it was true, at least. He had plenty of suspicions but no real clue as to what had happened to Ellie. He put the phone on speaker and placed it down on his bedside cabinet while he got out of his cold, wet clothes.

"No. It was a quiet one this morning. No foot passengers at all."

"You're sure?"

"As sure as day."

"Okay. Thanks, Feathers."

"Some weather we're having, isn't—" Thomas hit the end call button. The last thing he wanted was to get into a long, drawn-out conversation with Feathers.

He bundled up his clothes and placed them into the laundry basket. Isobel wouldn't be happy that he'd put items so filthy in there with no pre-washing, but there was no time to waste. He turned on the shower and waited until he saw steam filling the cubicle before jumping in. He shivered a little as the first beads of hot water hit his body.

I hope Dad's okay. Part of him felt guilty for enjoying the luxury of a hot shower, but he needed to get his head together in order to help Ellie and her mother. He looked down as the silty residue from the peat washed away. When he was happy that he wasn't going to get any cleaner, he turned the shower off and stepped out, rubbing himself down vigorously with a towel before getting dressed.

He left the bedroom and walked along the hall to find a cup of hot coffee waiting for him in the living room. Ellie was sitting bolt upright at the far end of the sofa and her mother had an arm wrapped around her. Two mugs sat in front of them on the table.

The bell from the entrance sounded, and Isobel got up and headed into the shop while Thomas sat down on the sofa opposite the mother and daughter.

"She hasn't said a word. What happened? What did he do to her?" Mairi asked.

Thomas looked at her for a moment and then turned to Ellie, who continued to stare straight ahead in a virtual catatonic state. "I'm going to call Jane. She might be able to help."

A doctor came with staff twice a week to the island. The doctor was a former resident, the son of one of the church elders, and he guarded and was responsible for many an island secret. He and his staff would visit those who were immobile in the morning and hold surgeries in the afternoon for any non-urgent problems. If something serious occurred outside of that time, the air ambulance was at hand to chopper patients to Glasgow. It was a rare occurrence, but it had happened. Jane had been called on more occasions than Thomas could remember, but even as he dialled the number, there was a part of him that wondered if he'd be calling for the air ambulance before the end of the day.

Ten minutes later, the retired doctor walked into the general store. The snow was still falling and she had to shake herself off in the entrance before traipsing into the living quarters. Thomas cut her off to have a quiet word before she saw the girl and her mother.

"So, what can you tell me?" she asked. As Mairi had been present when he'd phoned, Thomas had only given her the vaguest of details, but now he could go into a bit more depth.

He gave her a full account of how he and his father had found her and what had happened from there. Jane was an intelligent woman and easily read between the lines. When he was done giving her the rundown, he saw the question in her eyes and beat her to it. "We haven't found Duncan yet. In fact, I'm going to head over to see his mother and father now. If you could give me a call the second you get anything out of her, I'd appreciate it. I can't definitively say what's happened, but I've got a bad feeling that I'll be asking for help from the mainland before the day's out."

Jane sighed sadly. "Let's hope it doesn't come to that."

Thomas looked back towards the entrance to the living room. "Yeah. We can hope, I suppose."

*

Three loud knocks came on the door and Summer and Seb cast each other puzzled looks. As they walked down the hallway, they could hear conversations going on in both their children's rooms. "Normality's been restored at least. They can go back to ignoring us until mealtimes now," Seb said, and Summer laughed.

Seb opened the door to find Murdo standing there with a bottle of wine in his hand. "I completely forgot about this when you were around at ours earlier. I'd got it for when I came across and introduced myself."

"That's so kind," Summer replied. "There was no need, especially coming back around in this weather. Please come in," she said, looking at the sky behind him as the snowy deluge continued.

"Och, well, actually, I can't stop. I came around to see if I could take a wee peek out back."

"Err ... sure, but what for?"

"My cousin's widow. I check in with her once in a while to make sure she's alright. Turns out half a dozen of her sheep have wandered off. She only lives across the way, so I was thinking they might have drifted onto your property."

"Yeah, no problem. I'll come out and give you a hand," Seb said, grabbing his coat and slipping his boots on. "This happens a lot, does it?"

The pair left Summer on the doorstep as they headed across the yard. "Happens on occasion. All it takes is for one of the little ones to shuffle through a gap in the fence. That makes it bigger for the next, and so on. Before you know it, a handful of the little beggars have got loose." Murdo's mind drifted back to when missing sheep meant something else entirely. It had happened to him, to his cousin, and to everyone who kept animals on the island.

He opened the boot of his car and pulled out a bucket half full of sheep feed. He smiled at Seb and gave it a shake. "They respond to that, do they?"

Murdo laughed. "Beats a dozen sheepdogs, it does. You rattle this thing for a few seconds, and if they're in earshot, they'll come running."

The pair continued across the yard, past the stables, paddock and outbuildings and into the wide-open field behind the property. The snow continued to lie heavily, but tufts of longer grass still poked through. They stood there for a few moments surveying the white landscape.

"Probably not the easiest things to see in the snow."

Murdo chuckled. "No, they're not. If they find a patch of grass that isn't covered, they'll just carry on chewing. Before you know it, they'll be covered from head to foot and you won't see them again until it thaws."

It was Seb who laughed this time. "Maybe you should give your bucket a shake and see if any are around." Murdo rattled the pellets, and the two men scoured the field for movement. "Could they have gone into the forest?" he asked, looking towards the trees beyond the field.

"Ach, anything's possible, but sheep go where the grass is good. Chances are they'll be in a field rather than woods."

"Let's hope. We came across a hell of a sinkhole on our walk. I'd hate to think that they wandered out that way."

"A sinkhole?" Murdo turned towards the other man with surprise on his face.

"Yeah. It had taken some trees down with it. Was there ever any mining or anything on the island?"

Murdo shook his head. "Never anything like that."

Seb shrugged. "I'm guessing the torrential rain we had the other night was the straw that broke the camel's back. It was pretty deep."

"Well, I've lived here all my life, and that's the first time I've ever known of a sinkhole on the island. I suppose if you live long enough, you see everything."

"I suppose you do."

The men's eyes swept out over the field once more, and Murdo shook the bucket again. They waited a few more moments. "Ach, well. Doesn't look like they made it out this way. I'll go check out the other side of my cousin's place."

"Let me have your number. I'll give you a call if they show up."

Murdo nodded appreciatively and took out a piece of paper. "I'm an old man and don't have enough space in my head to be remembering numbers."

He showed the piece of paper to his new neighbour, and within a couple of seconds, the number was programmed into Seb's phone. "You be careful out on these roads now, won't you?"

They both looked up at the sky. "It won't last much longer," Murdo said authoritatively.

"How can you tell?"

"You get a feel for the weather when you've lived out here as long as I have. You will too."

"I'll take your word for that."

"Be sure to keep your fire and range stoked. Wouldn't surprise me if we get another power cut. That's usually the way around here."

"Brilliant. The kids'll be over the moon."

Murdo smiled. "They'll get used to it."

"Yeah. I wouldn't put money on that."

"I'd better be getting off. Thanks again."

"It's okay, Murdo." The pair walked back in the direction of the house and Seb waited at the door until Murdo climbed into his vehicle. The engine started and he was about to drive away when Summer came rushing out of the house.

He lowered the window. "Would you like to have dinner with us tonight?" she asked.

Murdo was taken by surprise, as was Seb, who remained a few feet away just looking at his wife. "Err...."

"Please. It's the least we can do for you saving us today."

Murdo chuckled. "I hardly saved you. You were just turned about, that's all."

"I'd love it if you came. We don't know much about the island other than what we've read. I bet you've got a thousand stories in that head of yours." She unleashed her killer smile, and with all the self-control in the world, it was impossible for anyone seeing it not to smile too.

"Well, that's very kind."

"About eight … assuming the roads are passable."

Murdo looked up at the sky. "You don't need to worry about that. This isn't going to carry on much longer."

Summer looked up too. "If you say so."

"Eight it is. I look forward to it." He nodded and smiled as the vehicle slowly moved away.

"I thought we were going to have a nice quiet few days, just us and the kids," Seb said as he walked up to her.

"We are. There's nothing that says we can't do a little entertaining. And he seems nice. We could get all the local gossip."

"It's like an illness with you, isn't it?"

Summer laughed. "There's nothing wrong with having an inquisitive mind."

"Uh-huh."

They remained in the yard for a few more seconds as they watched the car disappear, and then they both looked up to the sky as the snowfall became noticeably lighter. "Huh. He said it wouldn't last."

"That he did."

There was a loud bang from inside the house and they both looked at each other. "What the hell was that?" Summer asked as they started towards the door. Seb noticed the coloured lights on the Christmas tree were not flashing.

"My guess is the power's gone out again."

"This is going to be a long day." They heard another bang as a door slammed inside. "A long, long day."

7

Thomas brought his car to a stop outside the Macintosh house. It was a big stone-built place on the edge of the village. Like many people on the island, David worked in the oil industry. Sometimes he'd be away for a few weeks at a time; hence the fact that Duncan was given way too much freedom by his mother, who in turn gave herself way too much freedom to step outside the bounds of her marriage.

Cora was only a small island, but it held a lot of secrets, and Thomas was sure this latter one wouldn't remain secret much longer. He knocked on the door and Isla, David's wife, answered.

"Have you found him? Have you found our boy?" she asked as Thomas stepped inside. David appeared at the far end of the hall at that same moment.

"No. Not yet," Thomas replied. "We've found Ellie though."

"And?" David asked as he joined his wife.

"Look, can I come in and sit down?"

"Aye, of course."

They all walked through to the living room, where a real fire blazed away in the hearth. "We found Ellie out at the bothy. My dad got sucked into a bog, and I nearly followed him."

"Dear God. Is he alright?"

Thomas nodded slowly. "It's been quite a day already." He looked to Isla. "I don't suppose I could have a cup of something warm, could I?"

"Sorry. Of course. Where are my manners?" she said, immediately disappearing out of the room as the two men sat down opposite each other as the flames crackled away.

Cora had come a long way, but there was a part of it that would always be locked in the old ways. Like this, now. Like the woman being excused with busy work so the men could talk. It's what came from living as a patriarchal society for centuries. It's what came from church tradition never being questioned and just accepted as part of daily life. Change took a long time, and as archaic and unfathomable as these practises were by modern standards, as much as modern men like Thomas and David thought they were nonsense, there was another part of them that couldn't comprehend there was anything wrong with excusing the women to talk about important issues.

Mugs began to clatter from the other room, and the sound of water filling the kettle told both men that they would have a few minutes to discuss the important things before Isla's return.

"The power's down again, so she'll have to boil the kettle on the stove. We'll have a while, so now you can tell me what's happening. Where's my boy, Thomas?"

The other man let out a long breath and looked towards the doorway. "I probably shouldn't even be here."

"What are you talking about?"

"I mean that I don't have any real official capacity. I should be contacting the mainland and getting someone to come across to lead an investigation."

"An investigation?"

Thomas looked long and hard at the other man. He'd known David all his life, and they had never been close, but there was always mutual respect there. He could see by looking into the other man's eyes that there was no cover-up. He wasn't hiding him in the attic. He didn't know where his son was any more than Thomas did. He was also aware that if this was what he feared, and there was an investigation, and, God forbid, charges were pressed, then his inexperience and interfering in what was a matter for the police, the real police, could result in the case collapsing before it had even begun, but this was Cora. Cora looked after its own and dealt with its own. One way or another, Duncan would get what was coming to him.

"We found Ellie at the bothy," he said quietly.

"You already told us that."

He nodded, almost as if he was taking the time to collect his thoughts. "She's virtually catatonic, David. There are scratch marks on her arms, and her clothes had been ripped and torn."

The other man leaned back in his chair and stared towards the fire for a few seconds as the words sunk in. "Did ... did she say it was Duncan? Did she say it was him who did it?" he asked eventually.

"She hasn't said a word. I've got Jane over there now. I'm hoping she can coax something out of her."

"S-so it might not have been Duncan who did this? For all we know, Duncan might have tried to fight off whoever it was. He could be out there now, lying in a ditch."

Yeah, and the Fairy King could be raising an army to take over the island. "It's possible. Anything's possible. That's why I was hoping you could help me."

"What, help you search?" Thomas looked out of the window. The snow had stopped a few minutes before and the sound of water trickling down the drain pipes told him that it was already starting to melt as the clouds lifted. "Most of this will probably be gone in a couple of hours. I could get a team together, and we could—"

"Listen to me, David. I wondered if I could take a look in Duncan's room and maybe his computer."

A look of puzzlement swept over the other man's face. "Why?"

"I just want to see if there are any clues, anything that will tell us if he'd told anyone else about meeting Ellie at the bothy or—"

"You think one of his friends might have done this to him … to them?"

No, you moron. I think your idiot son's the only one who's responsible for this entire mess, and I'm hoping he was dumb enough to say something to one of his equally idiotic friends. "Exactly."

"I suppose it's worth a try at least."

*

"So, just a minor thing, but since you've invited a guest around this evening, have you any idea what we might serve him?" Seb asked as he and Summer unpacked two boxes that had remained untouched since the move. The children had stayed in their rooms apart from the odd shuffle into the kitchen, where they had grabbed a snack from the cupboard only to return to their rooms a moment later, making sure to slam the door behind them. The power was still off and this was their form of not-so-silent protest.

"Yeah. You could make your vegetable lasagne."

Seb paused the unwrapping of one of Summer's awards. "I see. When were you going to tell me about this?"

"I just did."

"Uh-huh. I know the kitchen is my department, and given your cooking, I'm more than happy for that to be the case. But the thing about making something like a vegetable lasagne is that it hinges on several important elements, and if any of them are absent, the said lasagne has little or no chance of being made in the first place."

Summer shrugged. "If you say so."

Seb shook his head. "It's all so simple to you, isn't it? You say something, and you think it's the equivalent of a genie just snapping his fingers."

"Hey, look, if you're going to get all PMS about it, I can phone up and cancel. I'll just say you've got a headache, or you're stressing about how much laundry there is."

Seb raised his left eyebrow and looked towards his wife. They had both grown up in households that had embraced the belief that there were certain things that men did in the house and certain things that women did and never the twain should meet. To any outsiders, Summer's barbs would seem cutting, but Seb knew she was trying to make him smile. He put the silver-plated trophy down and walked across to her as she stood there with her hands on her hips and a smirk on her face.

He grabbed her by the hips and pulled her towards him. Their lower bodies met, but he kept his head far back enough so he could see the expression on her face. "Are you questioning my masculine wiles?"

Summer sniggered. "Masculine wiles? Err … yeah."

"Oh really."

"Are you deaf, old man? I said yeah." They both smiled, and Seb leaned in, kissing Summer gently on the lips. When he pulled back again, her eyes were closed, and the smirk was gone, replaced with a lingering smile instead. At that precise moment, the Christmas lights flickered back on. "Did you make the electricity come back on?" she asked, opening her eyes.

"Course. When we've got rid of our guest tonight, I'll show you what else I can do."

Summer giggled. "It's a date."

He kissed her again, more briefly this time. "Good. Right now, though, we're going to have to put our hats and gloves on and head back out there."

"What are you talking about? We're unpacking."

"No. We're going shopping."

"What do you mean?"

"What do you think I mean? We need to go buy some ingredients. You wanted to head to the shop and meet people earlier today, and here's your chance."

"Yeah. That was before it got all North Pole out there. Can't you do it by yourself or take the kids with you?"

"You seriously think I want to spend time with those little bastards?"

Summer laughed again. "You make a fair point. Will they be okay if we leave them here?"

"The power's back on. They won't even notice we're gone."

"We're seriously going to leave them here by themselves?"

"We're not in London anymore. Nothing is going to happen. Nobody is going to walk in here and abduct them as much as we might want them to."

"Don't even joke about that."

"I wasn't."

"Okay. I'll come to the shops with you, but you've got to promise me that we'll make a concerted effort to get these boxes unpacked then. I don't want Murdo thinking we're living in a shanty town of boxes and rubbish."

"Well, maybe it would have been an idea not to invite him until we'd got them all unpacked. Or maybe it would have been an idea to—"

"Maybe it's an idea that you just shush your cakehole, stop whining like some prissy little bitch, and we get to the shops while they've still got food on the shelves."

Seb smiled again. "I don't know why you keep referring to it as plural. We're going to one shop. The one shop that sells food. You make it sound like we're heading to Harrods and Selfridges. We're going to Munro's General Store, and the chances are they won't have half the stuff I need to make lasagne, but will that matter to you? Nooo. I tell you what. Why don't you invite the rest of the village around while we're there?"

"Bitch, bitch, bitch. I'm getting my coat."

*

Murdo brought the car to a stop outside his cousin's house. He let out a small huff of a laugh as he turned off the engine. His cousin had been dead for nearly ten years, but he still referred to it as his house despite Donalina, his widow, being the sole occupant all that time.

A small triangle of sunlight shone through the clouds up above, illuminating the hill behind the property. There was a song a few years back that could almost have been an anthem for this island, well, for anywhere in Scotland. *Four Seasons in One Day*. When you grew up on Cora, you just took the changeable weather for granted, just another part of life. But as the islanders interacted with tourists and visitors to the island, they realised more and more how unusual it was.

A journalist actually wrote a piece on it that ended up in one of the Sunday papers. *The Island of Thunder and Snow*. Remembering back made Murdo smile now. It was a thing of great mystery and wonderment to the writer, having never encountered the phenomenon of thunder snow before. But for many inhabitants of the northwest coast of Scotland, the islands and an even larger number of people on the eastern coast of Canada, it was nothing out of the ordinary.

Murdo looked again towards the snowy white hill and knew that by the end of the afternoon, the chances were that there would only be a little snow left on the peak and probably nowhere else.

He climbed out of the car, and at exactly the same moment, Donalina opened the front door. "You didn't find them, then?" she asked, looking at the empty trailer.

"No. I'll call around. They'll show up."

"Come in. Come in," she said, opening the door a little wider.

Murdo entered and was nearly knocked over by the wall of heat that hit him. Radio Scotland was on low in the background, and the smell of peat was thick in the air. Murdo still cut his own peat, but William made sure that any of the older folk who couldn't had at least a small supply to supplement their coal and logs. Any of the teenagers who had been misbehaving were given peat-cutting duties as a kind of community service. It was how they preferred to handle things here, and it was always with the full consent of the parents. It was the Cora way. "I met the new incomers today."

Donalina paused as she closed the door. "Oh yes?" There was always an air of apprehension when so much as a tourist spent longer than a day or so on the island, so a new family settling here meant the local radar was operating at full pelt.

"Nice people. They've invited me around for a meal tonight."

"And you're going?"

"Well, aye. Of course I'm going. Why wouldn't I?"

"You don't even know them," she said, releasing the door handle and shuffling across to the range.

"And how do you expect me to get to know them without spending a little time with them?"

"From a distance."

Murdo smiled to himself. *She's still a funny old bird, alright.* "Well, if my body turns up hacked to pieces, you'll be able to tell Thomas who it was."

"D'you want this pan of soup over your head?" she asked, not turning around but just stirring it slowly.

"A bowl will be just fine."

She turned a little and gave him a smile before it was gone again just as quickly. "They say it's getting bad across on the mainland."

"What is?"

"What do you think?" she said, pointing to the window. "The weather."

"Well, I think we've seen the worst of it."

"Och, hark at Mr BBC World Service over here."

"You get a feel for the climate when you've worked outdoors all your life."

She took the pan off the heat and ladled the chunky soup into two waiting bowls before reaching into the bread bin and pulling out two crusty rolls. "There've been accidents on the motorways. They've closed some of the Highland routes, and blizzards have brought down lines."

Murdo's ears did prick up now. They often got short power cuts on the island, which were nothing unusual, but when there was major disruption on the mainland, that could cause longer-term problems on Cora. He looked across to the basket of logs that sat by the range. "You've got enough fuel to keep you going?"

"Aye. Don't you worry about me. I've got enough wood and peat and coal to last until the Rapture," she replied, placing the plates down on the table. Murdo grabbed the roll resting by his bowl, tore off a piece and dipped it in the soup, taking a big bite before leaning back in his chair. He chewed with his mouth half open, breathing heavily through his nose.

"Good," he said, dipping another piece of roll before doing the same again.

"Well, I hope to heaven you don't eat like that when you go visit your new friends tonight."

Murdo stopped chewing for a moment and looked across at Donalina. "What's wrong with the way I eat?"

She rolled her eyes and shook her head. "Ach! Will you look at yourself, Murdo? You can't eat like that in a stranger's house; they'll think we're all just out of the caves."

He followed her eyes and looked down at his jumper. Crumbs sat on the perch of his belly, and a single drop of soup had soaked into the wool. He leaned forward, wiped the soup away with his hand and watched as the small flakes of bread fell to the carpet. He looked up again guiltily. "Sorry, Donalina."

"At least the mice will have something to eat."

"I'll get the dustpan and brush."

"Sit yourself down and finish your food. You're just like Hamish. He always ate like a pig with no teeth too."

Murdo laughed and spooned more soup into his mouth. "I suppose it's been a long time since I've had to think about sharing a table with someone."

"You eat with me near on once a week."

"I mean—"

"You mean someone who matters."

"No, I—"

"Calm yourself. I'm just pulling your leg. What are you going to be wearing?"

Murdo looked confused. "Err ... well ... this."

Donalina shook her head. "You are not wearing that, Murdo Macleod. Your Mary would be turning over in her grave if she thought you were going to someone's house looking like a tramp."

"What's wrong with this?"

"Apart from the soup stain and the hole under your armpit, you mean?"

Murdo looked from one arm to the other, and then his eyes focused on the hole that, up until now, he had never noticed. "Err ... I'll put a different jumper on."

"You'll put a shirt on, for goodness' sake."

"Anything else?" he asked, looking a little hurt as he surveyed his garb one more time.

"Yes. You can polish your shoes and comb your hair." He took another piece of bread and dipped it in the soup before sulkily taking a bite and turning to look out of the window. "And don't pout. You're not a bairn."

"I don't know what you mean."

"Aye. Course you don't."

*

Thomas had found nothing useful in Duncan's room. They had even managed to log into his computer, but other than finding some material in the search history that made both men blush in the presence of Isla, there was no clue as to where the teenager might have gone. His last Facebook message had been over twelve months ago, having abandoned that platform for Instagram and TikTok. Other than the odd swap of a link, there was nothing there either.

"I suppose it's all FaceTime and Whatsapping these days," Isla said.

"Yeah," Thomas admitted sadly. "And I suppose we don't have his phone around here, do we?"

"Do you know a teenager who goes anywhere without their phone?"

"No. No, I don't."

"I must have tried him fifty times," David said.

Isla let out a small whimper, then another before breaking down into fits of tears. David climbed to his feet and wrapped his arm around her. Finding comfort in each other was alien to them, but at that moment, she leaned into her husband. "Where is he?"

The little shit's in hiding, trying to figure out what to do next, Thomas thought just as his phone buzzed. He retrieved it from his inside pocket and read the alert before turning to David and Isla. "There's a severe weather warning in place across on the mainland. Chances are, even if I called the police, we wouldn't be able to get them here in time for the afternoon ferry crossing."

"What about Search and Rescue?" David asked.

Yeah. That's for people who actually want to be found and rescued. Thomas looked out of the window. "Your idea about getting a search team together isn't a bad one, David. I'll head back to the store and see if Ellie's any closer to talking. In the meantime, if you hear from Duncan or you need to speak to me, you've got my number."

"And what about Search and Rescue?"

"I'll put a call in." It was a lie. At least, it was for the moment.

"I'll walk you to your car."

The two men went downstairs and stepped outside. The afternoon air was crisp but nowhere near as cold as it had been in the morning. "Listen to me," Thomas said, closing the door behind them as they walked up the garden path. "This could be a gift."

"What are you talking about?"

"I can delay putting a call in to the police on the mainland because there's no point. They won't be able to reach the afternoon ferry even if it sails. That gives us more time to find Duncan and find out exactly what the situation is."

"What are you talking about?"

Thomas exhaled a deep breath. "Duncan isn't bad, David. He's just a bit wild. Maybe there's a way that the police don't get involved in this, and maybe there's a way Cora's not thrown into the spotlight."

"I'm not following you. Stop speaking in tongues, will you?"

"I mean that as far as the police are concerned until Ellie says otherwise, there's one suspect in her attack."

All the colour suddenly drained from David's face. He had often been the first to criticise his son, but of all the things he believed Duncan to be capable of, this was not one of them. "There's no way my boy would—"

"I know. That's what I'm saying. If we bring outsiders into this, then it's all going to get out of hand very quickly."

"Listen. My son is out there somewhere, and whatever has happened, he's as much of a victim as Ellie. I can tell you that for nothing. He's not a—" He couldn't bring himself to say the word, but when he finally did, it was in a whisper. "A rapist, for God's sake."

Thomas raised his hands placatingly. "Nobody's saying that."

"Oh really?" The other man's shock had suddenly turned to anger. "Then what are they saying, exactly?"

"I'm saying that when we bring outsiders in, it gets taken out of our hands completely."

David stared long and hard at Thomas. "My boy wouldn't do that," he said again, trying to convince himself this time as much as the other man.

"Look. Will you get a group together or do you want me to do it?"

"Wh—where should I start?"

"The forest about half a mile away from the bothy. It's more sheltered there. There are plenty of hiding places and—"

"My son wouldn't be hiding. There's no reason for him to hide. He hasn't done anything."

"Okay. Maybe he hasn't done anything. Maybe he's hiding from someone … the same person who attacked Ellie. But whatever he's doing, we need to find him. I can convince Mairi that I can't get anyone to the island today, but if we haven't found Duncan by tomorrow, then regardless of how innocent he is, I'm going to have to put a call in."

David fixed the other man with another stare. "I understand."

"Good. I'll talk to you soon." Thomas climbed into his car and started the engine. David just watched as he drove away. A shiver ran down his spine, and suddenly, he wondered how well he knew his son at all.

8

The bell above the door jingled as Seb and Summer walked into Munro's General Store. "Mr and Mrs Richards," Isobel said, coming from around the counter and down the centre aisle to greet them. The small cafe through the arch and to the right was empty, but the smell of freshly brewed coffee drifted on the air towards them.

Two other villagers peeked around shelving units to see the incomers as they entered. Isobel had met them both before, but the first time, she hadn't known who Summer was. It was only after subsequent visits by Seb and the children that Luna had let slip that her mother was the internationally renowned best-selling author. From that point on, the gossip mill had begun to operate in full vigour.

"That coffee smells good," Summer replied.

"We're just here for mushrooms, peppers and stuff," Seb added.

"You'd like some coffee?" Isobel asked, the traumatic events of the morning now completely forgotten as she had a bona fide celebrity in her midst. She reached out, taking hold of Summer's elbow and gently guiding her through the arch into the small cafe.

"Err ... I'll just grab what bits we need then," Seb called out after them as he picked up a shopping basket.

"You do that," Summer replied, looking over her shoulder with a grin.

"I saw you on television the other day."

"Oh?"

"*The One Show*. I don't normally watch it, but I heard you were on."

"That's really sweet. Thank you," Summer replied as Isobel let go of her elbow and drifted to the other side of the counter, where she reached for a paper cup and poured the freshly filtered coffee.

"Cream? Sugar?"

"No thanks. I like my coffee like my men, dark and bitter."

Isobel looked at her for a moment then burst out laughing. "Och! I can tell I'm going to have to watch you. You've got a good sense of humour."

"You've met my husband then."

Isobel laughed again. "You're terrible."

"Aren't I just? How much do I owe you?"

"Och. You put your money away," Isobel said, squeezing the other woman's hand as she tried to open her purse. "Giving our new neighbour a hot cuppa on a day like today is just the decent thing to do."

"That's very kind. Thank you."

"Don't mention it." She placed the lid on the cup and handed it over.

"Well, I'd better go see if Seb needs any help with his list."

Isobel rushed out from behind the counter and matched Summer stride for stride as they headed back out of the cafe and into the shop. "What are you shopping for today?"

Summer shrugged. "You'd have to ask Seb. He's the one who's cooking."

Isobel stared at her for a few more seconds then burst out laughing once more. "Och, you," she said, pointing her finger.

"No, seriously. He does all the cooking."

The smile vanished from Isobel's face, almost as if Summer had started talking to her in a different language.

"It's true," Seb said, suddenly appearing from around the corner with a couple of items already in his basket. "It invalidates our home insurance if Summer so much as sets foot in the kitchen. And the less said about that whole child endangerment case the better. Those were tough years. But now we're up here, hopefully that's all behind us." He looked down at the coffee then disappeared around the next corner.

Isobel's brow creased further as she turned back to Summer. "He's joking."

"Och," Isobel replied, laughing politely.

At that moment, the bell above the door rang again, and the two women turned to see Thomas walk in. "Has she said anything yet?" he blurted, ignoring the woman standing by his wife's side as he rushed into the shop.

"Is it true?" asked one of the shoppers who had popped their heads out when Summer and Seb had arrived. The woman was in her sixties. She had a long nose and narrow slits for eyes.

"Is what true, Mrs Brown?"

"Ellie McBride."

"What about her?"

"She was in the family way and tried to take her own life."

"What is wrong with you? No, like most of the things you hear in this village, that's complete rubbish."

"Well, I heard—"

"I don't give a damn what you heard, and I'd appreciate it if you kept your rumours and your opinions to yourself." He looked in the older woman's basket. "Bread and milk. Is that all you're wanting today or will there be anything else?" he reached out to take her shopping, but she pulled it away.

"I haven't finished browsing yet."

"Browsing. Good grief, woman. We've carried the same product lines for the past twenty years. What do you think you're suddenly going to find?"

"Oh, I see. Aren't people allowed to look around your shop now? I remember you when you were in nappies, Thomas Munro, and a little more respect in your tone wouldn't go amiss."

"Yeah. I'll bear that in mind," he said, starting to walk away.

"Thomas," Isobel called after him.

"Yes?"

"This is Summer Richards."

Thomas paused before retracing his steps. "I'm sorry," he said, extending his hand. "Pleased to meet you."

"So, she gets a pleased to meet you, and you talk down to me like a beggar on a corner. Very nice," Mrs Brown hissed before marching away to resume her reconnaissance behind another shelving unit.

Thomas let out a long sigh and massaged his temple for a moment. "As I said, I'm really pleased to meet you, but you've caught me on a very busy day. Please excuse me," he said, nodding and disappearing into the back.

"I am sorry," Isobel said. "It has been a hectic day today."

"Really? I never envisaged things would get hectic here," Summer replied, smiling.

"Well, no. Normally they don't, but today's been one for the books."

"Sounds like it."

"Nice coffee?" Seb asked, reappearing around the corner with a half-full basket.

"Delicious," Summer replied, taking a sip.

"Did you find everything you needed, Mr Richards?"

"You seem to be out of Congolese soya beans. Do you know when you'll be getting another shipment?"

Summer hid a smile and took another sip of her coffee. "Och, well. My husband does all the ordering. To be honest, it's not something I'm familiar with. I can take a note if you like and see if he can get some for the next time you're in."

"That'd be great, thank y—"

"That would be completely unnecessary," Summer interrupted. She looked at the contents of Seb's basket. "What you have in there is all we'll need."

"So now you're a cook all of a sudden?"

"Let's just pay for what we've got and let Isobel get on with her work, shall we?"

"There's no need to talk down to me like that."

"Not this again."

"Oh, not this again, not this again. The world stops so everybody can listen to the great Summer Richards speak, but when I have anything to say, you're always cutting me off and dismissing me like I'm some kind of servant." Seb sniffed and looked like he was about to start crying.

Isobel's mouth fell open in shock, and she reached out, grabbing the basket. "Here, I'll put these through for you," she said, suddenly feeling sorry for Seb.

"Thank you, Isobel," he replied with a shaky voice.

"I'll be in the car," Summer said. "Nice to see you again, Isobel."

"Err ... yes. Very nice to err ... see you too, Mrs Richards."

"Oh please, call me Summer," she said, pausing at the entrance.

Isobel stopped too and turned to look at her. "Summer." She smiled and then continued to the counter.

Seb looked at her for a moment as well then turned his head sharply and followed the storekeeper to the counter.

A few minutes later, he reappeared from the shop and placed two carriers in the back of the car before climbing into the passenger seat. Summer turned to look at him, and he looked at her for a few seconds before they both burst out laughing.

"You are the pits," Summer gasped between heaving breaths. "What the hell are they going to think of us now?" There was part of her that was horrified but a much bigger part that thought it was hilarious. She and Seb had their own little secret world. Nobody had entry to it but them. Their children, their siblings, their parents, they all got the occasional glimpse, but full access was never granted. It was well over a minute before Summer had calmed down enough to start the engine. "That poor woman isn't going to know where to look the next time we head in there."

"It would all have been easily avoidable if she'd given me a coffee too."

"You are such a total child," Summer said, laughing again.

Seb reached for the cup in the centre holder and Summer slapped his hand away. "No. It's mine."

"Yeah," he replied, laughing and reaching out again.

She slapped his hand. "I'm serious."

"One day, I'm going to write a tell-all book about you."

"Sorry, darling. Publishers tend not to accept manuscripts written in crayon."

"And we laughed and laughed and laughed. I think *Life with the Ice Queen* is quite a catchy title."

"I'm confused. Who's the Ice Queen, you or me?"

"I always said you should be on the stage."

"What, sweeping it?"

"You've heard that one?"

"Yeah, I think it was pretty popular on the nineteen fifties music hall circuit."

"I'll take your word for it. That was before my time."

"Ha ... ha."

They travelled in a comfortable silence for a moment before Seb broke it. "What do you suppose was going on back there?"

"What do you mean?"

"I mean Isobel's husband and that whole thing that the nosey old witch came out with."

Summer shrugged. "You know what gossip's like in a place like this."

"Yeah, but the first thing he said when he walked through the door was, 'Has she said anything yet?' I mean what do you make of that? Has she said anything yet? It sounds—"

"It sounds like you're going to fit in well here. Trust me, in another few weeks, you'll be in there lurking with Mrs Brown and the rest of them in order to get all the latest gossip."

Seb couldn't help but laugh. "Now that's an image."

"Yup. We really need to get you a hobby sorted before that happens."

"Thanks. I love the faith you have in me."

*

It was already mid-afternoon, and the day felt like it was running away with Thomas. He looked out of the rear window of the kitchen as he made a cup of tea. He had managed to catch Jane Weston's eye briefly when he'd popped his head around the corner of the living room door but had stopped short of going in. Mairi still had her arm wrapped around her daughter, and the young woman remained unmoving, staring blankly into the fire.

He poured the boiling water into the pot and watched as it covered the bag. Despite the hot shower he'd taken earlier, he was still chilled to the bone from his trip to the bothy. He reached into the mug, plucking the corner of the teabag out with his thumb and forefinger. He lowered it again, raised it, lowered it, raised it, and then removed it completely, letting it splash on the waiting saucer before adding a dash of milk.

Thomas reached for the phone and dialled as he leaned back against the counter. It rang two, three times before his father answered.

"Dad."

"Thomas."

"Are you okay?"

"Yes. Had a long soak. I'll be back down shortly."

"No need for that. You should stay wrapped up and warm. Is Mam looking after you?"

"Your mam is fussing like always."

"Sometimes you need to be fussed."

The older man sneezed. "I'm fine," he said before sneezing again.

"You sound it."

"It's just a wee chill."

"Yeah, well, wee chills can get out of hand quickly."

"Bah! Don't you worry about me. Where are you with the case?"

The case. He's treating this like we're a couple of detectives. "I went around to David's place. Didn't find anything useful there, but he's getting a group together to go out looking for Duncan."

"Oh."

"I'm guessing you've seen the weather warnings for the mainland."

"Aye. It's meant to be blowin' a hoolie over there in parts as well. They've issued a danger to life warning."

Thomas turned to look out of the window once more. The sun had maintained a presence for some time, and much of the snow had gone. It would stick longer on the higher ground, but the village was getting back to normal quickly. "Aye, well, there's no way we'd get anyone across today anyway, so I thought it was worth trying to see if we could find him and get to the bottom of this ourselves."

There was a pause. "You mean without bringing the police in?"

There was another pause. "Well, right now, we don't really know what's happened ... I mean really. And something like this wouldn't be good for the island."

"You're a good boy, Thomas. You've always had a decent head on your shoulders."

Christ. I'm turning into my father, blethering on about what's best for the island. "Look. I'm not saying I won't put a call in. I'm saying there'd be little point in putting one in when no one can get across here."

"I think that's a wise deci—"

William's words came to an abrupt end. "Dad? Dad?" Thomas removed the phone from his ear and looked at the handset. The light was flashing. He turned towards the microwave to see the display had gone off.

"Thomas! Thomas!" The shout came from the shop. "The power's gone out again."

Yeah. I think I'd figured that out already. "I'll be there shortly." He removed the mobile phone from his pocket and looked at the bars. He had two. It varied depending on where in the house he was and, indeed, where on the island he was. A text message flashed onto the screen as he stared at it. "Finishing my Lemsip and I'll be down."

"Stubborn old so and so," he typed in reply and put the phone back in his pocket.

He was about to head into the shop when Jane appeared at the door. "I don't suppose there's any water left in the kettle, is there?"

"Aye. Help yourself." He watched her walk across and spoon coffee into a mug then pour boiling water over the granules. "So?"

"So?"

"Do we have any idea what's going on?"

Jane blew on the coffee for a few seconds before taking a careful sip. "No, in a word. To be honest, I've never quite seen anything like this before."

"She's in shock, right?"

"Well, yes, but there's something else too."

"What do you mean?"

"It's like she's been given a drug of some kind. Her pupils are dilated. Granted, they seem less so now than when I first got here, but—"

"Drugs? Oh dear God, this is worse than I thought. You think Duncan could have given her Rohypnol or something?"

"Well, no. The effects of Rohypnol would have worn off long before now, assuming that she was given it last night. No, this is something else. And...." she shook her head.

"And what?"

"It doesn't matter."

"Tell me."

"I don't know if you noticed the discolouration on her left cheek."

Thomas thought back. With everything else that was going on, all he'd been concerned about was getting Ellie back to the car, but now he thought about it, he did remember that one cheek was a little redder than the other. "Well, now you mention it, yes. What do you think it is? Do you think it could that be a reaction to whatever drug she was given?"

Jane shook her head. "It's not like any reaction I've seen. People can have all kinds of adverse responses to drugs, but physical ones don't tend to be limited to one cheek. That's the kind of thing I'd expect to see if someone had an allergic reaction to a substance they'd come into contact with."

"So what do you think happened?"

Jane shook her head again. "I honestly have no idea."

"I watched Duncan grow up. I never thought he'd be that kind of kid."

"Well, there is the possibility that he's not."

"What do you mean?"

"I mean you haven't found him yet, have you? There's a chance that there was someone else involved in this. There's a chance that someone did something to him too."

A sudden shiver ran down Thomas's spine. The thought had only briefly flashed into his head before, but now, with the talk of drugs, it suddenly held more weight. Drugs were not an issue on Cora. Underage drinking, yes. Drugs, no. "What the hell's going on here, Jane?"

She smiled sadly and leaned back against one of the kitchen counters. "I genuinely have no idea."

"I've never heard of anything like this before. Not on Cora."

Jane had moved up from Manchester fifteen years before. Despite being an incomer, she had fitted like a glove. She had relatives on the Isle of Mull and used to visit them regularly, so island life held few surprises for her, and having a former doctor on the island, who was still willing to get her hands dirty, added an entirely new dimension to the community.

She was held in the highest regard by William and the rest of the council. There wasn't a man, woman or child who did not afford her the esteem she deserved, but more than that, she was like a friend to everyone, devoutly religious, and though she struggled to believe parts of the legend that surrounded the community, she fell in line with William and the elders out of respect. Although not complicit in any of the wrongdoing, she subscribed to an agenda of wilful ignorance, which made her as good as one of them. "The whole world's gone to hell, Thomas. It was only a matter of time before the stench spread across here."

"But we've never had a problem like this before."

"You can say it as many times as you like. It doesn't change what's happened."

"No."

"Thomas! I can't get the till open," Isobel called out from the shop.

His shoulders slumped. "I expect you'll want to be getting off."

Jane smiled. "I'll hang around for a while and see if we can get something out of our patient."

"Thanks, Jane," he replied, placing his cup on the countertop and heading out of the kitchen.

9

The afternoon was vanishing quickly as Murdo stepped into the house. He had stayed longer at Donalina's than anticipated, and after his late lunch, she had insisted on grabbing one of her husband's shirts for him to wear so he wouldn't have to use his Sunday best and end up wearing a food-stained garment to church the following Sunday.

He placed the neatly wrapped bundle on the table and was about to head into the bedroom when he felt eyes on him. He turned quickly and saw Porridge sitting on one of the countertops staring intensely. "You're trying to give me a heart attack, y'wee brat," he said, placing his hand on his chest and chuckling a little.

He was about to head into the bedroom when his mobile phone rang. He reached into his jacket pocket and pulled it out, squinting at the screen momentarily before finally hitting the answer button.

"Gordon?"

"Aye, it's ... I was ... —eep. I can't—"

"Gordon? Gordon, it's a bad connection. Let me call you back on the landline." It was rare that anyone called him on his mobile phone at all. They were always a last-ditch attempt to get in touch with someone. He hung up and walked across to his other phone only to realise why Gordon had decided to use the mobile instead. "Dammit." He looked out of the window. There was still snow on the peaks but just patches here and there over the fields. It was not uncommon for it to come and go this quickly on the island. The salt in the sea air was one factor, but the fact that they were in the Gulf Stream also played a part.

He squinted at the mobile in his hand and tapped the redial button.

"Hel … Murd … that you?"

"Gordon. It's a bad line. The power's down."

"Mur … you see … eep? I'm … ee. Last … morni … nowh.…"

"Gordon. I can't make out what you're saying."

"…sheep. I've.…"

The line went dead, and Murdo tried to call back again, but this time, he couldn't get through. He hadn't spoken to Gordon in the best part of a month. He was more of a hermit than Murdo himself, but word had probably got to him that Murdo was looking for Donalina's sheep. That was the only thing that made sense. *He must have found them, but surely they couldn't have made it as far as his property. That's a good five miles at least. Maybe he was out for a walk or a drive and he saw them.*

He tried the phone again, but again, he couldn't get through. He looked at his watch. "Dammit all." He had been hoping to have a nap by the fire before heading out to the Richards' place, but now all his plans had gone up in smoke. "You be a good girl now, Porridge," he said, picking his keys up from the table and heading out.

*

It was dim in the entrance hall as Seb and Summer stepped inside. Summer reached for the light switch, and when nothing happened, both of them got a sinking feeling. "Oh crap. This is going to put them in a great mood."

A door slammed loudly from somewhere in the house, and the pair let out a long sigh. "How old do they have to be before we can seek emancipation?"

"I don't think it works like that."

"Too bad. Well, I'd better make a start on dinner. Without the microwave to help, I'm going to have to do things the old-fashioned way."

"Uh-huh," Summer said, slipping off her boots and coat. "I think I might take a bath."

"Don't worry; I'll take care of it all by myself."

"Take care of what?"

"The dinner."

"Thanks, honey."

"By myself. I'll do it all by myself, with no help from anyone at all."

"I might try those new salts I bought from that place in Covent Garden."

"That'll be nice for you."

"I know, right? When was the last time I could just lie back and take a bath? Buddy's assistant had me booked into these rooms that just had showers, and I tried to switch, but they were at capacity. I mean they get a lot of tourists in London Christmas week."

"That must have taken a toll."

"You have no idea," she said, heading down the hallway.

"So, I'll make a start on dinner then," he said again.

"Thanks, babe. Ooh, and could you pour me a glass of that Malbec that came in the Fortnum and Mason hamper from Buddy?"

"Course, darling. Anything else?" Seb asked as he took his boots off. "Do you want me to sand down each individual bath crystal so no jagged edges dig into you as you're scooping them out of the bag?"

"No, I'm good. Don't forget that wine, now."

"Unbelievable," he muttered under his breath as he took the two bags of shopping into the kitchen. He laid everything out on the countertop before grabbing the discussed bottle of wine from the cupboard. He retrieved a glass and then paused before taking another. He half-filled each one then returned the bottle before grabbing the colander from under the sink.

Even though the power was off, it wouldn't affect his ability to make a meal. They had a built-in electric hob and oven, but Summer had insisted the original solid fuel range was restored to its former glory. Not only that, but the back boiler had meant it could heat the water and radiators. One of Jezyk's men had spent days sanding away the rust and breathing new life into it. When he was done, even Seb had to admit it looked spectacular, and the heat it threw out warmed most of the house even without the radiators.

He heard shuffling and turned towards the doorway to see Luna. "Hi," he said tentatively, not sure if she was going to launch into another tirade about being dragged to the middle of nowhere.

"Hi," she said quietly.

"You okay?"

"Yeah."

"Okay. You hungry?"

"No."

"Your brother still in his room?"

"Yeah."

"You want to help me with dinner?"

"No."

"Okay. Good talk," Seb said, heading over to the range and throwing three logs in.

"Dad?"

"Yeah?"

She didn't reply for a moment, and he took the time to knot a couple of strips of newspaper and place them carefully beneath the logs.

"I'm sorry about earlier."

Seb turned to look at her and climbed to his feet. "That's alright, sweetheart. I know it's frustrating. I mean technology is everything these days, isn't it? It's how we stay in touch, it's how we play games; it's how we watch movies. Don't worry; we're going to get a couple of generators."

"It's not that. Well ... it is a bit, but not really."

He walked across to his daughter and guided her to one of the stools at the breakfast bar. "What is it then?"

"I had a nightmare last night."

Her words lingered in the air for a moment. Everybody had nightmares, but Luna had experienced particular problems. They went far beyond the territory of run-of-the-mill nightmares and into the realm of night terrors. Seb and Summer had found her multiple times in the living room or in the kitchen and once in the back garden. She was fast asleep but screaming at the top of her voice. Just remembering back now sent a shiver down his spine. They had sought therapy for her and it had taken a long time, but eventually they had got the situation under control. It happened in increments at first, but then one day it just stopped. The following weeks had been tense. They were all terrified that one event would be the start of it all happening again, but it never did.

The initial cause had been one that would give well-balanced adults, never mind an impressionable ten-year-old, torment. She had woken in the middle of the night to find a man in her room. He turned out to be someone with severe mental health issues who had escaped from the facility where he was normally housed and returned to his childhood home. He had climbed the garden wall, hopped onto the garage roof and finally slipped in through the narrow, open awning window.

Of course, none of this mattered when Seb had him on the floor, pummelling him into a state of unconsciousness. He and Summer were normally caring, liberal, decent people, but when there was any threat to their family, they became something else.

After that night, no one was ever allowed to sleep with their windows open again. A new alarm system was installed, and all the locks were changed, despite locks not being an issue in the first place.

Luna's night terrors had begun shortly after. The family moved house, convinced that would resolve the problem, but it didn't. The new property was a three-storey Victorian place, and it creaked and groaned more in one night than the occupants of a dozen old people's homes.

If anything, it made the situation worse, and in the end, Seb and Summer submitted and took Luna to see a specialist. The only reason they had delayed it that long was if word had got out, her life at school would have become miserable. Luna was aloof from the other children to begin with. Not in a snobbish way, but she was very creative, usually in her own little world, and this would have created a whole new set of problems.

It turned out that taking her to see Doctor Patel was the best thing they could have done. It helped with the sleep problems as well as a whole host of self-esteem issues.

It had been well over ten months since the last episode, but for Luna to say this now, hundreds of miles away from her therapist, made Seb feel sick.

"We didn't hear anything. Did you cry out? What happened? Why didn't you say anything?"

Luna exhaled a long breath. It was as scary for her to contemplate as it was for Seb. "It wasn't like before."

"How do you mean?"

"Well, before, you and Mum used to wake me up, and I'd have no recollection of how I'd ended up where I had or what had happened in the nightmare or anything. This time it was like I was conscious, and I saw what was happening, but I was frozen."

"Oh, Luna. I'm sorry, darling, that must have been terrifying," he said, placing his hand on his daughter's.

"I suppose it's a plus that I can actually remember it, right?"

Seb smiled weakly. "I suppose so, sweetheart. Did you tell Charlie?"

"No."

"Okay." Charlie had taken it badly when it had happened originally. He had almost entered a kind of madness himself, experiencing bouts of insomnia as he lay awake in bed listening for his sister. "That's probably for the best."

Luna sniffed. "That's what I thought. I'm really scared, Dad. What if it's all starting again?"

"Okay, let's look at this logically. Everybody gets nightmares, Luna. Everybody. The fact that we didn't have to wake you up screaming in the middle of the night suggests it was a nightmare and not what happened to you before. It's probably come about from all the changes. I mean this is a big, big move coming up here. You're away from all your friends, away from everything you're used to, your old routine. It's going to take some getting used to. The fact that you remembered the dream and were aware of what was going on is a big difference to what happened before."

She looked at her father for a moment and then nodded. "I suppose you're right," she said, wiping a tear from the corner of her eye.

Seb immediately went over to her, throwing both arms around his daughter and kissing her gently on the head. When he was sure no more tears would come, he went to sit back down.

"So, what was it about, this dream, anyway?"

"It was just so weird."

"Weird, how?"

"Well, like I said, I remember everything. It was like it was actually happening like I was in bed, and it was happening there and then, but at the same time, I know it can only have been a dream."

"Okay … so you were in bed, and then what happened?"

"Well, I was lying there, and the curtains were closed, but my room was bright."

"Yeah. I'm sorry about that. We've got some with lining somewhere. When we get all the boxes unpacked, I'll put them up."

"No, I mean in my dream."

"Oh, okay."

"But yeah, as well. The sooner we can get some proper curtains up the better."

"So what happened next?"

"Well, I was just lying there, and I could feel my eyes getting heavier and heavier, and I must have drifted off within a few seconds, but at the same time, I could feel them flicking open now and again, but this was obviously part of the dream."

"Alright, then what?"

"Then I saw a shadow."

"A shadow?"

"Well, a silhouette."

"Of what?"

"A figure."

"A figure? Standing outside your window?"

"Yeah."

I swear to God, Jezyk, if one of your men has been snooping around my house in the middle of the night and creeping out my kids, I'm going to sack the lot of you. "I think the lads had a couple of drinks when they finished last night. It's not out of the realms of possibility that one of them had too much and strayed away from the caravans."

"No, Dad. This wasn't a man."

Seb's brow furrowed. "Okay. You said it was a figure. What kind of figure?"

"Well, I suppose it could have been a man, but a really, really tall one. I mean really tall. And with really long arms and a funny-shaped head. No. Now I'm thinking about it again, it couldn't have been a man at all. But it was something, and it was in front of my window, and it was like it was sniffing at the air or something."

"Sniffing at the air?"

"Yeah. And then the silhouette got bigger as if it took a step nearer to my window. All the time, its head rose a little as if it was sniffing or searching for something. And all the time, I was just lying there frozen, watching all this happen. It felt so real, Dad."

"And then what happened?"

"Well, it seemed to stand there for ages, or at least it felt like ages in my dream. Then there was a sound, like a door closing on one of the caravans, and it turned in that direction then disappeared."

"I'm not surprised you were scared, sweetheart. I'm just sitting here listening to you and I've got goosebumps."

Luna giggled. "Like I say, it was just a silly dream. Oh. There was one thing though. Yeah, it definitely wasn't a man. When it turned, it didn't have a nose. It was just flat, almost like there was no face there at all."

"But you said the curtains were closed, so you couldn't see that for certain, could you?"

Luna thought for a moment. "No, I suppose not. Plus, it was just a stupid nightmare, and nothing ever makes sense in those."

"Ha. No." The goosebumps were still present on Seb's arm when he sensed a presence at the door, and his head jolted towards it.

"Is that my wine?" Summer asked, appearing in her robe.

"Jesus wept, Summer," Seb replied, reaching out for the counter for support. "You can't sneak up on people like that."

"Don't worry. You're well insured."

Luna laughed. "Oh, thanks very much," Seb said.

"So, what you been talking about?" Summer asked, walking across, picking up her wine and taking a sip.

There was a look in Luna's eyes that pleaded with Seb not to say anything. "The curtains in Luna's room. She struggled to sleep last night because the moon was too bright."

Summer looked puzzled for a moment. "The new ones we bought?"

"No. I haven't been able to find those yet."

"I told you to mark them clearly."

"Yeah, well, I must have forgotten. I'll get on to it."

"Honestly, Seb. I ask you to do one thing, and you can't even get that right," she said, heading back out of the kitchen.

"Have a nice bath, darling. Don't make it too deep. I'd hate you to drift off and drown horribly," he called after her as she disappeared once more.

Luna giggled again. "Thanks, Dad. I just didn't want it to become a whole thing again."

"Are you saying your mum overreacts?"

"How can you possibly interpret that from what I said?" Luna asked, smiling.

"Jesus! You are so much like her it's scary."

"You take that back."

They both laughed this time. "If it gets bad again, we'll have to tell her, but right now, as far as I'm concerned, this is just a nightmare. Everybody has them, and yes, they're scary and upsetting, and they can linger with you for a while, but something as simple as eating the wrong thing before bed can give you one."

"I suppose."

"If it happens again, you'll tell me, won't you?"

"Course I will."

"I love you, kid. Y'know that, don't you?"

"Yeah. I love you too, Dad."

"You want to help me prepare dinner?"

"No. Why would I want to do that?"

"'Cause there's no leccy, there's no phone signal, and there's nothing else to do."

"I'd rather read one of Mum's books than cook," she said, climbing to her feet and heading to the door.

"Thanks, sweetheart. I love how reciprocal the relationship between a father and his children is."

"If we're that much of a burden, why didn't you just get a couple of dogs?"

"Because I lost the coin toss, that's why. If it was up to me, I'd have two beautiful Labrador Retrievers called Charlie and Luna instead of what I've been landed with."

Luna laughed. "Thanks."

"Hey, the basis for any successful relationship is honesty."

"At least you gave us the names you were going to give them."

"Yeah. It was as a reminder of the life I could have had. Every time I call your names, they stick in my throat like screwed-up sandpaper now, as I think of how things might have been."

Luna laughed again. "Thanks again, Dad."

"You're welcome, darling." He watched her head down the hall then reached for the two bags of mushrooms he'd bought and emptied them into the colander.

"SEB!" Summer called out.

"Ugh. YEAH?"

"CAN I HAVE A TOP-UP?"

He shook his head and grabbed the bottle, heading down the hall. He entered the spacious bathroom to find Summer with her hair tied back and neck high in bubbles. She extended her glass, which only had a few drops remaining in the bottom. "Have I told you lately that you're the best husband a girl could have?"

"Does the fact that I've brought you wine have any bearing on that assertion?"

"Might have."

They both smiled as he filled her glass. She took a sip and smiled. "Y'know, you could lock that door and climb in here with me."

Seb paused for a few seconds and looked at his watch. "You do realise our dining table is still in bits and I'm going to have to put it together before Murdo arrives, don't you?"

The playfulness remained on Summer's face for a second longer then she shrugged. "Yeah, you're right. It'd look rude if you were still doing that when he got here."

"And, of course, there's the dinner to prepare as well. By myself. Just me."

"Uh-huh. Do me a favour, darling. Leave the bottle, will you?" she said, nodding to the wine still in his hand.

"Of course, precious," he said, placing the Malbec down on the side of the bath and heading to the door. "You will shout if there's anything else I can do, won't you?"

"Uh-huh," she replied, putting her glass down and sinking deeper into the bubbles.

Seb shook his head and trotted back down the hallway muttering to himself as he went.

When he reached the kitchen, he took the mushrooms and rinsed them under the tap, turning and tossing them in the colander to get rid of any excess compost. He looked out of the window as the sun continued to get lower and lower. He thought about all the work that there was still to do on the place. He thought about Jezyk and his men, and then his mind drifted to Emil.

It had been a long time since he had seen anyone as scared as that. Then Seb started to think about the conversation in greater depth. *I saw it standing by the fence post over there. Taller than me, much taller. A thin black figure in the darkness just staring.* A shiver ran down his back as he recalled the conversation he'd had with his daughter. She had used the same term. Not a man, but a figure.

Okay, Seb, nice work. You're managing to freak yourself out by the ramblings of a drunk and one of your kid's nightmares. He reached for the glass of wine and took a gulp, then another.

"SEB?" Summer shouted.

"For fuck's sake," he mumbled. "YEAH?"

"IS THERE ANY CAMEMBERT LEFT?"

"YEAH."

"BE A DOLL. FETCH ME SOME WITH SOME CRACKERS."

"I'M TRYING TO MAKE THE DINNER."

"GOOD POINT. DON'T LEAVE ANYTHING ON THE STOVE. IT'LL BE A NIGHTMARE TO CLEAN IF IT BOILS OVER."

Seb took another deep breath, grabbed his glass and drained it dry. "I swear to God. I'm going to be a raging alcoholic before Christmas is over."

10

William was such an impressive and imposing figure in the community that it was easy to forget he was getting old. But now, as Thomas watched him coughing, it was blatantly obvious that the fall into the bog had more of an effect than he'd let on.

"She's still not said anything?" he asked his son when the coughing fit finally abated.

"No."

"Strange. Very strange."

"That's not all."

"Oh?"

"You don't tell another soul."

"As God is my witness, I shan't, Son. What is it?"

"Jane thinks she was drugged."

"Drugged?"

"Aye."

William shook his head sadly. "Och. What is this world coming to? You don't suppose those men working up at the Richardses' place could be responsible, do you?"

"What makes you say that?"

"Well … drugs. We've never had any problems like that in the past."

"They've been working here for weeks, Dad. They've all been in here. They all seem like decent enough, hard-working men."

"Aye, they might seem decent enough, but drugs, Thomas. In my sixty-eight years, that word and Cora have never been mentioned in the same sentence."

"Look, we're getting ahead of ourselves. We still don't really know what's happened and until we can get Ellie to talk or we can find Duncan, we can't just jump to conclusions and start accusing people. Plus, that's not actually our job, my job to do anyway. I mean hell. I've already spent a lot more time on this than I should. I run a general store."

"Ach, you know you do much more than that, my lad. This is a community. We all do much more than is expected; that's how it works. How's Mairi?"

"How do you think she is? She's worried sick. She was droning on about getting an air ambulance to take Ellie to the hospital, but since Jane's examined her and convinced her there's no threat to her life, she's stopped going on about that, at least."

"That's something, I suppose. Mind, from what I've heard about what's going on over there, I doubt that an air ambulance could get up at the moment. The radio says there's been no end of accidents. Power and telephone lines are down. The trains have stopped, and people are trapped in cars on the motorways."

Thomas looked out of the window. There was a little snow on the higher ground, but that was all. "Let's hope we've had the worst of it because a night of that and it's a recovery party we'll have to send out for Duncan and not a search party."

*

Murdo knocked on the door and didn't wait for an answer but stepped straight inside. "Gordon?" he called, walking into the house a little further. White ashes from the hearth still threw out heat, but there was no sign of his friend. "Gordon?"

He went further into the house. Peeking around corners. When he was sure the other man was not at home, he walked back outside. Gordon still kept a few sheep himself, so the chances were that if he'd found Donalina's, he'd have penned them off or maybe even coaxed them into one of the outbuildings.

Murdo walked across the yard to the edge of the croft. Sure enough, there was Gordon's flock. *Strange. That's a lot less than he used to keep.* He followed the fence a little further along, keeping his eyes on the animals as they all huddled around a feeding trough. Nervous bleats played a steady accompaniment while the sheep continued to eat. He paused at the gate then looked across to the far end of the field. Two extra posts had been erected and barbed wire had been wrapped around in a haphazard manner, almost as if a rushed repair had been carried out.

Gordon was the last person in the world to rush anything. He always took great pride in a job done well, and the appearance of the patchworked fencing didn't sit easy with Murdo. It was just a couple of days until Christmas, and the sun would be down within the hour. Gordon's car was still parked outside the house, and soon the cold would start biting harder than ever.

"Gordon?" he shouted, turning, hoping he would see some sign of his friend. He saw nothing and retraced his steps, casting another glance towards the feeding sheep. When he arrived back in the yard, he checked the outbuildings, but the older man wasn't there. He walked across to the beaten-up Toyota and put his hand on the bonnet. *Stone cold.*

Murdo let out a long sigh and turned a full circle. "Gordon?" *Something really doesn't feel right.*

He finally climbed back into his own car and started the engine.

*

"Do you think the power's going to come back on?" They were the first words Charlie had spoken to Seb for hours. The twelve-year-old's eyes were narrow and a little swollen, as if he'd just woken from a nap.

Seb didn't answer for a moment. He'd actually enjoyed the last twenty minutes or so of peace and quiet. The wine had given him a happy little buzz. Radio Three was replaying the best concerts of the year, and currently, the Berlin Philharmonic were ten minutes into Beethoven's Choral Symphony. He'd dug out a few candles so he could see what he was doing in the fading light, and all was good in his little sphere of existence. He paused in mid-chop and laid the knife down, grabbing his glass and taking another drink.

The twins could sometimes be a handful, but Charlie was more like his mother than Seb, and when the mood took him, he could be difficult to tame. "I don't know, Son."

"I can't get a signal on my mobile."

"I know. We're all in the same boat."

"But...." He let out a long, sulky sigh.

"We're going to get some generators sorted out. You're the tech head in this family. How about tomorrow, we go online and figure out which ones are best going to suit our needs?"

"Tomorrow? You don't think the power will be back on until tomorrow?"

"I don't know, Charlie. But your mum invited Murdo around for dinner tonight, so even if it does come back up, we can't very well leave him to do some online shopping, can we?"

"Tch." It wasn't a word, just a click of disapproval from the back of his throat, and Seb felt sure it was a prelude to a prolonged barrage of teenage anger. Instead, Charlie turned and started walking away.

"Hey," Seb called after him, causing his son to return to the doorway.

"It's going to be a different way of life up here, but we'll get used to it, Son." Charlie just nodded and was about to turn once more when Seb spoke again. "What's wrong?"

"Doesn't matter."

Seb took another sip of his wine. "It does. What's wrong?"

"Amelia said she was going to call me tonight."

"Amelia?"

"Amelia Pankhurst."

Seb shrugged and shook his head. "I don't know who that is, Son."

"God, Dad. Way to show an interest in my life."

"Wait a minute. You like this girl?"

"Ugh. Forget it," Charlie said, about to walk away again.

"I thought you liked that Eve girl."

"Eve started going out with Nick. Not that it matters. Not that anything matters because we're all the way up here, and they're hundreds of miles away, and Eve, Amelia, Nick, they'll all have forgotten about me by New Year. And please, please don't tell me that I'll meet someone new up here, Dad, 'cause there are like five kids in the whole school."

"Actually, there are nearer seventy kids in the whole school, and you might meet someone, but even if you don't, when we've got this place finished, you'll be able to invite people up, and we'll be going down there pretty regularly. The world's a lot smaller than it used to be."

"Invite them up?"

"Yeah. We're keeping the new static caravan. We thought it would be good for when people come to stay. You could invite Amelia and her family up or Amelia and some other friends."

"You're serious?"

"You might be an obnoxious little bastard sometimes, but in general, you're a good kid, Charlie. It's not like this place will suddenly descend into a hive of iniquity if you have some friends coming to visit. When I was thirteen, I used to go down to see my friend Paul in Cornwall. My foster mum would put me on the train, and his family would meet me on the other side. We'd have a ball."

Suddenly, Charlie perked up at the prospect of being able to see his friends again. "I've never heard you mention Paul before. I'm guessing you're not still friends."

Seb reached for his glass and took another drink. "Paul and I were in the same home for a while. We were inseparable. He was adopted by a couple, and they had to move to Truro for work. We promised to stay in touch, and we did. And bear in mind, this was a long time before mobile phones."

"So, what happened to him?"

"He died of bone cancer at the age of sixteen."

A heavy silence hung in the air for a few seconds. "I'm sorry, Dad."

Seb shrugged. "It is what it is. You never know how long you've got in this world, Charlie. That's why you need to live life to the fullest and enjoy every second of it."

"Why did we move here then?"

Seb laughed and Charlie joined in. "Didn't you have fun with us out in the forest today?"

Charlie thought for a moment. "Yeah. That was pretty cool."

"I know everything's a bit chaotic at the moment, but it'll settle down, and we're going to have a lot more adventures as a family. Your mum's been working so hard to make this happen. I know you don't see it right this minute, but when we go whale watching in the summer and learn to kayak and surf and all the stuff that we always talked about doing when we lived in London, you'll understand."

"Whale watching?"

"Yeah. There's a guy who runs whale-watching trips in the summer months."

"That would be so cool."

"Trust me. There are lots of things that are cool about living up here."

"The internet going down isn't one of them."

"No. It isn't. We'll figure it out though. It'll take a little bit of adjustment from all of us, but we'll get used to it."

"Like I said before, I'm not sure I want to get used to this," he replied, gesturing towards the candles.

"Well, no. I'm not expecting you to. But when we get some generators sorted, the candles will be for full-on emergencies only. And I'll tell you what else, we're going to get a phone that doesn't need a power supply just in case too."

A look of confusion swept over the twelve-year-old's face. "You can get those?"

Seb laughed. "Yes, Charlie. All phones used to be like that."

"So, what, we'd need to look in antique shops or something?"

"Are you winding me up?"

"No."

"You can get them from Amazon. You can get them all over the place."

"So, why don't we have one already?"

"They're old-fashioned now, that's all. You can't see who's calling you. You can't store a load of numbers inside them. Technology moves on, but if the power goes down, they still work. So, we'll put one of those on the shopping list too, and you'll be able to speak to Amelia to your heart's content."

Charlie smiled. "Okay."

"See. There are solutions to all of life's little irritations."

"SEB!"

"Oh, for the love of Christ. What now? YEAH?"

"HAVE WE GOT ANOTHER BOTTLE OF THIS MALBEC?"

"NO."

"HOW ABOUT THAT AUSTRALIAN SHIRAZ?"

"I swear. Your mum is the only person I know who can have a conversation from five rooms away. I'LL BRING SOME THROUGH, DARLING."

"AND CAN YOU FETCH SOME BRIE TOO?"

"There's a lesson here, Son. When you're in a relationship, and your girl's down and missing you, never say something like, 'Don't worry, darling, the second you're home, all you'll have to think about is relaxing. I'm going to treat you like a queen.' Y'see, to you and me, it's romantic and a nice thing to say to make her feel better, but to her, it's a contract no different to the one Doctor Faustus made with the devil."

"Are you saying Mum's the devil?"

"No, Son. Your mum's real. She's a lot scarier than the devil."

*

There was a part of Murdo that felt silly for worrying about Gordon. If anyone could look after himself, it was that old warhorse. But seeing the quickly cobbled-together fence repair had made him feel ill at ease. He remembered back to the conversation he'd had with him on the phone. It was hard to understand much of it, but he was pretty certain sheep were mentioned. He had assumed that it was Donalina's sheep, but seeing the damage to the fence, he now realised that it was probably his own that he'd been calling about.

He brought his car to a stop outside Munro's General Store and climbed out. There were more people than usual in for this time of the day, presumably stocking up on batteries and the like. He looked towards the cafe as he passed by the arch but couldn't see William sitting at his usual table, so he walked to the back of the store.

"Hello, Murdo," Isobel said.

Murdo nodded politely. "I don't suppose William's about, is he?"

Isobel gestured towards the back. "Go through. He and Thomas are having a yarn in the kitchen."

Murdo passed the living room and saw Mairi, Ellie and Jane all sitting in front of the fire. *Strange*. "Isobel said I'd find you through here."

"What can I do for you, Murdo?" Thomas asked.

"Well, it's nothing, really. I was wondering if you'd heard from Gordon at all."

"Gordon Macleod?"

"No. Gordon Mackay."

Thomas's face creased for just a moment. "Wait a second," he said, reaching for a small pile of scrap paper stacked by the phone. "I'm sure I've got a note to phone him back. It's been a manic day today. I haven't had the chance yet." He finally arrived at the sheet he was looking for. "Here we go. Call Gordon about sheep." Thomas shrugged. "I have no idea what that means. ISOBEL?"

There was a short pause before Isobel appeared in the doorway. "The shop's busy. What is it?"

"This message from Gordon."

"What about it?"

"What's it about?"

"What does it say?"

"It says, 'Call Gordon about sheep.'"

"There you go then. Can I get back to work now?" Not bothering to wait for an answer, she about-faced and disappeared.

Thomas raised his eyebrows and shook his head. "Well," Murdo began. "I got a call from him, but the line was a bad one. He said something about sheep, but I thought maybe he'd found Donalina's."

"Donalina's missing some sheep?"

"Aye. Anyway, I went around to his place and there was no sign of him."

"Okay. And you're telling me this why?"

"I just wondered if you'd heard from him, that's all."

"What's troubling you, Murdo?" William asked.

"Nothing. I just—"

"Och, man. You and I have been friends long enough not to lead each other on. You didn't just come here for a blether. Now, what is it?"

"There was damage to his fence, but the repair looked like it had been done by a bairn."

"So what?" Thomas asked. "His sheep had obviously found a way through. He needed to stop any more getting out before he went to look for them, so he patched it up quickly. What's the mystery?"

"No. Murdo's right. That doesn't sound like Gordon at all. I've never known him to do half a job in his life."

"He's old, Dad. Time takes a toll," he replied and, right on cue, William sneezed.

"You're getting a cold?" Murdo asked.

"Just a chill."

In the few minutes they'd been chatting, the light had deteriorated further, and now Thomas switched on a lantern. "I tell you what. After we've closed up the shop tonight, I'll head around to Gordon's and check in on him. He should be back home by then, and I can find out what all this is about." He gestured to the note in his hand. "And I'll drop in and tell you the craic on the way back."

"Ah, well, I'm heading out tonight. I didn't want him calling me and worrying when he couldn't get through."

"Well, the way the storm on the mainland's sounding, I don't think anyone will be too surprised if the landlines go down too. You've got batteries for your radio and plenty of firelighters, Murdo?"

Murdo smiled and looked at William. "He was born to make a million, this one. I'll get a packet before I leave."

"Going out, you say?" William asked.

"Aye. Met the Richardses today. Seem like a nice family. They invited me around for dinner."

"Very nice."

"Here. What's with Mairi and her girl in the living room?"

"Long story," William replied.

"Oh."

William stepped closer to his old friend and whispered, "Might be looking at drugs and rape."

"Jesus, Dad," Thomas hissed.

"Ach, you don't need to worry about Murdo. Anything you say to him won't go any further."

"Is she alright?"

William shook his head. "Hasn't said a word."

A confused expression swept over Murdo's face. "How do you know what happened then?"

"She was meant to be meeting Duncan Macintosh last night. When she didn't come home, Thomas and I went looking. Found her out at the bothy. Her clothes were torn and she had scratches all over. Jane's been looking after her, but the poor bairn has been too traumatised to say as much as a word."

"And what does Duncan say?"

A thin self-satisfied smile crept onto William's face. There was nothing he liked more than having the inside track on a story, and this was a belter. "We don't know where he is. His dad and a few others are out looking for him now."

"Have the police been called?"

"Well—"

"Not yet," Thomas said, giving his father a chastising glare. "For a start, we don't really know what's happened. Everything is just guesswork, and on top of that, there's no way we could get anyone across to the island at the moment anyway. The way things are going, the ferry might not even sail tomorrow."

Murdo nodded. "I see."

"Don't say any of this to anybody. Okay?"

"I told you," William replied. "You don't have to worry about Murdo." He turned to his old friend. "You have a good evening, and you'll have to come in and tell us all about it tomorrow."

"Aye," Murdo said, smiling. He had no intention of telling William anything. He was a friend, but he was as much of a gossip as Feathers, and the Richardses seemed like good people. He didn't want anything he said to be twisted to make their lives hard. "I'll grab some firelighters for now, but I'll be in for my messages tomorrow."

"We'll see you then."

"Aye."

"Remember what I said, now, Murdo. Not a word to anyone," Thomas repeated as the older man left before he turned to his father. "I cannae believe you sometimes, Dad."

"I told you. You don't have to worry about him repeating a word."

The pair stood there for a moment longer as the room got darker and darker. The shop bell rang again, and Thomas let out another sigh on a day that seemed to have been filled with them. "I'd better go and give Isobel a hand before checking in with David. Why don't you head home to Mam?"

"It sounds like you're trying to get rid of your old man."

"No. I just don't want my old man to catch pneumonia. There's a fresh strain of COVID going around. The last thing we want is you being airlifted to Glasgow Royal."

"Aye, well, maybe I'll head back. You'll be sure to let me know if there are any developments, won't you?"

"I'll come and see you before I call it a night."

"Alright, boy. I'll see you later."

Thomas watched his father walk out of the kitchen then turned to look at the bright pink sky as the sun made its final descent. "Red sky at night, shepherd's delight. Somehow, I doubt that."

11

Seb had lit more candles as well as several lanterns to work by as afternoon had become evening. He had prepared all the veg, and even though the lasagne sheets advertised that no pre-cooking was necessary, he had them in a dish of boiling water with a few drops of cooking oil to make sure they wouldn't meld together. It had all taken longer than he had anticipated due to various interruptions, but he had enjoyed himself. The radio had provided excellent company and the wine gave him a happy glow.

"Well, somebody's been busy," Summer said as she appeared around the corner in jeans and a black blouse.

"Wow," Seb replied.

"Wow, what?"

"We've been married for eighteen years and you still take my breath away."

A broad smile swept onto her face. "That's not what you were saying when you brought me that Shiraz earlier. I heard you chuntering all the way down the hall."

"I'm allowed to chunter when you drag me away from my work. Plus, I didn't mean most of it."

"Oh yeah. Which bits?"

"The bit about how you think the world starts and stops with your say-so and you're a prima donna."

"I never heard that part."

Seb shrugged. "Just as well. Like I say, I didn't mean most of it."

"Most of it?" she asked, smiling. She walked across from the door and pecked him on the cheek. "Love you."

"You smell like wine." She grabbed hold of his face and kissed him on the lips, brushing her tongue against his before pulling away again. "You taste like wine too."

"So do you."

"This is just my second glass."

Summer grabbed it and glugged it back. "There. Now you can start your third."

"You're a bad influence. I was a decent, sober pillar of the community before I got mixed up with you."

"You were never any of those things. If you had been, I certainly wouldn't have been interested in you."

"So it was my bad boy image that attracted you?"

Summer laughed. "You never had a bad boy image. And like most of the female teachers at Weyland Fields High School, I first noticed you when you played Prince Charming in the school panto."

It was Seb's turn to chuckle now. He and Summer were both teachers at Weyland Fields. She taught English, and he taught everything from drama, humanities and civics to P.E. He'd only been at the school a few months when the teachers' pantomime was put on. All proceeds went to local charities, and the five nights it was on were always guaranteed sell-outs. It was loosely based around *Cinderella*, and Summer was cast in that role while Seb took the male lead. "So, I was just a piece of meat to you women?"

"Pretty much."

He kissed her again. "I can live with that."

She pinched a chunk of red pepper from the plate and threw it in her mouth. "You put the table together yet?"

"Yes, Summer, because in between preparing all the veg, making two sauces from scratch and acting as counsellor to our children, I've had all the time in the world."

She looked at the clock on the wall. "He'll be here in a couple of hours."

"Yes. I'm aware of that, Summer."

"Well, is there anything I can do?"

"You ask me this after spending hours languishing in the bath and then deciding to have a nap?"

"Well, is there?"

"You can try the tomato sauce."

Summer walked over to the range. The wooden spoon was still in the pan, and she breathed in deeply, salivating a little as she brought it up to her mouth. "Oh, God. That is so good. If we weren't already married, I'd propose right now."

"It's okay? Not too much garlic?"

"It's perfect."

"There's enough basil?"

"It's perfect," she said, dipping the spoon in again and taking another slurp.

"Okay. Leave some in the pan."

"I can't help it. You shouldn't be such a good cook." She turned back to look at her husband as she dabbed the corner of her mouth with a tea towel. "You said you were counselling our children."

"Hmm?" Seb replied, taking another bottle of wine from the cupboard and grabbing the corkscrew.

"Just a minute ago, you said you'd been counselling our children. About what exactly?"

"Y'know. Stuff."

"What kind of stuff?"

"Charlie's going to miss a call from a girl tonight."

"What girl?"

"Amelia, I think he said her name was."

"Okay. And what's Luna's problem?"

Seb popped opened the bottle and filled his glass before jamming the cork back in. "I told you already. She was having trouble sleeping last night because of the curtains." He took a drink as he felt Summer's eyes bore holes into him.

"What aren't you telling me?"

"What do you mean?"

"I mean I can tell when you're keeping stuff from me. Now, what else did Luna say to you?"

"She … err…." He was about to take another sip when Summer walked up to him, reached across and grabbed the glass.

"You and I don't have secrets, Seb. We always, always said we would be a united front as far as the kids go, and if we start keeping secrets, then we can't be united, can we?"

"She had a nightmare last night."

The air froze around them for a moment despite the heat from the range. The whole episode with Luna's night terrors had seemed never-ending at the time, but they'd gotten through it as a family. To hear this now quickly nullified the effect of the wine Summer had drunk up to this point.

"But…."

"Listen. This wasn't a night terror. She said herself that it wasn't the same."

"What was it then?"

He reached across for the wine, but Summer took a big gulp before handing it to him. "She said she saw a figure outside her window, and even though she knew it was a dream, she couldn't wake up, and she was frozen there just staring at it."

Summer's shoulders sagged. "Sleep paralysis then? Is this what we're going to be facing next? The poor kid. Why didn't she want to say anything to me?"

They had both read up on all kinds of sleep disorders when Luna had begun to have problems, so now Summer's mind began to work overtime. Seb reached out and took his wife's hand. "Listen to me. This is the reason. She didn't want you to freak out. Right now, it's just one bad dream. Everybody has them."

"But what if it isn't, Seb?"

"Then we deal with it."

"I should go and talk to her."

"No. You shouldn't. If she wants to talk, she'll talk."

"Maybe we should call her therapist."

"Well, for a start, we can't call anyone right now. But again, it would be jumping the gun. It was just a nightmare."

She shuffled her hand free. "I really hope you're right, Seb. I really hope you're right."

*

David had been vague with the details when he scrambled together the four other men that made up his search party. There was a part of him that refused to believe his son could ever be responsible for attacking someone in the way Ellie had been attacked. There was another part of him that felt guilty for not being more present in the home.

Is this all my fault?

It was already evening. Despite Thomas's assurance that there was no sign of Duncan at the mill or bothy, David's search team had scoured the surrounding areas before finally entering the woodland.

The five of them were spread out in a line. David himself, his closest friend Neeps, a nickname courtesy of his love for mince, tatties and neeps, and the three Ross brothers, Patrick, Jim and Rob. They had all maintained polite conversation during the search, mainly about what they had heard on the radio about the weather on the mainland. But as time passed, talk had become less frequent.

With the cold starting to bite, and stomachs beginning to rumble, all their thoughts began to drift towards food and the warmth of a good fire.

"I dare say if he was in here, we'd have seen some sign of him by now," Patrick said. He and his brothers were all in their fifties and still lived with their parents. They spoke and dressed like people older than their years, but they were diligent and subsequently the second port of call when David was putting the search team together.

"Aye. Maybe we should pick this up tomorrow," Rob agreed.

"Look," David began. "I know we're all tired, cold and hungry, but my boy's out here somewhere. He'll be more tired, colder, hungrier, and God knows what else. He could be injured. He could be unconscious. He could be… anything."

"DUNCAN!" Neeps yelled. They all stopped and listened as the final echo of his shout disappeared into the forest. "DUNCAN!" he cried out again.

There was no response, and the five men began to shuffle forward again. "DUNCAN!" It was David's turn to shout, but this time, they did not pause to wait for an answer, they just continued walking.

"Y'know, maybe we should head back, get some scran, and get a few more people together for a bigger search party. Fifteen or twenty pairs of eyes can see a lot more than five."

"Aye," Jim replied. "We could head around to our cousins' place. That'd be another four right there."

"And we could drop in on Angus Macneil and Innes, and—" A sound suddenly ripped through the darkness towards them, causing them all to come to a sudden stop. It was like nothing they'd heard before; a loud, echoing, hollow, high-pitched rasp soared into the frigid air.

They stood there glued to their respective spots for a moment, unable to continue as their brains tried to process what they had heard. Then, suddenly, a similar noise erupted from behind them, and they all turned in unison, shining their torches beyond the nearest trees and bushes, desperately scouring the forest.

Their blood ran cold as a third shriek to their left then a fourth to their right rushed through the trees.

"Wh-what is that?" Patrick asked, his voice shuddering like a frightened child about to start crying.

Nobody else spoke for a moment until they heard the sound again and swivelled once more to point their beams in the direction they'd initially been travelling in.

"Dear God, help us," Rob said. "You know as well as I do what that is."

Up until the night that Murdo Macleod had shot the strange beast that had visited his croft, no one had ever laid eyes on the legend known as the Deamhan Oidhche. Well, no one had ever laid eyes on it and lived. There were many who thought it invisible. A thing that came from Hell entered this world and left just as quickly. It was only on that fateful night that they realised it was a physical being. A monster of sorts, but a monster of flesh and blood that could be killed and stopped.

For three years, the islanders had lived with the certainty that the terror was over. But now the sounds that surrounded them told a different story.

"There was only ever one," Neeps cried.

"What?" David replied as he continued to search the darkness with his beam.

"There was only ever one."

"Look. Whatever's out there, it can't be that. That thing was killed three years ago."

"Then what the hell is it?"

"I don't know, but I suggest we start heading back to the cars. You're right. We need more people out here."

"What are you talking about, man?" Jim asked as they all did an about-face and started retracing their steps, almost breaking into runs as they continued to look around the woods. "We can't come back in here."

"My boy could be in here."

"If your boy's in here, he's—" Jim stopped himself from saying the word, but everyone knew what he meant.

"We need to get every man with a shotgun, a rifle or even a pitchfork out searching. We need to—" The chilling sound erupted again to their right. It was travelling with them. They all panned their torches across, but there was no sign of anything.

Another squalling, prolonged, high-pitched, rasping howl echoed to their left, prompting them to finally break into a sprint, regardless of the dangers of tripping over divots or exposed roots. They carried on for just a few seconds before David slowed down.

"What are you doing, man?" Neeps asked, slowing down as well.

"I can't. If Duncan's out here, I can't leave him."

Neeps grabbed hold of his friend's arm and forced him to start moving faster. "You've just said it yourself, *if* he's out here. We don't know where he is, and something catching us won't do anything for his chances of being found. Now run."

12

Duncan was sure his eyes were open, but he couldn't see a thing. There was part of him that felt like he was in the deepest sleep he'd ever been in. *Where am I? What's going on?* He tried to lift his head to search for some small beacon of light, but the effort was too much. *What's happening?*

He could feel his breathing was shallow. His head felt like it was wrapped in a giant fuzzy blanket. He tried to think, he tried to reason, but every time he did, it felt like he was falling back into sleep. *Mum. Dad.* He managed to think the words, but he couldn't say them. *Why can't I speak? Am I dreaming? Mum. Dad.*

Again, no sound left him. *Sound.* He lay there for a few more seconds, and, finally, something registered. *Drip. Drip. Drip.* It wasn't the sound of a tap or a leaky pipe. It was louder, had more of an echo. A few more seconds passed and the fuzziness encasing his head dissipated as he recognised the hard, cold feel of stone beneath him.

He swallowed, but his throat was dry and it made a painful clicking sound. He tried to take a breath in through his mouth, but he couldn't open it. *What's going on?* Duncan desperately tried to search his memory for any clue as to how or why he was in this situation, but the harder he tried the further away any kind of answer was.

He tried to shift his body but couldn't. He waited a few seconds then tried to move the fingers on his left hand. He couldn't. A few more seconds passed, and then he tried to move the fingers on his right. *Yes.* It was a tiny victory, but he could feel the stone ground beneath him as his fingertips gently tapped against its surface.

From tapping them up and down to waving them side to side, he gradually managed more and more movement. His fingers stretched his hand and now his wrist was moving too. Centimetre by centimetre, he was regaining control of his body. *Try the left fingers again.* He tried, but still nothing. He managed to bend his elbow slightly at first, then a little more. Eventually, he raised his hand to his face. His forehead felt cold and clammy. He traced a path further down then recoiled a little as he felt something sticky covering the lower part of his cheek and mouth. The thought of such a substance covering his lower face suddenly repulsed him, and he scraped at it, digging his nails underneath. He sucked in a giant breath of air as the sticky jelly-like substance peeled away from his mouth, lower chin and neck. It felt like removing a large sticking plaster, and it explained why he'd only been able to manage shallow breaths through his nose. In fact, if it wasn't for the nose ring his parents had so vehemently objected to, he may not have been able to even do that. But as it was, the tiny hole it had pierced through the strange concoction had allowed him to breathe just a little.

He felt around further and found more residue of the substance stuck to his bridge and his left cheek too. It was pure chance that one of his nostrils had been left clear. He sucked in another deep breath, and the oxygen helped unfog his mind a little more. *Torch. My torch.*

Duncan reached down into his right pocket and slid his hand in, retrieving the penlight. He pushed the rubber button on the end and, still not fully in charge of his body or his faculties, panned it around while he tried to figure out how he had ended up in this situation.

The beam diffused as it travelled around the vast cavern, and Duncan started to breathe faster as fear took a tighter grip. *I'm underground or in a cave or something.* He closed his eyes tight and desperately tried to recall how he might have ended up there.

He took another deep breath, and now fragments of memories were beginning to return. He had met Ellie at the Norse mill. They started kissing, and then she heard something. He went outside to check, and then he heard a sound. Then … *what then?* He concentrated as hard as he could, but all he could remember was a blurry image of Ellie running away, screaming. *No. That's not all. There was something there, standing between me and her. A figure.*

For the first time since waking up, Duncan realised there was a terrible smell surrounding him. He now managed to lift his head a little and turned it as he panned the torch around. He was on a narrow ledge of some kind, raised off the ground. He groaned as he lifted himself a little further and cricked his neck.

He had a reputation in the community, and not a good one. He was a wild boy, the nearest thing Cora had to one anyway, but as the beam of the torch focused on a garden of bones, antlers and carcasses stretching the entire floor of the cavern and beyond, much further than his torch could reach, he let out a childlike scream. "Help. Someone, help me. PLEASE!" It was pointless and ridiculous, and hearing his echoing shouts bounce back just made him feel more terrified, but his mother had been the one to rouse him from fear-filled nightmares of abandonment when he was younger. His mother had been the ever-present figure while his father worked away. His mother had always been there, but as much as he willed it, she was not there now. She was not with him, and she would not answer his frightened cries for help.

He let out a fear-filled shuddering breath and watched the beam of the torch jerk and judder as his hand began to shake. Then he heard a sound and realised he wasn't alone down there. Suddenly, more than anything in the world, he wished he was.

*

"DUNCAN!" It was more of a screech than a scream. Both Mairi and Jane let out stifled cries of their own as they had slowly been drifting with the heat and hypnotic glow of the fire, but now the warmth of the room became inverted as the horrific wail rose from deep down inside Ellie.

"My poor girl," Mairi said, shuffling across the sofa to place her arm around her daughter. "What did he do? What did he do to you?"

Feet thundered down the hall, and a second later, Thomas burst into the room. He had been to Gordon's place only to find what Murdo had found—nothing. He had just returned and was finally starting to help Isobel in the shop. Ellie's cry had stopped as soon as it had started, but now, rather than being in a catatonic haze, her eyes were wide and full of terror. Her body was rigid, and she leaned forward on the couch, cobra-like, ready to spring up at any second.

"What's happening?" he asked, looking at Jane rather than Mairi, who was desperately trying to soothe her daughter.

"I don't know," Jane replied.

Thomas walked around and knelt down in front of Ellie, blocking out some of the light from the fire, but not too much that he couldn't see tears streaming down her face. "Ellie. What happened last night?"

"Leave her alone. Can't you see she's traumatised?" Mairi replied, holding her daughter a little tighter.

Thomas ignored her and carried on with his questioning. "You shouted Duncan's name. What did he do? Do you know where he is?"

"Duncan," she whispered this time, momentarily pulling her gaze from the flames and fixing on Thomas before moving her eyes back to the fire.

"Yes. Duncan. You were with him last night. Now, where is he? What happened to you?"

"Duncan," she said again as the shop bell rang once more.

"My poor girl. My poor girl," Mairi said, stroking her daughter's arm. "What did he do to you?"

The three adults just looked towards the teenager, hoping some answer would come, but the longer they stared the more they realised that it was less and less likely. For the time being, anyway.

"Thomas," Isobel said from the doorway.

"What is it?"

"You're needed in the shop."

"Yeah. You'll have to manage by yourself."

"I've been managing by myself all day, but it's not that."

"Then what is it?"

"Just come, will you? Someone's got to run this place," she snapped as the bell rang again.

She could be heard muttering by them all as she disappeared back down the hallway. Thomas rose to his feet. "If she speaks again, shout me. I won't be a minute."

It was dark in the hallway as Thomas entered, but the shop beyond was lit up like a beacon. Battery-powered lanterns and lamps were positioned all around the shop floor to light the way for the customers. If this was any other place, it would have been closed for health and safety reasons until the power was back on, but word had spread that the ferry probably wouldn't be arriving with supplies the next day and, depending on how bad the storm got on the mainland, it could be even longer than that.

He entered the shop to find it busier than it had been in a long time. There was a noticeable murmur that wasn't usually present, however, as potential shoppers gathered in the aisles in small groups discussing the day's events, which had in their entirety or not filtered down. He let out a sad sigh as the gossip mongers quieted a little as he appeared.

"What is it, Isobel?" he asked his wife as she emptied the proceeds from another transaction into the open till. She had a table calculator by her side as she totted up the required change.

"There you go, Lizzy. You be careful on the way home. The temperature's dropping again."

"I will. Thank you."

"Mrs Morgan. How are you?"

"Isobel. What's so urgent?" Thomas asked irritably.

She nodded towards the far end of the counter, and he turned to see Annie MacNeil, Angus's wife, standing there with a furrowed brow. Annie was his cousin. In fact, Angus was his cousin once removed as well, but he had always been closer to Annie.

"Judging by the look on your face, you're not here to make my day any shorter, now are you, Annie?" he said as he walked across to her. When he got near enough, he could see in the light of the nearest lantern that her face was pale and drawn. "What is it?"

"I…." She looked around the shop to see at least a dozen pairs of eyes on her, desperate to hear another piece of gossip to keep the mill running in full flow.

"Come back here with me," he said, inviting her around the counter.

She followed him into the back, and they could almost sense the disappointment in the air as they walked out of earshot. Thomas felt sure this was something to do with her husband's drinking. Since that night three years ago, it had got worse and worse. A couple of times, she had been seen around the village with bruises, which she had explained away by unlikely falls, but everyone knew the real cause.

They walked along the hallway, and he flicked on his torch. When they entered the kitchen, he lit a couple of candles too. The bell above the door rang once more, and Annie looked almost apologetic as she spoke.

"It's Angus," she began.

"I thought it might be. What has he done this time?"

"He's not come home."

Thomas looked puzzled. "What do you mean?"

"He went around to see John and Joseph last night. Sometimes they drink too much, so he stays over. He never bothers to call. He doesn't care if I worry or not, but…. Look, that doesn't matter right now. The point is he went around there and he didn't come back."

John and Joseph were brothers who had both married in their early twenties. They'd gone to find their fortunes in Glasgow only to get divorced and make their way back to their parents' croft where they continued to live even after their mother and father had died. Just like Angus, after that fateful night when the Night Demon had finally been laid to rest, they had begun to drink more heavily too. It was not unheard of for them to go on benders lasting for several days before finally coming up for air again. "Okay, have you managed to speak to John and Joseph?"

"I went round there."

"And?"

"No one answered the door."

"If they were sleeping one off, Annie, you might have needed to give it a while."

"I must have knocked for fifteen minutes or more. Their car and ours were parked out front, but there was no sign."

"Angus took your car?"

"Aye."

"How did you get there?"

"I cycled."

"And how did you get here?"

"Cycled."

"Good grief, Annie, you must be frozen."

"I'm alright. I'm just worried about Angus."

"So, you've come here straight from there?"

"Aye."

"Don't take this the wrong way, Annie, but why did it take you so long?"

She stared into the flame of one of the candles. "I love him, Thomas. I said that vow for better or for worse, and I meant it. But the drink takes a hold of him sometimes. When he's blootered, he can be a bastard. For all I knew, the three of them could have been steamin'. At home, it can be the afternoon, sometimes even the evening before he's approachable, and I didn't want to risk going earlier. He's got a temper and then some. If you catch him the wrong way.... Anyway, I'm not here to talk about that. I'm worried. He's never disappeared like this before."

Thomas shook his head. "In my life, I've never known a day like this."

"What do you mean?"

"Ach. Ne'er you mind. Come on. The pair of us'll head around to John and Joseph's place and see if we can't figure out what the devil's going on."

"I told you. They're not there."

"No offence, but the amount of time it took you to cycle from there to here, they could have woken up, cooked a three-course meal and started round two."

"What about my bike?"

"Don't you worry about your bike. I'll put it in the back of the car. Now give me a minute. I need to speak to Jane then—"

"Jane?"

"Yes."

"What's she doing here?"

"Well, you must be the only person on the island who doesn't know. Look, I'll fill you in when we're in the car. Just give me a minute and we'll be on our way."

*

The beams of the flashlights danced through the forest as the five men ran. Whatever beasts were making the bloodcurdling sounds did not falter in their pursuit. The haunting, howling rasps played a regular fanfare as they tried their hardest to escape.

"Waaaggghhh!" The earth rushed towards David as his foot got caught in a looped root. All the wind left his lungs as he collided with the ground. Neeps immediately came to a stop to help his friend, but the three brothers began to run even faster, deliberately or subconsciously taking advantage of the other man's misfortune. No one was sure, not even them, but nonetheless, five torch beams became three as the brothers picked up the pace and weaved in and out of the trees in the hope they could escape their pursuers.

Patrick glanced over his shoulder. He could just about make out the arcs of light from the other two torches as Neeps helped his friend back to his feet. No more demonic sounds rose from the darkness for the time being, and hope began to rise in the siblings' guts as they continued in the rough direction of the vehicles.

*

"Y'okay, David?"

"No. Not any part of me is okay," he said, brushing the forest floor detritus from his front before panning his torch around.

"Aye. Come on. Let's catch up to the others. The bastards didn't stop for a second when you went down."

The pair resumed their race, but now the other three rays of light could only be seen intermittently through the trees up ahead. The ungodly noises wailed again, but this time they were not to their sides or to the back, they were up ahead.

The two men skidded to a stop as a howl of a different kind filled the air this time. It was followed by another, then a third in quick succession. Low-pitched gurgling growls could be heard through the terrified shrieks, and a certainty that this would be their last day on this earth seized Neeps and David.

*

Everything happened in no more than the blink of an eye. One second, Patrick, Rob and Jim were charging through the forest, the next they were on the ground. Two of the torches they'd been carrying had gone cartwheeling through the air, finally coming to rest on the forest floor at different angles, revealing much of the theatre of play as the terrifying demonic creatures that tackled them rose from the shadows.

A fourth beast stood on the periphery of the light, almost as if it was supervising proceedings, while the other three figures loomed ever larger over their struggling prey as they pinned them to the ground.

*

"Sweet God, no!" It was Rob who cried out like a tormented child as the creature's mouth opened like no animal he had ever witnessed. He had not even been able to begin to take in the strangeness and size of the rest of its body. Its skin had the look and texture of well-worn leather. Its black, soulless eyes lit up white like evil tractor beams as they caught at a certain angle in the diffused glow of the LEDs. Its claws, whose sharpness and length he could only guess at, sent shards of pain jolting through him. All of it was overwhelming, but the worst thing was the mouth, opening up, down and out like an ever-expanding hole revealing dagger-like teeth and issuing a gust of warm stench so foul he would have thrown up if he wasn't frozen in horror. Even his breath caught in his throat as he beheld the demonic creature that straddled him.

He could hear his brothers crying and screaming like infants being torn away from their parents by devilish child abductors. In all their years, they had never made such heart-breaking and horrifying noises. He could feel them pounding against the earth close by as they desperately tried to break free, but it was no good. They struggled, but, like him, they were transfixed, seized by the terror of the monsters that were about to snatch their very lives away.

Each man was convinced he was about to have chunks of flesh ripped from him like wildebeest caught in the grasp of a starving lion.

*

A cry of sadness left Jim's lips. It was the cry of a little boy lost in the woods alone with the terrible and terrifying stories he'd heard passed down from generation to generation. But he wasn't a boy, and these were no longer stories. What was happening was real. It was real, and it was worse than all the stories he'd heard about the curse of Cora.

The creature pinning him down moved its head a little closer. He felt his stomach churn as he swallowed its thick, stinking breath. He could feel it as its putrid exhalation burned against his face in stark contrast to the cold night surrounding him.

Dear God. He'd heard a plea to the almighty from one of his brothers a few seconds before, but now it was he who dared to ask for help and forgiveness.

A guttural hiss began in the back of the monster's throat as strands of thick, stringy saliva caught in the periphery of torchlight and stretched between the beast's lower and upper razor-sharp teeth. The hiss got louder, and, inexplicably, a childhood memory of sitting in a dentist's chair while having a suction device shoved into his mouth flashed into Jim's head. The sound was eerily similar, and although his fear of dentists and what they did while you were trapped in their chair was a lifelong one for him, it was nothing compared to the fear he felt now.

*

Patrick had rasped tortured cries but had been unable to let out the full-bellied scream he had intended. The weight of the beast on top of him pushed all the air from his lungs, and now he lay there petrified, just watching everything unfold in the overlapping arcs of light.

Then the bizarre hissing sound that was emanating from his attacker and those of his brothers came to an eerie and sudden stop, allowing a chilling silence to cloak the entire clearing for a moment before each of the beasts vomited a thick, sticky, translucent liquid in unison.

He only caught a split-second image of what was happening to his siblings out of the corner of his eye as the hot, gelatinous excretion covered his nose, mouth and much of his face. It burned like salt on an opened wound for just a moment, and then gradually, he began to drift. The creature's mouth was still wide open as the final drops of the strange fluid dripped. Then finally it closed, not like a human would close their mouth, but almost like four corners all folded in at once, hiding the broken yellow knives behind.

"Jim. Rob." Patrick thought he had said the words, but he couldn't be sure. His senses drifted. He felt like he couldn't breathe, but, strangely, he didn't need to at the same time. The weird concoction that the creature had spewed seemed both suffocating and life-giving, but his body was numbing more with each and every second. He felt like he was drifting on a warm cloud deeper and deeper into sleep. *Jim. Rob.* Now he was sure he didn't say the words. He could just about feel his lips, but they were painted in a thick warm glue. *Jim. Rob.*

He drifted further and further. *Is this what dying's like?* It felt like that warm place somewhere between sleep and wakefulness, and he was completely oblivious to the discomfort as he felt himself start to be dragged across the forest floor.

13

Thomas navigated the narrow country lanes way faster than Annie was comfortable with, but this had been one of the most bizarre days of his life and there was still no sign of it being over. As promised, he had told his cousin about Jane and Ellie. He was not worried about the content of his conversation going any further because the one thing he was sure of was that Annie knew how to keep a secret.

He brought the Volvo estate to a stop outside of John and Joseph's place. The cars were still parked out front of the small croft house. It had once been a picturesque cottage. Their father had painted it white for their mother. But now the paint had chipped and flaked. The door and sills had not been cared for either, and age had taken a toll giving the property a ramshackle appearance.

There were no lights on despite it being dark outside. Yes, the power was out, but there was not a man, woman or child on the island who did not understand the importance of having candles, lanterns and the like.

"I told you. They're not here," Annie said.

"Hmm," Thomas replied, getting out of the car.

"Where are you going?" Annie asked, following him.

"Just having a wee look around," he replied, flicking his torch on. He walked up to the door and tried the handle, but it was locked. *Strange.* It was a rare thing for anyone to lock their doors on the island. He then walked around the property, occasionally flicking the beam of light in another direction to look for any clues, but none were forthcoming.

"I'm worried, Thomas. There's something not right."

Their travels took them to the back door, which Thomas tried, this time to find it open. "You stay here," he said, stepping inside. "John, Joseph, Angus," he called as he walked in through the small kitchen.

Bottles were strewn over the countertops, and it smelt like a bar after closing time. He continued to the living room, but there was still no sign of the three men. He moved the ray of the torch around and focused on a half-full ashtray. He stepped a little closer and hovered over it with his hand. There was no heat, suggesting the final stubs to be extinguished in it had been a little while back at least. He continued to search and saw the case for a pornographic DVD lying on top of the player. *That explains why the front door was locked anyway.*

An empty whisky bottle sat in the middle of the coffee table, surrounded by three glasses. He walked across to the fireplace and bent down, carefully reaching out his hand. *Stone cold. This hasn't been lit today.*

It had been too cold a day not to light the fire. There was a coal bucket and a pile of logs next to it, so there was no excuse. A sound made him jerk around to see Annie standing behind him.

"I told you to wait outside."

"It's like a fridge in here."

"What time did he leave you yesterday?"

"About five o'clock."

Annie's torch shone towards the case on the DVD player, but that was one conversation Thomas wanted no part of. He continued out of the living room and into the hall to find the door to the cupboard under the stairs wide open. He shone the torch inside, and a little part of the puzzle fell into place. Like their father, John and Joseph had been keen fishermen. The back wall of the storage cupboard had mountings for half a dozen rods. Three were still there, but three were missing. He shone the torch a little further around.

The only time he had seen the brothers happy was when they were sitting on their tackle boxes on the banks of the river, and now, as he continued to pan the torch around the small room, he realised the boxes were missing too.

"They went fishing," he shouted, only to find that Annie had crept up behind him. "They went fishing," he said more quietly this time.

"When, though?"

It was a good question. Everything he had seen suggested that no one had been present in this place all day. Had they gone out at first light? Or, in a drunken stupor, had they decided to catch themselves a fish supper the previous evening and not returned?

He retrieved his smartphone and sighed as the readout displayed no bars. "We'll head round to David's place. He took a group out in search of Duncan earlier. Maybe they stumbled across them. Hell, maybe they recruited the three of them."

They went back out to the car, but there was little hope in Thomas's mind that what he had suggested may actually have happened. Too much about this day was not sitting right with him, and far at the back of his mind, there was a little voice saying that none of this was a coincidence.

*

Duncan had remained frozen since hearing the eerie, low-pitched noise. It was the kind of sound one made when on the cusp of a nightmare, caught in between a dream and abject horror. He raised his head and angled the torch as best he could. He still hadn't regained full movement, and his mind was still foggy, but each second free from the viscous brew that had coated his face brought him nearer to normality.

His eyes followed the beam as it travelled in the direction of the sound. He sucked in a painful draft of fetid air as he focused on the bodies scattered around him. They were all still. John, Joseph, Gordon, Angus. Each lay there immobile, each with the same translucent gloop spread over their mouths and noses.

Everybody knew everybody on the island, but there were degrees. Duncan knew Angus, Joseph and John, but when spoken by their parents, the names were always followed with derisory comments. Gordon was virtually a hermit, but he was a cousin or an uncle of his father's, and he had once spent Hogmanay at their house.

"Gordon. Gordon," Duncan called, but there was no response other than a distant murmur from one of the others. "Gordon?" The teenager breathed in another breath and mustered all his strength. He rolled onto his side, and his body groaned as if waking from a hundred-year slumber. Drip, drip, drip continued to echo somewhere in the vast cavern as he shuffled rhythmically towards the other bodies. "Gordon," he called again and again. An internal mumble came from one of the other men, almost as if they were trying their hardest to communicate but couldn't.

The journey of just a few metres over the cold black rock seemed to take forever, but eventually he reached the other men. Duncan managed to scramble to his knees, and it was only then that he realised the fear and panic that had consumed him up until this point had been nothing but a dry run. Fearful tears ran down his face and his whole body trembled as he moved the torch to discover Angus's right leg had been torn off. "God, no, please. God, no, please. God no, please." He repeated the words over and over as if, somehow, they would set him free from this horror, but there was no escape. What he had seen could not be unseen.

There was far less blood than he would expect for such a wound, and, along with his leg, the trousers had been ripped off fully. Duncan studied the gory mess that had been left behind. It was not as if an axe or saw had made a clean cut, but the stretched cords of muscle and sinew, along with the shattered bone, suggested the leg had been snapped and then ripped away from the body.

Duncan turned his head and threw up violently. He had managed to resist doing so after smelling the vileness surrounding him, but this sight was too much. He looked at the other bodies. For the moment, they were whole, but he was sure that was just a temporary state. Then he caught movement in the light and his heart began to pound even faster. He slowly reached out and pressed down on Angus's chest. Du … … … dum. Du … … … dum.

It's a heartbeat. But it can't be. He moved the torch back to the wound. There was a trace of blood leading away from it, but not the massive amount one would expect with such an injury, and it was all still bright red as if it had just happened, which didn't make sense because if that was the case, then surely it would be gushing.

Duncan shuffled around and placed his hand on Joseph's chest. Du … … … dum. He did the same with the other two men and got the same result. Then he recalled the strange dreamlike state he had been in when he had come around. He could still feel the effects of it. *It's that stuff. It does something. It puts you in a coma or something.*

He slowly climbed to his feet, and the world seemed to spin. He closed his eyes until the dizziness was gone then opened them again, casting the beam over the ledge and the vast bone yard. *A lot of those are human bones.* If any confirmation was needed, among them lay clothes, rucksacks, and a whole host of other items exclusive to the kingdom of man but now as useless to their owners as the air around them.

Duncan finally realised what this was. This was the lair of the Deamhan Oidhche. Up until this moment, it had been a story told to scare children into being good. Cora was a strange place. Even though he had been brought up here, it was easy to figure that out. There was a way things were done, and stories passed down from generation to generation were to be revered no matter how ludicrous they were, but now this legend carried weight. The weight of a thousand skeletons. Maybe even more.

He continued to search the graveyard then paused on a skull. It was a little like that of a human but elongated. He followed the ladder of bones down its broken ribcage and beyond to its legs. The thing must have been over seven feet tall. A shiver rippled down his spine as he moved the torch to an identical creature, then another and another. Now he could see a dozen fragments of similar beasts floating on this sea of bones, and a memory flashed into his head.

He was at the Norse mill. He'd gone out to check on the noise that had disturbed Ellie, and he had seen a black outline set against the white of the moon. It had been of a tall, thin figure with a stretched body and long arms. Razor-like claws were silhouetted in the blue-white glow, but before he'd had the chance to move his torch towards it, he was on the ground, and something hot was spewing over his face. Then ... blackness.

His breath shuddered once again. *I have to wake the others and get out of here. I got in here. There must be a way out.* He turned, searching the walls for a crack or a hole, but it was only when he heard the bones rattle behind him that he realised there was something in the darkness waiting.

*

David and Neeps stared at each other in the arcs of light from the dropped torches as they reached the spot where the Ross brothers had vanished from view moments before. Granted, there had been a pause between them seeing the initial attack and their eventual response, but now it was as if Jim, Rob and Patrick had vanished into thin air.

They were grown men, but the two friends felt previously unchartered levels of dread as the loud, high-pitched sounds exploded around them once more. "Oh God, David, it's back."

"It?" David cried. "You saw as well as I did, there was more than one of them."

"I don't understand," he said as both men turned in a circle trying to get a fix on where the sound had come from.

"It's clear that night wasn't the end of it." They had lived with the legend of the Night Demon their entire lives, and, yes, fear had been drilled into them, but it was nothing compared to what they were feeling now.

"Y- You heard the stories as well as I did. It was shot. It was sealed up. There's no way any man or beast could have survived."

"Aye, well, it did," David replied, turning, searching, silently praying that, somehow, somebody would come to their rescue, but knowing all the same that such ideas were for children, not grown men.

"Maybe it's not a beast at all. Maybe the stories of that night were just that, stories. Maybe there's nothing worldly about this thing and tonight it's come back with others to make sure we all pay for what we did."

"Quiet man. There's no such thing as ghosts or spirits or demons or—"

Another terrifying sound erupted from the darkness, stopping David from going on, rendering him still. He closed his eyes, no longer wanting to scour the night for the source of the noises. Instead, all he wanted now was for this to be over.

"Well, do you want to tell me what the hell that is? 'Cause it's not anything I've ever heard."

The sound of pounding feet made the ground shake beneath them as they wielded their torches like swords, desperate to fend off whatever was approaching.

"RUN!" David cried, and both men began to sprint again, not sure if they were heading towards danger or away from it but certain that staying put would mean certain death. All thoughts of their fallen friends were gone as they fled for their own lives, out of the cones of light from the fallen torches and into the darkness beyond the rays of their own.

"They're behind us. I can hear them."

"Aye. Just run. Run as fast as you can and don't look—" Whoosh. Thud. "Aaarrgghhh AAARR—"

Neeps' stride faltered for just a second. There was a part of him that wanted to help his lifelong friend, but there was another part that was sure the only way to help was to get back home and raise the alarm. *I'm sorry, David. I'm sorry, David.* "I'm sorry, Dav—" Thud. Blackness.

*

"Y'know, there's like twenty minutes until Murdo arrives," Summer said as she handed Seb another Allen key.

He tightened the bolt locking the table leg in place before lining another one up with the corresponding slot. "Well, my darling wife. If we hadn't spent the best part of a quarter of an hour looking for the fittings to go with the table, I'd be done by now, wouldn't I?"

"So, this is my fault?"

"I'm not saying that."

"What are you saying then?" she asked, taking another sip of wine. Candles surrounded them in the dining room as Seb worked.

"I'm just saying that if I'd have disassembled the table, I'd have taped the envelope of fittings underneath to make sure we had easy access to them when they were needed."

"Oh well, excuse me, Mister Hindsight. I'll remember that the next time you're off on a drunken weekend and I'm left at home trying to prepare for the biggest house move of our lives."

Seb let out a sigh. "Hindsight doesn't even enter into the equation. You don't need hindsight to know that when you take a table apart, you're going to need all the bits you remove from it to put it back together again. And that drunken weekend was your brother's bachelor party, which we'd known about a year in advance, and it was the first time I'd been away from my family for more than a night in about two years. And furthermore, if I remember, and I'm sure you'll set me straight if I misquote you, but you said, 'Just have a wonderful time, darling. You deserve to chill out and have some fun.'"

Summer sniffed. "Yeah, well. Fuck you."

Seb burst out laughing and climbed to his feet, pulling Summer towards him and kissing her on the lips.

"Eugh. Gross. You'd better not be doing any of that lovey-dovey stuff in front of our guest or he'll be up chucking your world-famous lasagne all over the place."

"My sweet little girl," Summer said. "Always so lovely to see you. What brings you out of your room? Is your bed on fire, darling?"

Luna smiled, and Seb chuckled as he got back to work on the table. "I just thought I'd check that you were both still standing and not passed out drunk in a corner somewhere. There are already two empty bottles on the kitchen counter."

"For your information, neither of those were full to start off with … I don't think. And furthermore, it's Christmas, and I'm on my official wind down. It's been a mad twelve months. I'm allowed to chillax."

Luna shook her head disapprovingly. "I'm amazed you can still speak without slurring your words."

"You don't have to worry about that, sweetheart," Seb said. "Your mum's a high-functioning alcoholic. There's no way anyone can tell when she's drunk or not. Her decisions may be impaired, but to talk to her, you'd never know."

Luna laughed this time. "Exactly," Summer added. "Listen to your father. I'd had half a bottle of vodka when he asked me out. Why the hell do you think I'd have agreed otherwise?" The teenager laughed again as Summer looked down at her legs and frowned. "Where are your jeans?"

"That was the other reason I came out. Can I borrow some of yours? I've spilt Pepsi over mine."

Summer frowned again. "Haven't you got any clean ones?"

"Err…." She looked towards her father doing her best not to get him into trouble.

"I've been meaning to do a load of washing," he said, hoping that would be enough to bail him out.

"Oh, you've been meaning to do a load but thought what's the point because Summer's coming home."

"That's not—"

"Dad's been working really hard, Mum. He's been putting furniture together and decorating and all sorts."

Summer looked at her daughter and then at Seb. "This is a conspiracy. Go into my wardrobe."

"Thanks, Mum. You're the best," Luna said, disappearing down the lantern-lit hallway.

"And don't put pins in them this time. Just roll them up at the bottom."

"Okay, Mum."

Summer took another sip of wine and watched as Seb continued to assemble the table. "I saw you put the bathroom cabinet up."

"Uh-huh."

"I think you should take it down tomorrow."

"What? Why?"

"You were right. It's going to collapse, and I'd never forgive myself if one of the kids got hurt."

"Meaning you could forgive yourself if I got hurt?"

Summer shrugged. "The social services can't take you away from me."

Seb laughed, but the good humour was gone in a heartbeat as a loud knock sounded on the front door. "Oh shit. He's early."

"Well, that's just downright rude."

"You're going to have to take him into the kitchen and give him a drink or something while I finish off in here."

"Leave it to me," Summer replied, closing the door behind her.

Seb listened as Murdo's greeting carried down the hallway. There was nothing he'd have liked more than to get an early night, snuggle up in bed next to Summer and read a good book before finally drifting to sleep, but it wasn't even eight o'clock, and something told him there was a long way to go before he could afford himself that little luxury.

14

Isla answered the door before Thomas had finished knocking. She had a cigarette in one hand and her phone in the other. A waft of nicotine-filled smoke drifted towards him as he stepped inside with Annie following close behind. "Have you found him? Have you found my Duncan?"

"Actually, I've not been looking for him, Isla. I was hoping I could have a word with David though."

Isla led them both down the dark hallway to the candlelit kitchen. There was a glass of whisky on the table next to the ashtray, and she tapped her cigarette, releasing some of the glowing residue, before grabbing her glass and taking another drink. "I haven't heard a word from David since he went out earlier."

"Did he manage to get a search party together?"

Isla let out a huff of a laugh. "Oh, aye. It was a regular posse. Neeps and the Ross brothers."

"And you haven't heard anything from him since?"

She gestured to the phone, which she'd now set down on the table next to the bottle of Scotch. I can sometimes get a bar, but if he's in the forest, chances are he won't have anything."

"I would have thought he'd have been back by now."

Isla nodded towards Annie and, with no pleasantries, asked, "What's she doing here?"

"Her husband's gone missing too."

"Missing? You're sure he's not intravenously hooked up to the giant bottle of Bells above Sandy's bar?"

Thomas and Annie shot each other a look. As unlikely as it was, it was a possibility. Sandy MacDougal's pub was in the village, and it would have been a hell of a trek from the river to there, but if the three of them had decided to go on a Christmas bender, it was not out of the realms of possibility that they had visited there or White's guesthouse where one could also go for a drink to warm one's cockles.

"We'll drop in and see if they've shown up."

"They?"

"John and Joseph were with him."

"Ach, well, my cousins haven't spent a day sober since their ma and da passed. And why are you out looking for wasters like them instead of my Duncan?"

"Well, for a start, Isla, none of this is my actual responsibility. I try to help out when it's needed and—"

"Aye, well, it's needed now. My boy needs help now."

"Och, well, I'm sure we won't be keeping you any longer, Isla," Annie said. "You'll be wanting to get out there as well to look for him."

Thomas did everything he could to suppress a smile, but it was hard. "I ... I ... have to stay here in case he comes back."

"Well, we'll leave you to that then," Annie said, heading back out of the door and down the hall.

"Tell David to come and see me the moment he gets back."

"The last I heard, my husband didn't take orders from shopkeepers."

"The last I heard, Isla, we all looked out for one another on this island, and something's going on today that I really don't like the feel of."

"What do you mean?"

"I mean ask David to come and see me when he gets back."

Thomas left Isla alone in the kitchen and heard the bottle clank against the glass as more whisky was poured into it. "Honestly," Annie said. "The brass neck of the woman, daring to accuse anyone else of being an alky when she's half-jaked herself."

"It's worth us dropping into MacDougal's and White's just on the off chance."

"I'm not hopeful."

"No. Nor am I, Annie, but it's on our way back to the shop, and they might have heard something."

"I suppose."

*

There was a big part of Duncan that didn't want to turn around. The clatter of bone against bone told him all he needed to know. Something was heading towards him across the vast lake of debris. It was probably the something that had attacked him; that had attacked the others and put them into this strange coma-like state. It was probably the thing that had ripped Angus's leg from his body as if it was no more difficult than pulling a wishbone.

Another frightened breath shivered from his throat as he turned and lifted his torch. A pathetic sob left his mouth as the beam illuminated a line of parting bones as something black glided through them like a shark fin slicing through water. Duncan remained there in frozen dread as he just watched it all happening. The movement stopped as he lost sight of it due to the ledge's overhang.

Then, as suddenly as it had begun, the sound stopped, but this didn't ease his fear, it magnified it tenfold.

The silence but for the distant echoing drip, drip, drip made goosebumps ripple up and down his arms. There was another clatter followed by a blurring image shooting from below as a single lithe figure erupted from the darkness.

It landed just a few metres in front of him, and instinctively he backed away, doing his best to keep the torch in his trembling hand pointed in the direction of the ungodly thing. *It really is a demon.* More memories of the previous evening came flooding back to him now, but this creature did not possess the size and stature of the one he had seen. Quite the opposite. It barely came up to his chest. It was like a miniature version of the beast that had attacked him, but that made it no less scary.

The fact that it had jumped the ten-plus feet from below and still managed to rise past the tip of the ledge told Duncan it had scarily powerful muscles, despite its meagre frame. Its black, soulless eyes seemed to squint, and it recoiled as the artificial light of the torch shone directly towards it turning its eyes white for the briefest moment as they caught in the glare. It let out a high-pitched screech from the back of its throat as it took a step forward, then another.

Duncan was mesmerised. Two thin, narrow slits for nostrils sat above its mouth, which opened, revealing perilously sharp yellow teeth. As it took another step towards him, its lips peeled back further and a hiss began in the back of its throat. *What the fuck is this thing?*

Its thick, tough skin had the appearance of well-worn leather. Talon-like claws extended from its unnaturally long arms. Its feet were long and thin, and as it carried on towards him, he saw them bend in the middle as if they had an extra joint.

Another loud hiss emanated from the back of the creature's throat, and a large glob of the sticky fluid like that which he had removed from his face was spat forth and landed just a couple of feet in front of the beast. It let out a high-pitched wail of frustration, and it was in that instant that Duncan became convinced this creature was the offspring of the fearsome monster that had attacked him the night before. *It makes sense. The thing that I saw was huge. This is tiny. But still … it jumped up here, no problem.*

It hissed loudly once more, angled its head up and a second expulsion of the clear gelatinous solution was fired through the air, again landing well short of its target. A shallow moan sounded from one of the other men, and Duncan understood that he might not enjoy the same good fortune he had the first time. If he didn't want to end up like the others, he only had two choices, run or fight.

In the absence of a way out, he raised the beam of his torch and shone it directly into the monster's face. Again, the demon pup recoiled from the bright glow a little, raising one of its arms to shield it from the light. Duncan continued to back up, looking around desperately for something, anything that he could use as a weapon. Fear continued to course through his veins faster than blood, but his will to live was suppressing it enough to stay upright and look for chances.

Then he glimpsed it for just a split second before the creature moved forward again, blocking it from view. A patch of black on the wall to the right of the cavern darker than the rest. It was an opening. *It might lead deeper into the cave system, but it might be a way out too.* Indecision wracked him for a few seconds as he carried on edging away and the thing continued forwards.

Duncan's back hit something solid. *Fuck! Nowhere left to run. This is it. This is it.* He could feel his brow crease. He could feel the burning sensation behind his eyes as he desperately tried not to cry.

The beast began to hiss once more and the teenager angled down his torch. In response, the creature lowered its arm and tilted its head back as a fresh batch of the coma mix gurgled in its throat.

Duncan jerked the flashlight up again, and the demon pup recoiled once more, defending itself against the rays with its arm, but that wasn't enough to protect it from the powerful shove as Duncan charged forward. The young creature fell back with both arms flailing. A screech of surprise and pain left its mouth, and it just managed to strike before it hit the stone floor of the ledge and watched its prey leap off into the pit below.

It was Duncan's turn to let out a cry of shock and pain now as he disappeared up to his belly button in the sea of bones. Sharp edges tore at his clothes and flesh as he regained his balance and started to wade in the direction of the opening. He angled the beam of his torch to see that, before he had leapt, his attacker had managed to claw four bloody divots from his stomach. The heat from the wound was intense, but it numbed as the adrenaline continued to surge. It was only a few seconds before there was another loud crash behind him, and he spun around to see an explosion of bones as the creature dry-splashed into the death pit.

The distributions of the skeletons, antlers, carcasses and bones were uneven. In some places, they were piled up to chest high. In others, they were shin deep, but to get to the other side would mean surfing, trudging and wading.

It's no good. I can't outrun it. He continued to move forward no matter how hopeless it was. His left hand carried the torch, and his right brushed over the surface of bones and skeletons until, finally, he grabbed something that resembled a weapon. It was a femur, half a metre in length. One end was almost club-like and the other was spear-shaped where it had been snapped.

Duncan stopped and turned to see his pursuer was now just a few steps away. He brought the torch up again, shining it directly into the monster's face. It raised one of its long arms defensively to shield itself from the glare, and as it did, Duncan leapt at it, parrying the monster's arm and bringing the club end of his makeshift weapon down like a sledgehammer. There was a loud echoing crack followed by an ear-piercing howl as his victim shrieked in pain.

Crack! Howl. Crack. Howl. Crack. Silence. The beast moved back. Blood as red as his own streamed down the side of its head, and suddenly it wasn't the strange, wild, vicious beast intent on killing him anymore. It was a small wounded animal, desperate to escape to somewhere quiet to die.

Its fearsome eyes were not as dark or penetrating. Its small but powerful body was hunched over as it backed away, forcing a trail through the lake of bones.

Duncan stood for a moment with his torch in one hand and the makeshift club in the other. He just watched as the thing retreated quietly, beating an urgent path through the hellish scrapyard.

The beast stopped just below the ledge, and whereas before it had vaulted up and beyond with ease, now it couldn't even render the power to free itself from the sea of skeletons surrounding it. Instead, it fell back, its black leathery body in stark contrast to the dirty white around it. It opened its mouth wide, and Duncan expected another ear-piercing shriek to echo throughout the cavern, but all that came out was a shallow, pathetic sound almost like a dying lamb's bleat.

Even from this distance, he could see the creature's chest rising up and down as it greedily sucked in its last breaths and then.... Silence but for the drip, drip, drip from elsewhere in the cavern.

Duncan looked at the end of the club as it too dripped with blood then raised his gaze towards the dead beast. *They're not demons. They're not supernatural. They're just ... things. Something from another age or another place or whatever. But they die. They die just like we do.*

He looked back towards the ledge and the other men. *It will take them time to wake up, time I might not have. If I get out of here, though, if I get help, then we might all stand a chance.*

He turned around towards the opening in the cavern wall. It was black beyond it, and now the lethargy from before had left him completely as a fresh surge of adrenaline pumped through his body. He continued to climb, step, and frantically clamber until he reached the opposite ledge. This was lower, just over chest high, and he scrambled up, freeing himself from the graveyard once and for all. He glanced back, and now he could barely see the outline of the beast he had killed. He turned towards the tunnel and fear of what lay beyond enveloped him. On the one hand, it could be the way out as he hoped. On the other, it could lead him into the bowels of this place and even more of these things.

Duncan squeezed his eyes shut for a moment, and when he opened them again, he did everything he could to push the fear that welled inside him as deep down as possible. He looked at the wound on his stomach. It appeared worse than it was. They were welts rather than deep cuts, and although painful and grisly, they were not life-threatening. Finally, he began his journey into the unknown.

*

"This place has certainly changed since the last time I was here," Murdo said, looking around the large dining room.

"You knew the people who used to live here?" Summer asked before taking another bite of lasagne.

"Everybody knows everybody on this island. It lay abandoned for years. It was a cousin of mine who owned it. When they passed, the house went to the daughter, who'd moved away from the island forty years before and never came back. Didn't speak either, as far as I know. She held on and held on to it before finally putting it on the market."

"Well, I'm glad she did. It's everything we've always wanted," Summer replied, her teeth glistening brightly in the candlelight as the five of them sat around the large dining table.

"Oh yeah," Charlie added. "Why would you want to live in a place with Wi-Fi or electricity when you can have this?"

Murdo laughed politely.

"You'll have to forgive my son. He's still adjusting."

Murdo nodded. "Aye. Dare say this is different to what you're used to. We have a few smaller power cuts up here, but this one's because of the bad weather they've got on the mainland. I heard on the radio that over sixty thousand houses were without electricity. The storm's still raging over there, and at least eight people have died already."

Charlie was suddenly wracked with guilt. "Eight people?" he asked.

"Aye. I can't remember a storm like that in a while. We just got a little taste of it earlier, but, thankfully, it backtracked soon enough."

"The snow didn't last long."

"We're in the Gulf Stream and the salt in the sea air means it's rare that the white stuff sticks. We had quite a flurry, but when you've lived here long enough, you'll get a feel for the weather."

"A feel for it?" Luna asked.

"Aye. Often you can see it coming."

"See it coming? Like how?"

"I dare say in your city, your view of the sky had a lot of interruptions. Here you can see what it holds. You can see if the clouds are heading your way. You can see what they're carrying. You can see how many there are. As I say, you'll get a feel for it."

The five of them ate quietly for a few moments before Seb spoke. "So you live by yourself, Murdo?"

Murdo finished chewing and took a drink of wine before answering. "Aye. My Mary died four years back."

"I'm so sorry."

There was a pause of a few seconds as discomfort blanketed the room before Summer, who had lost count of how many glasses of wine she'd had, broke the silence. "What happened?"

Seb and the children looked at one another despairingly as the cringe factor edged up another notch.

Murdo just sat there for a moment before reaching for his glass and draining it.

"I'm sorry. I shouldn't have asked." Summer extended her hand and placed it over the older man's while Seb rose to his feet and refilled his guest's glass.

"No," Murdo replied eventually. "It's alright. Nothing stays a secret on Cora. She died suddenly. It was a heart attack."

This was the excuse he had stuck to all this time. It was the reason placed on the death certificate, and who knows, it may even have been the case. He could hope anyway. He could hope it was sudden and she felt nothing. But he had felt plenty. The pain of losing her. The pain of having to collude while William called in favours so the burial went ahead with no questions asked.

"I'm so sorry," Summer said, tightening her grip around his hand.

"Och, well. We've all got to go some time."

"I'm sorry, Murdo," Seb added, and the older man looked up and nodded towards his host appreciatively.

"Too bad you couldn't have met her. She'd have liked having a celebrity as a neighbour," he said, smiling and trying to lighten the mood.

Summer removed her hand and picked up her fork once more. "I'm just a hack who struck it lucky."

"You have to forgive my wife, Murdo. If she didn't possess false modesty, she'd have none at all."

They all laughed, even Summer, and just like that, the sadness lifted from the room. It didn't take Murdo long to realise that he liked the Richardses. Other than running into the odd tourist here and there, he'd not spent much time with outsiders, but in the short period he'd been with these people, he'd felt more than comfortable. They had welcomed him into their fold without hesitation. When they had said they were sorry for his loss, it hadn't been something they just said out of necessity. They had meant it.

He believed that when the meal was over, he would be finishing his drink and heading home. He had never socialised with urbanites before. Instead, the dishes had been cleared away and they adjourned to the living room with its Christmas tree not lit but glittery all the same. Here, finally, the children came alive as the games were brought out. It had been a good sixty years or more since Murdo had played a game, and as the rules of Pictionary were explained to him, it was hard to hide the smile on his face, even in the shadows of candlelight. Yes, the Richardses moving to Cora might just be the best thing that had happened to Murdo Macleod in a long, long time.

*

It was nearly nine o'clock by the time Thomas and Annie returned to the general store. They had visited the pub and the guesthouse and even spoken to the patrons therein but had gleaned no further information about the whereabouts of Angus and the others.

To Thomas's surprise, the store was still open, and Isobel and his daughter, Tara, who had been missing for most of the day, were serving behind the counter. It was now official; according to Feathers, the ferry would not be running at all the next day, and there was a chance it would be cancelled the day after as well.

The shop was already out of fresh milk, but they always kept a good supply of long-life and powdered. The fresh bread was gone too, but bread mix, flour and yeast were bountiful on the shelves. Just as Thomas and Annie entered, Tara stepped out from behind the counter with another box of supplies to restock the shelves.

"Hi, Dad," she said, raising her eyebrows as if to warn him that her mother was on the rampage again.

"So, you've decided to return," Isobel called across the shop floor, and several of the patrons looked around and smiled. Thomas and Annie walked down the centre aisle as another customer laid their shopping out on the counter. "Where was he then, drunk under a bush?" It was obvious that the reason for Thomas's absence had been no secret and laughter fluttered around the shop floor as the two of them headed behind the counter.

"No," Thomas replied. "There's no sign of him."

The smirk left Isobel's face. "And you've checked all the—"

"We've checked everywhere, Isobel."

"You've checked—"

"We've checked everywhere," he repeated, more sternly this time.

Even in the lantern light, she could see how troubled her husband's face was and though her irritation and anger had been building all day and a rant was well overdue, all thoughts of that were now pushed aside.

"Annie, why don't you go into the kitchen and make us all a pot of tea, eh?"

"Aye," Annie replied, disappearing into the back.

"Tara. Come and serve for a minute, will you?"

"I'm putting the stock out."

"Aye. The stock'll wait for a minute. Just come here." She guided her husband into the back before their daughter had even reached the counter. "What is it? What's wrong?"

Thomas shook his head. "I don't know."

"What does that mean now?"

"It means I don't know, Isobel. There's something about today that's just nattering away at me. There's something not right."

"Ach, you're just tired. It's been quite a day, and with that poor girl still in our living room, your head must be going around in circles. That could have been our Tara just as easily."

"Like hell it could," Thomas replied, and they both smiled briefly.

"What is it then?"

"Duncan's missing. Angus, John and Joseph are missing, and I know you say that's no great loss, and I'm liable to agree with you, but that doesn't change the fact that they're missing all the same. There's no sign of Gordon either and I went round to Isla's place before I came here, and David and the others still aren't back. There's been no word."

Isobel exhaled a deep breath and reached out to take her husband's hands. It had been a frustrating day for her, managing the store almost single-handedly on what had been one of the busiest days they'd ever experienced. They normally opened from nine in the morning until eight in the evening, but they'd be trading some considerable time past that today.

"Look. It's been a long one, but there's nothing more to it than any other day; it's just all happened at once, that's all. A perfect storm, if you will. The power's gone down. The mobile signals are patchy at best. Duncan is probably in hiding after what he's done, but he'll show up sooner or later, it's not like he can get off the island. Angus, John and Joseph are going to turn up pished somewhere, like they always do. David is a proud man. The shame of what his son might have done means he'll want to get to him before anyone to hear the truth for himself. All of this has happened on the same day in a place where the ferry being ten minutes late is normally a subject of hot gossip. And to top it all off, you think you're responsible for solving all these riddles when you're responsible for nothing. You're just trying to do your best for everyone, for the island, just like you always do." She tiptoed up and kissed him on the cheek. "You're a good man, Thomas Munro. There's no better on Cora."

Thomas leaned in and kissed his wife. "I thought after today I was going to get an earful."

Isobel smiled. "Well, there's still time left. You still might before it's over."

Thundering feet drummed down the hall. "Thomas. You need to come quickly," Jane said.

"What is it?"

"It's happening again."

"What? What's happening?"
"It's back, Thomas. The Deamhan Oidhche is back."

15

The tunnel system beyond the cavern was labyrinthine. Duncan had twice taken a spur, which had led him to a dead end, only for him to double back and start again. There was a big part of him that was scared he would never escape this place. He wanted to cry out and scream for help, but he barely let out as much as a loud breath as he couldn't be sure what else was down there with him. He had high hopes as he headed up an incline where dried blood had painted one of the walls. He reasoned that it might be the route where the creatures entered with their prey.

It turned out to be another dead end, though, and black wisps on the wall of the tunnel where the cave-in had occurred suggested that this may have been the original doorway to the underground lair of the thing the islanders called the Night Demon.

He headed back down again until he found the junction and tried another path. This time, a little hope lit in his heart from the outset. A faint but distinct breeze travelled from the blackness towards him, displacing some of the rotten air. *This has got to be the way. Got to be.*

"No." It was a sad, pathetic cry that left his lips as the torch caught what appeared to be another dead end in its beam. But as he got closer, he realised the slope led up to a much smaller gap than the rest of the tunnel, but a gap nonetheless. He got down on his hands and knees and crawled through. There was space of about a foot above him and to each side. It wasn't tall enough for him to walk, even in a crouch, but it was ample enough for him to crawl.

After twenty metres or so, the tunnel deepened further, allowing him to stand. Now the breeze was far more evident, and he realised that it wouldn't be long before he would be outside. Hope gave way to excitement, and as he finally reached the entrance to the underground cave system, a giddy laugh left his mouth.

He shone his torch around a little. He was in a trough of what looked like a massive sinkhole. He'd seen similar ones on YouTube that had devoured whole streets. There were no buildings or roads for the ground to eat here, but trees lined the sides of the caved earth, and a large murky pool stretched out beyond the ledge he was standing on.

Duncan panned his torch around, looking for the easiest and quickest route out. One appeared to be as good as another, and as the moon peeked from behind a cloud, he decided to switch off his torch. In all likelihood, he would need both hands to climb, and holding the torch would be more of a burden than a help.

He clawed at the ground, digging his fingers into the soft earth, giving himself purchase to ascend the steep banks. Each centimetre he put between himself and the cavern made him feel a little freer, a little less afraid. Twice he grabbed handfuls of soil that disintegrated between his fingers, and he slid back down, but, finally, he reached the top, heaving himself over the side and pressing his face against the cold, damp earth.

Duncan began to cry. He still wasn't out of the woods, quite literally, but at least he was out of that hellish cavern. When he had gathered himself and wiped his tears away, he turned a full circle. All he knew was that he was in the forest. He had no idea which direction he should head off in, but the forest wasn't massive, and at some point, he would emerge and be able to find his way back home from there.

Eeny, meeny, miny, mo. He was about to set off when he heard a sound to his left and ran to a nearby tree for cover. He crouched down, listening intently. *What is that?* He couldn't quite make it out. It was like the ground was churning. Snapping twigs and rustling leaves got nearer and nearer, and, finally, staying low, he peeked out. An ice-cold shudder ran down his spine as more memories of the previous evening flashed in his head.

Three creatures, far taller than the beast he had killed, were heading towards the sinkhole. The one in front pulled a single body behind it. The other pair dragged two each as if they were nothing more than sacks of coal or peat.

The first figure paused before reaching the bank and raised its head, sniffing at the air. *It can smell me. Oh, God! It can smell me.*

*

Laughter erupted in the room as another round of Pictionary came to an end. Summer had chosen Murdo as her teammate, and the pair of them were way out in front.

"Oh, man. All this winning is making me thirsty. Who wants a top-up?"

"I wouldn't say no," Murdo replied.

"Losers fill the winners' glasses. That's the rule," Summer said, waving hers in front of her.

"I don't think that's a rule at all," Charlie replied.

"I really don't think that's a rule at all," Summer mimicked before bursting out laughing.

"Shall I get you some coffee, Mother?" Luna asked, smiling and already knowing the answer.

"No, but you can get me some more wine." She handed her daughter the empty glass. "And how about some snacks too? Chop, chop the pair of you."

"Dad's on our side. How come he doesn't have to help?"

"Your dad's old. He gets a special exemption."

The pair disappeared into the other room with the empty glasses, and the adults all watched them go. "Och, you've done well in this day and age to raise two bairns the likes of them."

"You wouldn't want to buy them, would you?" Seb asked, making Murdo chuckle.

"No. I've got enough on my hands with Porridge."

"Porridge?"

"Aye. It was my Mary's cat, and she looks at me as if I'm just a bad smell most of the time."

"Yeah. That's cats," Summer said. "We should get one."

"Don't you think we've got enough on our hands?" Seb replied.

"It could be fun. A family needs animals."

"Uh-huh. I don't have a problem with that, but I've already got two kids who hate me intermittently. Can't we get a dog or at least something that might pretend to like me?"

"Oh, sweetheart, you never need to worry about that. I'll always pretend to like you."

Murdo chuckled again. "I can't remember laughing as much as I have tonight in a long time."

"I'm glad," Summer replied. "It's been lovely having you here. But the night's not over yet. We agreed this was going to be the best out of five, and Seb and the kids are terrible losers, so we need to give them a chance at least."

"Ha!" Seb huffed.

"Excuse me. What was that in aid of?"

"I'm a terrible loser? Who refuses to play Monopoly because she loses every single time?"

Summer shook her head irritably. "Monopoly's a game for children and the uneducated."

"Yet still you never win. What does that tell you?"

"You talking about Monopoly?" Luna asked with a smile on her face as she entered the candlelit room with a tray of drinks.

"How did you guess?"

"It's impolite to listen in on someone else's conversations," Summer said.

"So why did you insist on staying in the lobby when we went to see the new Spiderman movie until that man and woman had finished arguing?"

Summer grabbed one of the glasses from the tray. "Y'know, there used to be a golden age when children were seen and not heard."

"And that would be what you call changing the subject," Seb said, causing Murdo to laugh out loud.

"Okay, Dad. Me and Charlie have been talking."

"Okay."

"We think you should be the match umpire."

"Wait, what?"

"We think we'd just be a better team. Y'know, with the twin thing and everything." Luna laid the tray on the table and took a can of Sprite then grabbed a handful of crisps from one of the numerous bowls.

"You're firing your own father from the team?"

"We just think your strengths would be put to better use in a scoring capacity."

Summer howled with laughter, covering her mouth because even she didn't realise she could be that loud. She rocked back in the chair as her entire body shook.

"Did you put them up to this?" Seb asked as he looked accusingly at his wife. Summer couldn't speak. She just shook her head as tears streamed down her face. "This isn't funny. Your children have just thrown me off their team. That's the kind of behaviour you'd expect from a pair of sociopaths."

"It's just that your drawings are a bit ... substandard."

Summer let out another ear-splitting shriek as she nearly spilt her wine. Seb looked over to Murdo, who was in hysterics too. "Substandard?"

"Not everybody can draw, Dad."

"Where's your co-conspirator?"

"He went to put the bottles in the recycle bin. We were running out of space on the kitchen counter."

"Very funny. There were about four."

"Anyway. I lost the toss, so I was the one who had to tell you."

"I suppose it beats winning the toss and being the one to tell me." He looked across at his wife, whose entire frame was still convulsing. "I can't believe this."

"Oh, come on, sweetheart," Summer said, leaning forward and wiping the tears from her eyes. "It's not like they don't have faith in you. They said you'd make a good umpire." She tried to say it with a straight face but erupted into laughter again.

"This isn't over," he said. "I'm going to the toilet, and when I come back, you and your brother have got some explaining to do." Seb headed out of the door, following the glow of candles as he travelled down the hallway to the bathroom. Waiting there was a large LED rechargeable lantern, which made him squint a little due to its brightness as he turned it on. He placed it down and then availed himself of the facilities. When he was done, he washed his hands and looked in the mirror, chuckling a little. Everything Luna said was true. He was a terrible artist, and he didn't really mind being thrown off the team. He was just enjoying having his family together again, and with Christmas just being a couple of days away, this was a great way for them all to bond.

He finished up, dried his hands and walked back down the hall. "Here's our umpire," Summer said, still giggling to herself as he arrived back in the living room.

"You're enjoying the fact that the kids have dumped me way too much."

"We haven't dumped you, Dad. We just—"

"They haven't dumped you, darling," Summer interrupted. "They just think your drawing is substandard." She laughed again as the words left her lips. "You should be happy that we've instilled a winning attitude in both of them."

"You and I are going to have words when this evening is over, Wife," Seb said.

"Ooooooh!" Summer fired back in a mocking tone before laughing again and taking another drink.

"Where's your brother, anyway? I thought you said he was just putting the bottles out."

"He was," Luna replied.

"He's probably too ashamed to come back in here after what you've done to your dad."

"Yeah. I'm sure that must be it."

"Charlie. CHARLIE!"

"He's probably stuffing himself with the last of the pickled onion crisps."

"What? My pickled onion crisps?"

"I think they're for everyone, Dad."

"No, no, no, no. When we were in Tesco on the mainland last week, I asked you what you both wanted, and I made sure I bought plenty so we didn't run out over Christmas," he said, climbing to his feet. "You both made your choices, and neither of them was pickled onion. In fact, I distinctly remember Charlie saying that he didn't know how anyone could eat pickled onion crisps."

"Yeah, well, I think he's got a taste for them."

"Well, he can get a taste for another flavour," Seb replied, leaving the room. He headed down the hallway in the other direction now and paused outside the kitchen door before leaping in. "Got y—" He stopped as he found the room empty. A puzzled expression painted his face. The recycle bin was just at the side of the house. It would only take a few seconds to deposit the bottles into it and return. "Charlie?"

He walked back down the hallway, past the entrance to the living room where laughter was still ringing out and into his son's room. There was no sign of the youngster. Seb's brow creased and he headed to the bathroom to see if somehow his son had slipped in when he'd returned to the others. Nothing. He headed back past the lively conversation, around the corner and along the hall to the master bedroom to see if he was in the en suite bathroom, but the place was in complete darkness. "Charlie?" Finally, he went back to the kitchen and walked to the door. He could see the glow from the torch around the side of the house. "Charlie. What's the holdup?" he asked as he stepped outside.

There was no vocal response, and the light didn't move. Seb's brow furrowed further as the puzzle deepened. "If you overheard me talking to your sister, I was only joking, Son. I've never been able to dr—" A frigid shudder shot down Seb's spine as he saw the torch lying on the floor next to a broken bottle. "Charlie?" he called again, turning his head in every direction, peering into the darkness. "CHARLIE!" He grabbed the torch and panned it around. "CHARLIE!" He listened hard for some clue as to his son's whereabouts, but nothing was forthcoming. "Fuck." Seb turned and ran back inside. "Summer, Charlie's gone," he shouted as he ran through the kitchen and down the hall.

He had already put on one of his boots when she and the others came out of the living room. "Very funny," she replied. "You've managed to coerce our son into pranking us because—"

"This isn't a joke, Summer." He picked up the torch. "I found this and a broken bottle out by the bins, but there's no sign of Charlie."

The smile wavered a little on his wife's face before it was back again. "Yeah. Very funny. You almost had us for a minute."

"Are you serious, Dad?" Luna asked. Seb just stared towards her and nodded. "Mum?" She grabbed hold of her mother's arm.

"Okay. Let's think about this logically," Summer said, finally realising that her husband wasn't joking. "There was broken glass, right? So, he dropped a bottle and he went to look for a brush or something. He'll be in one of the outbuildings."

"And how will he find anything without a torch in the middle of a blackout?" He turned to Murdo, whose face had become ashen in the space of a few seconds. "I'm still not getting a signal. Where's the police station?"

The old man looked a little taken aback for a moment before shaking his head. "We ... we don't have one. There's no crime here."

"Well, I'm telling you, there's been a crime now. We need to find a way to get a message to the mainland."

"There's still a call box in the village."

"Summer, go with Murdo and Luna and call the police, Search and Rescue, just call everybody."

Despite having had a lot to drink, she suddenly felt stone-cold sober. "This can't be happening. Seb, this can't be happening."

"It's happening, Summer, and I need you to—" The sound of a car pulling up outside stopped Seb in mid-thought. They all looked at each other wide-eyed before Seb opened the door and rushed out.

William Munro climbed out of the passenger side as the others caught up with Seb. "I'm sorry to interrupt your evening," he began. "I'm here to see Murdo."

"Listen to me," Seb said, ignoring what he'd said. "Thank God you've come. We need to call the police."

"The police?"

"The police?" Thomas echoed, climbing out of the driver's side.

"My son's gone missing. He was taking some bottles out to the bin, and he just vanished."

"Murdo. Can I speak to you?" William asked.

"Hello. Did you hear what I just said?"

"I heard you, Mister Richards. Maybe we could all go inside for a moment."

"Fuck going inside. We need to call the police, and I need to find my son."

William turned to Murdo once more. "I think you should come with us. We've got others gathering at MacDougal's."

"Have I suddenly turned invisible?"

"What's going on, William?" Murdo asked, stepping forward.

"It's back, Murdo. It's happening again."

16

Duncan stayed statuesque in his crouched position. He was convinced the creature had not only smelt him but spotted him too. Although he only had the moonlight to see by, it appeared as though it was looking straight at him. Its head rose, and it sniffed the air once more. *This is it. I've escaped from down there only to be killed up here.*

It remained there sniffing for a few seconds, which to Duncan seemed to last an eternity, before all three creatures continued down the embankment, dragging the bodies with them. Up until that point, even though he wasn't aware of it, he'd been holding his breath, and as the final one disappeared down the slope, he exhaled deeply. He was far from safe, but at least they hadn't seen him.

Duncan kept his eyes on the sinkhole as he retreated further into the darkness, slowly at first, but then faster and faster until he was sprinting at full speed through the forest. Tears were running down his face as the whole ordeal finally began to catch up with him. Every rebellious teenage instinct inside him was gone now. All he wanted was to be held by his mother and father. He wanted to hear their voices, see their faces. He wanted his family. He hoped Ellie was okay. The fact that he hadn't found her down there with the others could only have been a good sign. But all he could think about for the moment was his own welfare and escaping this Godforsaken forest once and for all.

*

No one present had been able to believe the words as they came out of Ellie's mouth. What she had seen and experienced was a nightmare, but it was a nightmare that they'd all hoped had come to an end three years back. To hear it had returned brought with it a feeling of despair that the islanders had not experienced in the longest time.

Now, her account of what had happened had resulted in the closed sign finally being turned on the door of Munro's General Store. Thomas had asked questions for a while as Ellie had become more and more lucid then, finally, gone to find his father. It was almost as if William had devised a plan for if this day ever came, and within minutes, he was knocking on doors around the village.

They were putting a posse together to hunt this thing down just as they had that fateful night three years ago. But as the minutes ticked on, much to Thomas's sadness, he realised that William was still more interested in guarding the island's secrets than the safety of its population. *He'll never change.*

The fact that it had returned after everyone had been convinced that it had been laid to rest added weight to the argument that it might not be a mortal being, as had been surmised from the blood trail they'd followed. Maybe demons bled just like everyone else. The only difference was they couldn't die. But regardless, something had to be done; otherwise, how many more villagers would become casualties of this creature?

William had instructed that word should go round that every fit man with a weapon should meet at MacDougal's and, just as they had three years before, explosives should be taken from the quarry to seal whatever hellish hole this thing had emerged from this time.

Now, Ellie, Mairi, Jane, Annie, Isobel and Tara all sat in the dimly lit living room, watching the flickering flames in quiet disbelief. The men of the village were getting ready for the hunt and the women would wait for their return. It was the old-fashioned way. It was the way things always had been on the island, and even though they were well into the twenty-first century, it would probably be the way they would remain for a while at least.

"Should I make us a fresh brew?" Isobel asked.

"I'll give you a hand," said Jane, rising from the sofa and grabbing the empty mugs from the coffee table. They headed out into the kitchen and Jane went about rinsing the mugs while Isobel filled the kettle.

"Truth be told, I just wanted to get out of that room," Isobel admitted.

"Join the club. I really can't believe this is happening again. Why now? Why after three years? Things were starting to get better."

"The Lord moves in mysterious ways, Jane."

"Huh. Somehow, I don't think the Lord had anything to do with this."

"No. No, I think you're right."

"Do you have any more candles? I think these are about to burn out."

Isobel laughed. "Och, candles are one thing that we'll never sell out of in this shop. We'll have spare candles while there's air to breathe." She crouched down and pulled a box out from the cupboard under the sink.

Jane grabbed three, lighting them one by one and letting some of the hot wax drip onto saucers before pushing each into place. "We kept it quiet for the longest time, but there's no way we'll be able to keep this under wraps."

The council and the villagers had been complicit in cover-ups of staggering proportions in the past in order to keep the secret. An odd tourist going missing or even the odd villager over the space of a few years could be explained away. But Duncan, Gordon, Angus, John, and Joseph all in the same twenty-four hours, and those were just the ones they knew about. How could they keep something like this secret?

"That'll be something for William and the council to decide," Isobel replied.

Jane shook her head as she emptied the teapot and placed four fresh bags in. "This is too big."

"Watch what you're saying now, Jane. If this comes out, then every last one of us has got plenty of dirt on our hands."

"Blood on our hands, don't you mean?"

"What's done is done, and there's no undoing it."

"You're right. There is no undoing it, but at the same time, there's no keeping something like this a secret."

"Maybe that's true, or maybe it isn't, but it's for other folks to decide. Not us."

"I went along with it for the longest time, and I thought, three years ago, I could lay all the guilt to rest, but it's reared its head again. Maybe God does have a hand in this. Maybe this is happening to give us all our chance at redemption, to come clean, to admit what we've done."

"Now, Jane Weston, you just watch what you're saying. All we've done is survive."

"No, we've done much more than that. We stayed silent."

"Silence isn't the same as a lie."

"Now we're talking semantics."

"We're talking facts."

"There'll have to be a reckoning after tonight. We can't let it all start again."

"Well, that's what my husband and William are taking care of now, isn't it? This thing will be laid to rest tonight once and for all, and all our secrets will be laid to rest with it."

"Whatever happens tonight, however it plays out, this is the beginning of something new, not the end of something old."

Isobel placed the kettle on the stove and gave Jane a long stare. "You don't mind keeping an eye on the water, do you? I think I'll go sit back down."

Jane watched as the other woman disappeared out of the kitchen. It hadn't taken her long to fit in on this island, but now she realised she was more of an outsider than ever.

*

Duncan wasn't sure how much ground he'd covered, and he was equally unsure about where he'd end up when he finally left the trees … if he ever left the trees. But suddenly, a scream that he knew would haunt him for the rest of his life sliced through the forest like a scythe. It was a wail of pain. But not the kind of pain caused by a broken limb or a deep cut, this was the kind of agony that would never heal. It was the torturous pain that came with the loss of a loved one.

Thump. Smash. Strike. A replay of the scene in the cavern flashed into his mind as he continued through the woods, and, despite his fear, a small pang of sadness for what he'd done hung with him for a moment. But then he was back to the race, the race for freedom, for safety. The race back to his parents. *I just want to see them again. I just want to be back with my family.* Just the previous evening, there was a part of him that felt sure he hated his mother and father, and he couldn't wait to escape this island once and for all and them with it. But now he knew this was a lie. He loved them, and the thought of not seeing them again was as big a fear as being recaptured by those things.

The trees began to thin out and fresh tears poured down his face as a large, wide stretch of croftland came into view. In the light cast by the moon, he could see the sheep over at one end, already lying down for the night. In the distance, he could see the lights of the village.

I'm coming, Mum. I'm coming, Dad.

*

"Mum! Mum, what's going on?" Luna cried as her father's tone and body language became more aggressive.

"There are things on this island that don't concern outsiders," William said, placing a hand on Seb's chest and forcing him back a little.

"Well, my son's just gone missing, so everything on this fucking island concerns me right now."

William turned to his friend once more. "We could use your help, Murdo."

"Murdo, what is this? What's going on?" Summer asked as the beam of the headlights showed tears had already begun to stream down her face.

Their visitor turned back to William. "They've got a right to know."

"No."

"Yes, Dad," Thomas said, causing his father's jaw to fall open a little. Never had his son contradicted him publicly.

"You don't know what you're saying, Thomas."

"No, I do. I should have called the police first thing this morning when we found Ellie. I was trying to protect the island, trying to protect our oh-so-precious way of life like you always taught me. And now I suppose the rest of it is on me because of my inaction."

"Inaction? You've done everything you can."

"Yes, Dad. I've done everything I can, and it hasn't been anywhere near enough." He turned to Seb and Summer and looked at them solemnly. As if by magic, the outside lights suddenly came on.

"The power's back," Luna said, stating the obvious but grateful to latch on to some small fragment of reality she understood.

"If you know something about my son, I—"

"I'm sorry, Mister Richards," Thomas said.

"Don't do it, Thomas. I'm warning you, don't do it," William ordered before descending into a coughing fit.

It was at that moment that Thomas understood more than ever that he was as guilty as anyone for the things that had been done in the name of Cora, the secrets that had been kept. He had always held his father up as someone more than human, this heroic figure who kept the island running, who kept the evils of the outside world at bay, but he was just a man, a frail one at that now. He had no magical powers other than being able to instil fear of what might happen if the secrets of Cora became exposed. And yes, after tonight, life would never be the same again. "There are only so many secrets you can keep, Dad. They grow inside you like a cancer, and one morning you wake up and you don't know where they end and you begin. You become all about the secrets, and you just forget to live life. Well, not anymore." He turned to Seb and Summer. "I'm sorry. If your boy's been taken, in all likelihood, he's dead."

"What? No. NO," Summer screamed as further tears streamed down her face. She turned to her husband. "What are they talking about, Seb?"

Seb turned to Murdo. "What are they talking about?" But the old man just looked down to the ground. "Will somebody tell me what the fuck's going on?"

"I'll tell you, but you probably won't believe much of it," Thomas said.

"Well, that's always a good start. Just start talking," Seb demanded, taking Summer's hand as she latched on to his arm. Luna was glued to his other side, crying hysterically too.

"This is a mistake, Thomas," William wheezed.

"Enough, Dad," he replied before turning to the heartbroken family. He thought carefully about how to phrase what he was saying before he began. "For the longest time, there was a predator on this island."

"Ha. If you're going to tell the story, call it what it was. It's a demon," said William.

Thomas took a breath to stifle his irritation before continuing. "We don't know what it was, but we know it attacked deer, livestock and people. It didn't just attack them; they vanished, almost as though they'd never even been there in the first place."

"Name me an animal that can do that?" William piped up again.

"Enough, Dad. Three years ago, Murdo shot it, and we managed to track it back to its lair. We got some explosives from the quarry and we blew up the entrance. We thought we'd buried it forever. We thought all of this was behind us. For three years, we experienced something approaching normality on this island, but nothing can ever be normal when you've held on to secrets like this for so long." He glared at his father. "Last night, four of our people disappeared. And I'm sorry, but it sounds like that's what's happened to your boy too."

"I don't accept that," Seb replied. "This has only just happened. There's absolutely no proof that he's dead, and I don't care what tales and superstitions and folklore have ruled you on this island. We come from the real world, and when someone goes missing, you look for them rather than just chalking it up to the boogieman."

"Look, Mr Richards, we're heading into the forest now to see if we can find any sign of this thing and put it to bed once and for all." Thomas shook his head. "I don't understand how it could have survived that night. It was bleeding. It was sealed in. It should have just starved to death if it didn't bleed to death first. It doesn't make sense, but here we are anyway."

"I'll tell you how it survived," William replied. "Because it's the Deamhan Oidhche. It's not of this world."

Thomas shook his head once again and took his mobile phone out. "No signal. Can I use the phone in your house, please?"

Seb just gestured towards the door, still in shock, still trying to comfort his family as the insane revelations of some previously unheard of mystery beast rattled around in his head. Thomas disappeared inside, and Summer finally stopped crying long enough to speak again. "Tell me what's really going on, Murdo. Please."

"It's the Deamhan Oidhche, I tell you," William said once more.

Murdo let out a long, sad breath. "Whatever it is, what Thomas told you is true. It was the thing that took my Mary from me." He turned to look at William accusingly. "I kept what I knew quiet in the name of the island."

"It was for the greater good."

"Was it, William? I don't think so. I think it was so you and the elders could keep this place a sanctuary from the mainland. I think it was so Cora would remain one of the last places in Britain to observe the Sabbath and remain untouched by—"

"The evil that's spread everywhere else like a virus."

"You talk of evil? What is it we've done by keeping this a secret for so long? How many families have lost loved ones with no clue as to what happened, with no closure?"

"I'll be in the car," he replied, heading back to the idling vehicle.

"I'm sorry," Murdo said, turning to the heartbroken family. "I'm so sorry."

"This is bullshit," Summer replied, wiping her eyes. "This isn't happening."

"Listen to me, Murdo," Seb began. "You seem like a decent guy. If this is all some big yarn you're spinning to protect some fucking paedo who just happens to be a church elder or something, I swear to you I will crush this entire island to rubble. This is my fucking family we're talking about. Now, the ringmaster's in the car, he can't hear you. Tell me the truth."

A stifled sob left Murdo as he remembered back to his Mary. He knew exactly what the Richardses were going through. "What Thomas told you was the truth."

"No. No," Seb replied, shaking his head. Suddenly, fear gripped him like a vice as his mind flashed back to Emil. He had dismissed what the big man had said as ramblings of a drunk who was clearly damaged goods to begin with. But now his words rang true. He turned to his wife and daughter. "I want you two to go inside. When that bloke's finished with the phone, call the police yourself. Call Search and Rescue. Call the army; call the fucking *Daily Sport* or whoever will pick up the phone. I'm going out to look for my son."

Summer grabbed her husband tighter. "You can't leave us. We need to stay together."

"I've got Wi-Fi," Luna said, looking at her phone. "I'm going to Whatsapp everyone in my contacts and tell them we keep having power cuts, Charlie's been abducted, and we need help. This is no joke." She spoke the words as she typed them, and before any of the adults could say a word, the message was sent.

Summer began to scramble in her pocket for her phone, and through her tears, she sent a similar plea for help to everyone on her contacts list. "Good. I'm going to get my jacket," Seb said single-mindedly, shaking his arm free from Summer. "Fucking monsters and demons, my arse. I've never heard such crap."

Murdo looked at Summer and Luna despairingly then back towards the car where William sat. "I'll have to go with them. I'm so sorry about Charlie. I really mean that."

"We don't know anything. You can't make assumptions. He—"

"They never find them. I never found my Mary."

She had tears running down her face and fear in her heart, but when she spoke, Summer meant every word. "I'm sorry about your wife. But we're going to find my boy. I promise you that."

*

Seb could hear Thomas talking quietly on the phone as he entered the house. He plucked his coat from the hook and headed straight into the kitchen, where he grabbed a twenty-five-centimetre Damascus carving knife. He placed it in his belt and then realised it would slice into him if he crouched or bent, so he removed it and slid it into the slot between his belt and the back of his jeans.

All the candles were still lit, but that was the last of his concerns. He picked up the nearest torch and started heading out when he heard the phone return to the cradle.

Thomas rushed out of the living room to cut him off. "Get out of my way," Seb said. "My wife and daughter have raised the alarm and—"

"Yes. Me too. The winds have eased off a little, but the swell is going to be an issue. It's probably going to be the day after tomorrow at least before the police can get over here."

"You've phoned the police?" Seb asked, mockingly.

"Yes, Mr Richards. I left out the bit about the legend of the Deamhan Oidhche, but I said we had missing persons, including a youngster."

"Well, can't they send a helicopter or something?"

"All the airports are currently closed. The nearest Search and Rescue chopper that could get off the ground is based in Stornoway, but there's a trawler that's in trouble about sixty miles north of Lewis, so we've got no idea when they could get here and, to be honest, even if they did, it would be of little use, but…."

"But what?"

"I don't want to get your hopes up, but I've just found out the boy who went missing last night has just turned up."

"And?"

"He's pretty banged up, but he's alive and back at my place."

"Then what are we waiting for?" Seb asked, grabbing his car keys.

"Mr Richards." Seb paused and turned. "People listen to my father. They always have, and that hunting party that's assembling right now will be heading into that forest with one aim and one aim only, and that's to seal up whichever hole that thing crept back out of."

"Yeah, well, they can fuck off if they think they're going to do anything that stops me from seeing my son again."

"I'd feel the same if this was my child we were talking about, but I just want you to know I have no authority. I won't be able to do anything to stop them other than try to reason with them."

"I'll fucking reason with them all right."

"Despite what you might think, I'm actually trying to help you."

Seb stared at Thomas long and hard. "Where had the boy been since last night?"

"I don't know anything. I'm going there to talk to him right now."

Seb nodded. "Listen to me. My wife and kids, they're nice people. They're good people, and they've made me raise my game. But I was brought up differently to them. If anybody gets in the way of me finding Charlie, I won't think twice. I'll fucking end them."

"Seb." He turned to see Summer and Luna standing in the doorway.

He ignored the shocked expressions on their faces. "The missing boy's turned up. Thomas here is taking me to see him now."

"Then we're all going."

Seb shook his head. "I really don't have a clue what's going on tonight, but I'm not letting either of you step into harm's way."

"It's not your choice to make. And for what it's worth, this is my son we're talking about, and if you think for a second I won't fight just as hard for him as you, then you don't know me as well as I thought you did."

"And who's going to look after our daughter?"

"No one," Luna replied. "I'm coming with you."

"Like hell you are."

"He's my brother." She sniffed back more tears. "My twin brother, Dad. And right now, there are just the three of us who are prepared to do whatever it takes to get him back."

"She's got a point," Summer said.

"Look," Thomas began. "This is wasting time. I'm heading to the shop. You can come with me or you can choose to stay. It's up to you."

"He's right."

Frustration was painted all over Seb's face, but it was true. Every second counted, and each one that passed made Charlie seem a little further away from them. He threw Summer the keys to the Range Rover. "Go start her up. I'll be there in a couple of minutes." He began to head out of the door.

"Where are you going?"

"To get something a little more robust than a kitchen knife." He didn't wait for an answer. The outside light was already on and he marched straight across to the outbuilding where the builders kept their tools. A minute later, he was heading back across to the house with a six-hundred-millimetre crowbar, a hatchet and a claw hammer. He wasn't sure what he was going to face, but whatever it was, he felt confident he could do some serious damage with the items he'd selected.

When he got back to the house, the candles had been extinguished, and it was empty. The sound of a vehicle pulling away outside made him speed up a little. The only people he trusted were Summer and Luna. He couldn't even be sure that he wasn't heading into a trap at the general store. He knew his thoughts were paranoid, but the last few minutes had merited paranoia.

He threw the tools into the back of the car and climbed into the passenger side. Summer immediately pulled away. He could see the silver streaks still running down her face, and he looked into the back, expecting to see his daughter crying too. Instead, she sat bolt upright with a determined look on her face. By her side were a selection of torches and lanterns. "We're going to find him," she said, the thin veneer of strength cracking a little as she continued. "We're going to find my brother."

17

The silver Volvo estate had headed straight to Murdo's place, so Seb, Summer and Luna arrived at Munro's General Store before Thomas. Cars were parked all over the square as men from around the village and surrounding crofts had gathered for the hunt. All they were waiting for was the master of ceremonies to kick off proceedings, but in the interim, they stayed in MacDougal's bar.

Seb banged on the front door to the shop, making the glass rattle in the frame. A roar of laughter went up from inside the pub, and that just made him even angrier. *How can anyone be laughing on a night like this?*

Isobel looked more than a little unnerved as she answered the door. She didn't open it at first, merely shouted through the glass. "We're closed, Mister Richards."

"Your husband told us to come here."

"Where is he?" She looked behind him, searching out the darkness for Thomas.

"He's on his way."

"Maybe you should just wait in your car until he's here."

"Listen, lady. You can open this fucking door right this minute or I'm going to break it down. It's entirely up to you."

"I really don't appreciate—"

"My son is missing, Mrs Munro," Summer said. "Open this door now or I swear I won't be held responsible for what happens next."

"I ... I...." She didn't know what to say. Instead, she unlocked the door, opening it wide for the three visitors to enter.

"Where's the boy? The boy who went missing?" Seb demanded.

"In-in the back," she stuttered, gesturing to the strip curtains behind the counter.

Without even waiting for an invitation, the three of them marched down the centre aisle of the shop and disappeared into the back, following the hushed conversations to the living room. "You're the one who was taken?" Seb asked, immediately focusing on the teenage boy who had an older woman glued to his side. Everyone in the room, including the scared teenager, looked taken aback by the influx of three strangers and the directness of their question.

"I ... I'm Duncan," the teenager replied. His face looked strange. Most of it was pale, but there was an area around his mouth, cheeks and nose that was red as if he had some kind of rash. The girl sitting on the arm of the sofa had a similar red splodge on her cheek.

"Who took you?"

"My son's been through—"

"I'm not talking to you." He turned towards Duncan once more. "Who took you?"

The boy shook his head, still finding it difficult to believe that he had made it back to safety. "It's not what they say. They're not demons. They're animals, just like any others. Well, not just like. They hunt and they kill, but they can be killed too."

"What are you talking about?" Summer asked as Isobel came into the room behind them.

"Careful what you're saying now, Duncan. At least until you've spoken to Thomas and William," Isobel said.

The teenager looked at her briefly and then turned back to the attractive woman who'd spoken to him. "Duncan? Your name's Duncan?" Summer asked. The teenager nodded. "Listen to me. My son was taken tonight. We need to find him."

"They don't kill their prey straight away. They keep them alive ... fresh."

"What are you talking about?"

"When I woke up, there was this stuff over my mouth and face," he said, gesturing to the red patches on his skin. "I don't know what it is, but I think it puts you to sleep. Only, not a normal sleep. There were others in the cavern." He turned to his mother. "Gordon, John, Joseph, Angus. They'd...." His face contorted in horror and revulsion.

"They'd what?"

"One of Angus's legs was gone. But he was still alive. I felt his heart, and it wasn't beating normally. But he was still alive. They all were. As soon as I got out, I heard something, and I hid. Those things were taking more people into their lair."

"Your father's been out looking for you most of the day," said Isla. "Nobody's heard from him or the others he was with. Do you think it could have been them, Duncan?"

Duncan's face saddened. "He was looking for me?"

"He was worried sick. We all were." It was a lie. Most people had thought that he was a rapist or at least a potential rapist. Even his mother had experienced doubts.

"It ... it could have been Dad. I don't know. It was dark. I couldn't see much."

"You said Angus had his leg removed?" Isobel asked, horrified.

Duncan nodded. "It was as if it had been torn off."

"Sweet Lord. Annie went across to MacDougal's to ask all the folk if they'd seen him as they arrived. I'd best go across and tell her."

"He's still alive though. They all are."

"If he's lost a leg, he won't be for long."

"Well. It was weird. It was as if it was hardly bleeding. Like the blood had coag-coag-coagul—"

"Coagulated?" Jane asked.

"Yeah," Duncan said.

"Okay. Tell me exactly where this place is, Duncan." Seb demanded.

"I-I'm not sure."

"You've got to have some idea."

"Well," he screwed his face up trying to remember. "It was in the forest. When I got out, I just ran and ran. I can't really tell you which direction. I just wanted to get away as fast as I could."

"For fuck's sake, can't you—"

"Can you remember anything?" Summer asked, interrupting her husband's rant before it got into full swing. "It's really important. Please, think."

"All I remember is it was in a huge sinkhole, and there was a—"

"Sinkhole?" Summer echoed, looking first at her husband and then towards Luna.

"Yeah. There was a big pool of water and there were—" Before he finished his sentence, Seb, Summer and Luna were back in the hallway and heading towards the door.

Before they'd made it halfway through the shop, they could see that the Volvo had pulled up and William was already heading towards MacDougal's to greet his army of volunteers. As horrific as all of this was, there was a part of the elder and head of the island council that was loving every moment. He was in charge, the man of power. Everyone was looking to him as they had during the dark times.

Thomas and Murdo were about to walk into the shop when Seb beat them to it and led the exit.

"Where are you going?" Thomas asked.

"We know where our son is," Summer replied, and Seb gave her a hard stare.

"Well, tell us, and we can—"

"No offence, mate, but I trust you and your father about as far as I can throw you. If I tell you, the chances are we'll never see Charlie again." Seb grabbed the keys from Summer and pushed past Thomas, nodding briefly towards Murdo as he climbed into the car. Summer ran around to the passenger side and Luna got into the back before the engine roared to life and the Range Rover sped away.

"We've got to help them," Murdo said.

Thomas glanced furtively across to MacDougal's. The noise coming from inside told him there were a lot more people in there than usual, and after his father's comments and actions earlier on, he couldn't blame the Richardses for their hesitance to trust him. He looked at his shop longingly then grabbed his mobile phone. "Come on," he said to Murdo as the pair of them walked back to the car.

They climbed in and he started the engine. The rear lights of the Range Rover could just be seen as they headed out of the village. Thomas used the hands-free function to call home as he eased off the handbrake.

"Cora four, four, two, three."

"Isobel. I don't have much time. Put Duncan on the phone."

"Where are you? The Richardses were just here and—"

"Put Duncan on the phone. Now."

A shuffling sound was followed by Duncan saying, "Hello?"

"Listen. I could lose my signal at any moment. I need you to tell me everything you can as quickly as you can."

There was a pause on the other end of the line. "Duncan? Duncan, are you still there?"

"Y-yes."

"Where did you escape from?"

"I … I don't know, exactly. Somewhere in the forest. There was a hole. A big sinkhole. And there was like a pool of water."

"The Richardses mentioned seeing a sinkhole when they were out for a walk earlier today. I bet they're heading straight to it," Murdo whispered.

"Okay. What else can you tell me, Duncan?" Thomas asked.

"I saw three of them."

"Three?" The temperature in the car plummeted with this stark revelation.

"They're not what you think. They're not what anybody thinks. They're flesh and blood. I killed one."

"You killed one?" Thomas and Murdo exchanged confused glances in the dashboard light.

"It was small. It barely came up to my chest, but it was strong and fast. I managed to kill it though. They die just like you and me. They've got Gordon, Angus, John and Joseph, and they were taking more down there when I escaped."

"Wait a minute. What do you mean they've got Gordon, Angus, John and Joseph?"

"They don't kill you. They keep you alive."

"What are you talking about?"

"I saw them taking others in. I think they might have my dad."

"In? Into this sinkhole?"

"It-it leads to a cavern, a huge cavern that's full of bones. It's like a sea of bones. Years and years' worth."

"Listen to me, Duncan. Are you absolutely sure that Gordon, John, Joseph and Angus were all still alive?"

"Yes. I felt a heartbeat. They squirt this stuff on you. I think it sends you into—"

"Duncan? Duncan? Dammit." Thomas looked across at Murdo, who was now staring down into the foot well. "What is it?"

"If that's true. If all that's true, then that means I could have saved her. I could have saved my Mary."

Thomas shook his head. "Duncan's just been through a huge ordeal, Murdo. We've got no idea if we can take anything he says as true. He'll be in shock. His mind will be all over the place."

"And if it is true?"

"Look, we can't think about that right now. Let's deal with one thing at a time. We've got a head start on the mob that my dad will have scrambled together. You know these people as well as I do. They're not going to listen to reason. All they'll want to do is seal up whichever hole that thing came out of again in the hope that, this time, it doesn't reappear."

"Things. You heard Duncan. There's more than one of them."

Thomas looked across at the older man once more. "Like I said, we can't really—"

"He sounded like he had all his senses to me."

"I suppose we'll find out soon enough."

Thomas sped up a little, and now he could see the red lights of the Range Rover as it turned back onto the Richardses' property.

It was only a few seconds before they were pulling onto the same road, and when they came to a halt, Seb and the others were standing there waiting for them. "If you're trying to stop us—"

"We're not trying to stop you from doing anything," Thomas said, interrupting Seb. "We're here to help."

"I'm going after my son."

"We're going after our son," Summer said.

"Look," Thomas began. "That angry mob that my father put together will be heading into the forest soon. The one advantage we've got is that you know where this thing is, but I can guarantee they'll happen across it at some point."

"Why should we trust you?" Seb asked.

"I suppose that's a good question."

"And what's your answer?"

"Because we can't go on like this. I grew up with this thing. We all did. We grew up with it, and we grew up with the secrets surrounding it, but it can't go on. I can't let it go on. I don't want my daughter to grow up like me, lying to the world. You must have noticed it when you got here. There's something not right with this place."

"How can you say that when you're a part of it?"

"Because for the longest time, I lived in my father's shadow and I obeyed him like a dutiful son. That's what we were taught in church. It's the way people have been brought up on this island for generations … for centuries. Honour thy father and mother, but mainly thy father. All of this … all of it has to end. The Deamhan Oidhche, the secrets, the lies. It all has to stop."

"Aye," said Murdo. "I'm as guilty as anyone. Guiltier. I went along with it to protect the island, protect our way of life, but my way of life ended the night I lost Mary. Everything I loved died that night, but I maintained the lie because that's what was expected." He turned to look at Seb and Summer. "I'll go with you. We'll get your boy back, and maybe, when I see my wife again, that might go some way to her starting to forgive me."

Seb regarded them both for a moment. "Okay. But I'm warning you that if I think for a second you've got another agenda—"

"Seb, stop. This is wasting time," Summer said, and her husband nodded. He walked to the back of the car and opened it up, grabbing the assortment of makeshift weapons he'd selected.

"You make sure you keep your doors locked," Murdo said, looking towards Luna.

"Na-ah. I'm coming with."

"I don't think that's a good—"

"We've already had this discussion," Summer said. "If these things can snatch anyone at any time, then what's to say she's any safer in the house than she is out with us? How would she be safer alone than with us?"

"Och. I've never heard of them entering a house."

"No," Thomas agreed. "I've never heard of it either."

"It doesn't matter," Luna replied. "Charlie's my brother, and nobody's going to stop me from looking for him."

"But you're just a bairn," Murdo said.

"Yeah. A bairn who can run faster than you, so if I were you, I'd just worry about myself."

Murdo stared at her for a moment in the ray of the outside lights and then laughed and nodded. "She's like her mother is this one."

"Tell me about it," Seb replied, walking back around and handing Murdo a torch. "The builders have left all sorts of tools, axes, hammers, everything you can imagine. Go into the stone shed at the back and take what you want."

Murdo handed the torch back. "We've brought our own." He and Thomas walked to the back of the Volvo and opened it up. First, they slipped on their thick wax jackets, and then each removed a double-barrelled shotgun. They grabbed a handful of shells each and placed them in their deep pockets then broke the shotguns and loaded them ready. Finally, they clipped powerful waterproof torches to their coats and lowered the hatchback.

Suddenly, Seb, Summer and Luna fully comprehended the term bringing a knife to a gunfight. Luna looked down at the claw hammer she held. Summer glanced at her hatchet, and Seb measured the weight of the crowbar in his hands. "I don't suppose you've got another couple of guns back there, have you?"

"We haven't, but trust me, if you're not used to them, they're as dangerous in your hands as they would be in an enemy's."

"I suppose. And the angry mob from the village, will they have them?"

"Some of them will; some of them won't, which is why it's important that we get to that sinkhole long before they do."

18

Isobel had left out the grimmest detail when she had told Annie about her husband. She had merely said he was badly injured but still alive. William and some of the other island councillors had listened to her conveyance of what Duncan had said, but none of them were convinced.

"By his own admission, he was scared, he didn't quite know what was going on, he was in a daze and, other than his torch, he was in the dark," William stated confidently, and the other men around him agreed.

"Aren't you listening?" Annie asked. "He said that he checked and they were still alive."

"He said he put his hand on his chest and detected a faint beat," William replied.

"Well, isn't that enough?"

"Annie, he's just a boy. He wouldn't know the difference between a rumble of gas escaping the body and a heartbeat."

"Och. That's nonsense and you know it."

"I'll remind you who you're talking to. Watch yourself, girl."

"I'm no girl. And I know exactly who I'm talking to."

"Annie," Isobel protested.

"I won't be silenced like some wee bairn. That's my husband down there. Those are his friends. They used to be all your friends too," she said, raising her voice and looking at some of the other men who were now listening in to the conversation.

It was true. Until the drink had taken them, John, Joseph and Angus had been respected on the island rather than being the punch lines that they had now become. But it was because of the island that they had ended up this way. Cora produced two types of men. Those who took the terrible secrets they held in their stride and those who were eaten away by everything they did and everything they knew. Her husband and his friends were not the only ones this had happened to, but many managed to keep their torture hidden from view.

"Maybe if you spoke to him, William," Isobel suggested, trying to ease the tension.

"I don't need to speak to him. We have all the information we need. This sinkhole Duncan spoke of is obviously how this thing came back into our world, so that's what we're going out there to look for, and by our Lord's name, we're going to close it up for good this time."

"Will you listen to yourself?" Annie hissed. "Came back into our world, indeed. You speak of these things as though they're the spawn of the devil himself. They come from no other world but our own."

"I'm sure the incomers will be more than happy to listen to the theories of some housewife," he replied with a cruel smile, which prompted sniggering from the elders standing around him. "But we've lived your years and a lifetime more. We know what this is. Reverend Enoch knows what this is, and if he were here now, I dare say he'd have something to say about the matter. Three years ago, we laid this demon to rest, and now it's back. Does that sound like something born of flesh and blood to you?"

Annie shook her head again with irritation and disbelief. "The police are coming. You said so yourself. Do you really think all the secrets this island has kept are going to stay secret now?"

Anger flared in William's eyes and he descended into a coughing fit. He had been thinking of little else since hearing the news that his son had made the call. Part of him still couldn't believe Thomas would betray him for nothing but incomers, but that was a problem for tomorrow. He turned to Isobel. "Take her away from here. We have work to do."

Isobel possessed a rebellious streak. That's what came from being married to someone who always tried to do the right thing in the face of archaic traditions. But there was another part of her that couldn't fail to fall in line when one of the elders spoke either. She placed her arm around Annie. "Come on, Annie. Let's get back."

The other woman shook herself free and raised her finger, pointing it accusingly. "I'm telling you now, William Munro. If you do this thing; if you sign the death warrant of my Angus and the others, I'll share every sordid little secret I know about you and this place. Everything."

It was more than anger that flashed on his face now. It was unbridled rage, and he unleashed a backhanded slap, silencing the entire room. The atmosphere could have been cut with a knife, and Annie moved a hand up to her cheek, rubbing it gently. She looked around at the elders standing next to William, who were equally surprised, then towards the other men. She knew them all. She was related to several. All of them stood in silence, not daring to say a word no matter how much they disapproved. "Take her away," William growled, glaring towards Isobel.

There was no pause this time. Isobel guided Annie through the parting crowd and to the exit, but before they left, Annie broke free of her grasp and turned around to look at the assembled mob. "Angus isn't perfect. Neither are John or Joseph for that matter, but who of us is? We all know why they've turned out the way they have. If you blindly follow William's orders, you'll all have blood on your hands. The three of them are alive, no matter what he tells you."

"Get her out. Get her out, now," William ordered before starting to cough and splutter once more.

She pointed towards William and the elders standing by his side. "If you're going to listen to a bunch of scared old men above your own conscience, then damn the lot of you." Her steely gaze locked on a handful of familiar faces before she finally turned and left.

The door swung shut, letting in an icy draft and an even more chilling sense of foreboding.

*

"Do you really think we're doing the right thing, Seb?" Summer asked as the five of them entered the forest.

"What do you mean?"

She glanced towards her daughter, who was leading the march in between Murdo and Thomas. "I mean bringing Luna out here with us."

"Considering what's happened, I think she's as safe out here as she is anywhere right now."

"I don't know, Seb."

"Err ... you do know everybody can hear what you're saying, don't you?" Luna said, causing Murdo to let out the smallest of chuckles. "It's not like it's even up to you."

"We're your parents, and you're a minor. Of course it's up to us."

Luna stopped and turned, causing her two companions to do the same. "This is my brother, Mum. My twin brother. And yes, sometimes he can be the biggest pain in the world, and sometimes I'd give anything for him to disappear, but ... not really, and not like this." Tears started streaming down her face again. "I need to do this. As scared as I am right now, I'd be more scared if I wasn't with both of you." She looked at them in the moon's glow then turned and carried on.

"That told you," Seb whispered, and Summer forced a smile through her own tears.

"I feel sick to my stomach."

"We're going to find him."

"We don't know that."

"Yes, I do. I won't rest until I've found him."

"What if that cave system goes on forever? What if the—"

"What-ifs won't help us, Summer. Let's just deal with what we know and what we see."

"Your husband's right, Mrs Richards," Thomas said. "Three years ago, there wasn't a man, woman or child on this island who would dare enter this forest after dark, especially at this time of year. Hell, in winter, barely a person would set foot outside. We need our wits about us right now and we don't need to be thinking about things outside of our control. It won't be long before the woods are alive with a bunch of bevvied-up fearties with shotguns, and I want to be out of here before that happens."

They carried on in silence for a few minutes until they reached a ridge. "Wh-what's this?" Luna asked.

"It's not unusual to find pools of fog or mist in some of the dips at this time of year," Murdo replied.

The moon shone down into the clearing between the trees making the foggy haze glow white. It was beautiful and terrifying at the same time. "And we've got to go through that?" Summer asked.

"You tell me," Thomas replied. "You were the ones who said the sinkhole was this way."

Seb took his torch out and shone it around. Even in the dark, he recognised the path they had taken. It was well after finding the sinkhole that they had gotten lost. "Yeah. It's this way."

"It's eerily quiet," Summer said.

"Aye," Murdo replied. "It's like the forest knows it should lie still at this time of year."

"No offence, Murdo, but that really doesn't help."

"Sorry. It's a long time since I've been out this way."

"So, we go on then," Thomas said, leading the way down the shallow incline. The others all paused for a moment before they followed.

"This is weird. I've never seen anything like this before," Luna whispered, suddenly feeling like anything could be in earshot.

The thick mist came up to chest height. "It's like being in a lake of fog," Summer agreed, catching up to her daughter, sharing her unease.

Murdo was suddenly transported back to the night he'd shot the creature that now terrorised them once again. A soupy haze like this had hung low over his property and the surrounding area that night as well. A similar fog had appeared two dozen more times since, but never with the same threat as then and now. "You spend long enough up here and you'll see plenty more."

The group advanced through it slowly like swimmers in shark-infested waters, fearing the worst and expecting to see something travelling towards them at any second. Luna jumped as she felt a nudge against her hand, only to realise it was her mother, desperate for the warmth of her daughter's touch.

Seb stayed behind them. If there was going to be an attack from the rear, at least he'd be able to give them a little more time. He still found it difficult to believe what had supposedly happened. His son had been taken, and that was the full extent of the truth he knew, but the words of Murdo, Thomas and Duncan, as far-fetched as they seemed, possessed the ring of truth. *Then there's Emil.* He chastised himself for not being more understanding or willing to believe, or at least willing to listen.

He'd put the whole episode down to being nothing more than the ramblings of a drunk. But out here, in this strange mist, he realised anything could be true. Then another chill ran down his spine. *Luna's nightmare. Was it a nightmare or did it actually happen? Was she on the cusp of sleep and that thing had appeared at her window only for her to write it off as a dream? Shit!* Seb sped up a little bit now, wanting just a minimal gap between him and his family, causing Summer and Luna both to jump a little as they sensed a presence behind them.

The warmth and happiness of the evening they had spent together was a distant memory now. This had fast become the worst night of their lives, and there was serious competition for that title.

"Stop!" Thomas whispered, bringing his left hand up like a squaddie on a manoeuvre in enemy territory. For a few seconds, no one understood why he'd brought them to a halt, but now they heard it too. Whumph. Whumph. Whumph.

"Oh shit! Where's that coming from?" Summer cried, pulling Luna into her.

"Keep your voice down," Thomas ordered as he and Murdo both brought their weapons up. Whumph. Whumph. Whumph.

They all turned as the sound changed direction. Whumph. Whumph. Whumph. The moonlight's glow was not enough to see beyond the circle of trees that surrounded them and they both flicked on their torches again. The others did the same, angling the beams around frantically in order to get a fix on the sound. Whumph. Whumph. Whumph.

"What the hell is that?" Seb asked, tightening his grip around the crowbar and ushering his wife and daughter to get behind him as he became a human barrier to the shifting sound.

"Is it in the fog?" Summer whispered.

"Nae," Murdo replied. "It's in the trees."

"Get behind me, sweetheart." She stepped in front of her daughter, offering a second line of defence. The sound continued, and despite their torches shifting around like searchlights during a prison break, no clue as to what was causing the sounds materialised.

"We should try to get out of this dip," Thomas said, and, slowly, they all began to move again, but their eyes continued to scour the trees to their right.

Whumph. Whumph. Whumph.

"Oh, Jesus. What is that, Seb?" Seb didn't answer. Instead, he slowed down to a stop once more. "What the hell are you doing?"

"Just keep going," he ordered. "When you're on the other side of this dip, I'll come, but right now, I'll give them something to focus on so you can get out." He glared into the darkness, angling his beam all around.

"Like fuck you will," she replied, grabbing his arm. "We stick together. You stay here, we're all staying here."

"Look. It's a nice sentiment," Thomas said, but your wife's right. "They say safety in numbers for a reason."

Reluctantly, Seb began to move but could not peel his eyes away from the forest.

Whumph. Whumph. Whumph.

It had only been a matter of seconds since they'd first heard it, but, somehow, it felt like this current scene had been playing out on an endless loop. They all sped up a little as the noise continued to their right; then there seemed to be a pause, and they all stopped. The strange sound itself was terrifying, given the context of the situation, but as strange as it was, silence was even more frightening.

They all turned to the vague direction from which they had heard the noises emanating, again shining their torches, although none of them really wanted to see the source of the noise. Then it started again, only now it was getting closer.

"What is that, Mum?" Luna asked, her voice shaking as all the determination and bravado from before was gone. "It's in the fog."

It was a truth none of them wanted to hear, but the time for denial was long past as the strange rhythmic beat continued towards them. Murdo and Thomas raised their shotguns once more. Seb brought his crowbar up, ready to swing. Summer held on tightly to her hatchet with one hand while ushering her daughter further behind her with the other.

"What the hell was that?" Seb cried as a shadow broke the surface of the fog for the briefest moment. "What is it?" he asked again, but still no answer came. He looked towards Thomas and Murdo, who, although pointing their weapons, looked as scared as the rest of them in the periphery of the torchlight.

Suddenly, a fast-moving figure broke through the surface. WREEE! The deafening screech made them all scream a little, even Murdo, as they watched the owl rise and its huge wings flap above them. Whumph. Whumph. Whumph.

The quintet remained frozen for a moment, chastising themselves for something so natural, so graceful being the cause of their fear; then, one by one, they lowered their torches and weapons as they peered into the darkness in the direction the magnificent creature had disappeared.

"Did you see the wingspan on that thing?" Summer said.

"Hard not to," Thomas replied.

"I say we get out of this place before anything else decides to buzz us."

"Seconded," Seb replied.

They made it across to the other side of the dip without incident, acutely aware that life went on in the rest of the forest and that was something else they had to take into consideration while continuing their mission.

"Well, that was something," Summer said as she began to scale the shallow bank on the other side.

"Aye," Murdo agreed. He would never let on, but his heart was beating faster than it had in a long time, and if it wasn't for the desperation of the situation, he would have taken a break.

An unearthly rasping shriek ripped through the forest. "That was no fucking owl," Seb said.

It was followed by another, then another, before a chorus of hellish screeches sang out in unison. "Oh God," Summer cried.

"Yeah. I think he might be on a night off."

"Come on," Thomas said, "we need to keep going."

19

The sounds tore towards the forty-strong troop, causing them all to fall silent. Some had heard this noise before, but not many. Calum, Innes and Doug all looked at one another in the periphery of the torch and lantern lights. It had been three years this winter since they'd entered these woods with an air of hope.

Murdo Macleod had managed to wound the thing, which they had been sure was unwoundable. He had drawn blood from the beast that had terrorised them for generations. By doing so, he had given them a sense that their nightmare could be brought to an end, and for three glorious years, it had been. Its return, though, had them plummeting into nothing short of despair.

They'd all felt sure that it was over. That the legend of the Night Demon would be just a story handed down from generation to generation. That, through time, it would become less and less real the way so many things did as days, weeks and years passed.

Time was the best healer, and unease had lived with them that first year, but when winter came around and with it came no disappearances, no horror, everyone, especially those who had trekked into the woods on that fateful night, breathed a little easier. The following year, when it failed to appear again, they felt sure the terror had ended. Hearing that Duncan had seen not just one but three of these things made them all feel as though God had played a trick on them, that it was some kind of punishment for all the bad they'd done in their lives.

The inhuman cries gradually faded, and the posse began to move once more. "It's true what Annie said," Doug muttered, not loud enough to be heard by anyone but his two closest companions.

"Aye," Innes replied. "It might have been true. But true or not, there's nae point dwelling on things we can't change."

"But we can change it, though, can't we?"

Innes glanced back nervously to make sure no one could overhear them. Many of those who had assembled in the pub had taken a drink. Most had taken more than one, but he and his two friends had remained stone-cold sober. They knew better than anyone that they'd need their wits if they were to survive the night. His eyes finally came to rest on William and the five elders who surrounded him. For as long as Innes could remember, the six of them had decided what had happened on this island. They had made decisions on behalf of the community. A thousand lies had been born from their secret meetings, all in aid of keeping Cora's business just that.

"No. We can't," Innes replied, unconvinced.

"Angus, John, Joseph. It could have been us as easily as it was them," said Doug.

"Aye, but it wasn't."

"But it could have been."

"They turned to the drink, and when that's got a man, it's got him."

"Och, will you listen to yourself, Innes? We could have helped them. The three of them reached out to us, but we fell in line with Munro's orders. We were told never to discuss that night again, lay the whole thing to rest, and that's what we did."

"He had a point. No good could come from speaking of that night or the time before."

"No. We could have helped our friends."

"That time's past now. There's no point talking about it," Calum interjected.

"Well, no. That's where you're wrong, isn't it? They're alive. They're alive, and if we do what Munro's telling us to do, they won't be, and that'll be on us. And not just them. You heard what was said. Duncan saw Gordon and others. Five of them. David took another four men out with him. It's a bit more than a coincidence, don't you think, that the boy saw another five bodies dragged into that pit?"

"Oh, man, will you listen to yourself, Doug? You've got the word of a doped-up teenager to go on that they had so much as a heartbeat."

"Look. I know Duncan's a bit of a wild one, but he's no druggie. I don't care what rumours have started today, but I've no reason to believe he's spinning a yarn. Annie was convinced, and from what I saw, so was Isobel. The fact that Thomas is out here in spite of his father, and Murdo too, tells me that they believe what Duncan's had to say as well." The chilling, distant screeches rose into the air once more, silencing their conversation and that of others for a few beats before they continued their march through the forest. "And there's the bairn too."

"What do you mean?"

"The incomers' boy. Are you willing to have his blood on your hands as well?"

"Let it rest, man. There'll be no blood on our hands. We're trying to stop—"

"There's already blood on our hands, and if we do this thing at the word of a bunch of old men for the idea of a place that died long before that night, there'll be even more."

"What do you mean died long before?"

"I mean it's them who've kept this lie going," Doug said.

"We've all kept it going," Calum replied.

"That we have, but it was at their orders. You have to obey the elders and the church. That's what we were told right through growing up. That's what we've told our own kids. And I've had enough. Do you really want your boy, Calum, or your girls, Innes, to blindly go on carrying this island's secrets because a group of old, scared men no wiser than any others, in fact a damn sight more foolish and blinkered than most, demand it?"

"Be careful what you're saying now, Doug."

"No. I won't. You heard what was said in MacDougal's. The police'll be coming. Aye, not tonight, maybe not even tomorrow. But they'll be coming. This time, not all the stories are going to be straight."

"What do you mean?"

"There's the Richardses. There's Annie. Hell, there's Murdo and Thomas. The fact that they're not with us tells a tale in itself. This thing is unravelling like a ball of yarn, and by the time it's done, it'll roll out flat. The Richards woman. She's not just anyone. She's famous. Christ, my missus was watching her on the telly the other day."

"So, she's got money and she's written a few books. Good for her. It doesn't change anything," Innes replied.

"It changes everything. When someone with money and fame says something, everybody listens."

None of them spoke for a moment while the truth of what Doug said sunk in. He was right, and his friends knew it, but going against tradition, going against the established order of how things were run on the island was taboo. From an early age, they had been indoctrinated, and, like any fundamentalist beliefs, it was hard to shake themselves free from the tradition of obedience.

A loud thud resounded to the side of them, followed by muted laughter and the bark of two dogs who had been brought along for the search. The three friends looked across to see one of the men had tripped over and landed flat on his face. His friends dragged him to his feet, still laughing and wiping his front free of the forest floor detritus that had attached itself. His name was Marcus, and he was William's nephew. He'd been one of the first to arrive at MacDougal's and he'd knocked back three drams in quick succession before most of the others had even appeared. When they did, he joined them for another whisky, washed down with a pint of bitter, and now he was paying the price.

"Will you look at that," Innes said, disgusted. He turned to Doug. "So, say we do this your way. How do we go about it? We're no wiser as to where this sinkhole is than anyone."

"It's very simple. When we do find it, we go in. We find Angus and the others; we get them out and then they can do what they want with that cave. I really don't give a toss."

"You want to go in there? With those things?"

"I don't want to, Innes. I want to be back at home with my feet up in front of the fire. I *have* to. If I let them seal Angus, John, Joseph, Gordon and the Richardses' boy in there, plus whoever else they may or may not have, I won't be able to live with myself."

*

The terrifying sounds had resounded in a fanfare somewhere to their left. It was impossible to judge how far away they were or how many they had heard. More than one? Certainly. One hundred metres? Three hundred metres? Five hundred metres? There was no way of telling. It depended on too many unknown factors.

They had left the lake of mist behind. Luna walked between her mother and father, glued to their sides. Thomas and Murdo took the flanks. Their beams continued to search the forest, but rather than feeling relief at emerging from the soupy fog, the trees now seemed to rear up like monsters themselves. Behind any one, there could be something lurking. They had heard the sounds some distance away, but that wasn't to say there weren't more of the creatures hidden nearby.

They had not spoken since shortly after the confrontation with the owl, realising silence was their friend, but as more memories of that morning came flooding back to Seb, he broke the silence with little more than a whisper. "It's up ahead."

"You're sure?" Thomas whispered back.

"Yeah. Can't you smell it?"

"He's right," Luna said. "I recognise that tree. And I'd recognise that stink anywhere." She angled her torch towards a giant pine that had fallen in some long-forgotten storm.

They carried on, slowing a little as they approached the wide open crater, knowing that they were nearing the home of the things that had made those bone-chilling shrieks minutes before. When they finally reached the edge, they all shone their torches down and recoiled at the foul stench that rose from within. The beams reflected on the murky brown pool of water and then slowly travelled across to the cave entrance, which stood out blacker than black in the glow of the moon.

"Oh Jesus," Summer said, clutching Seb's arm. "If he's in there, he's going to be so scared."

"Well, from everything Duncan told us, it's more likely that he's going to be unconscious, and let's just be grateful for that."

Summer sobbed. "Is this really happening?"

Seb took her hand and squeezed tightly while Luna held on to her other arm.

"I suppose we'd better make our way down there," Thomas said, trying his hardest to speak without his voice trembling as much as the rest of him was.

"How should we do this?" Seb asked.

"Maybe if Murdo stays up here while we head down, so he can cover us in case something comes out of the entrance or something appears up here. And then I cover him while he joins us."

"I don't like that idea," Summer said. "I don't like the thought of Murdo being up here by himself. What if one or maybe two of those things are around? He could be overpowered before he even gets a shot off."

"Okay," Seb said. "I'll stay up here with him."

"No, Dad," Luna pleaded, letting go of her mother and taking her father's arm. The full weight of this journey was beginning to catch up with her, and as sure as she was that she wanted to do everything she could to find her brother, there was another part of her that was just a terrified twelve-year-old girl who had come to the same conclusion as her father about the thing loitering in front of her window the previous evening. "We should all stick together."

"Look. You head down with your mum and Thomas. I'll stay up here with Murdo, and when you're down, we'll come and join you. Nothing's going to happen, sweetheart. I won't let it."

She clutched him a little tighter for a moment before finally letting go and taking hold of her Mum's hand like a little girl entering a house of horrors. Thomas nodded to Seb, and he returned the gesture before the store owner carefully began to descend the steep embankment. He slipped once, twice, three times before finding a firm footing and gesturing for Summer and Luna to follow him.

They both hesitated, looking towards Seb and Murdo before each taking a breath and stepping into the gaping hole. They finally let go of each other's hand and spread their arms out, still keeping a tight hold of their makeshift weapons and torches but balancing like tightrope walkers at the same time as they made their descent.

Thomas first took Luna's wrist and helped her to the safety of the large jutting boulder about halfway down before doing the same with Summer. "Okay," he said. "That was the hard part. It should be a stroll from here."

"Yeah," Luna said, her voice shaking wildly with exertion and fear. "We just head down the embankment into the massive cave system, hoping we don't run into any man-eating demons along the way, rescue my brother and your friends, then do the whole thing in reverse. Sounds like a doddle."

Thomas let out a small laugh, as did Summer before planting a firm kiss on her daughter's head. "She gets her sense of humour from her father."

"Are you ready?" Thomas asked, returning his gaze to the entrance.

"Yeah," they both replied.

"Okay. Just watch where I'm putting my feet."

*

There was a big part of Seb that wanted to be side by side with his family, but he knew that if anything happened to Murdo, they were as good as finished. In fact, if anything happened to either of the armed men, it was over. He glanced across to the old crofter, whose eyes followed his powerful torch beam down into the pit.

Seb brought his head up and panned his own flashlight out towards the trees. Every shadow, every shape oozed threat. It seemed impossible to distinguish between a tree limb and an actual arm, a sprouting branch and a spindly outstretched hand. He was not a man to scare easily or let his imagination run wild, but out here in a dark forest with so much at stake, danger lurked everywhere. Evil was no longer an abstract concept. It was real and lingered in the darkness, waiting for any of them to let their attention lapse for just a moment.

It would spring out and seize them as it had Charlie. Seb knew he couldn't let that happen. His family was his life, and he would sacrifice his own safety in a heartbeat to protect those he loved. He slowly rotated his wrist, feeling the weight of the crowbar in his hand. *Nobody and nothing threatens my family.*

*

It was too steep to make a direct descent to the narrow ridge that jutted out beneath the mouth of the cave, so they had to climb down at an angle. In daylight, it would have been tough, but with just torch and moonlight to guide them, it was far harder.

The earth was loose and frequently shifted beneath their feet as they descended further and further.

"Wah!" Summer cried, skidding as loose soil slipped underfoot. She froze, managing to keep her balance but needing to steady herself before continuing.

"Are you okay, Mum?" Luna asked, staring at her shadow as it loomed ever larger on the brown pool below her.

"I'm fine, sweetheart. Just slipped, that's all."

"Be careful. It's seriously—MUUUM." Before Luna could do anything to stop it, and before Summer had the time to react, the teenager lost her footing and slid down the embankment, knocking her mother's feet from beneath her.

The pair twisted and rolled, dropping from the edge of the bank and into the dirty pool below.

"Shit," Thomas hissed, stopping dead and panning his torch towards the water.

"Summer, Luna," Seb cried, breaking his vigil of the woods and starting down the bank.

20

The three friends continued along in relative quiet. Others more than made up for their lack of conversation. They'd heard no further beastly sounds, and the rest of the group had become more confident and rowdier as their trek into the woods continued, but now a thin mist hovered in the forest. It was not unusual, especially at this time of year, but it was the last thing they needed. Anything that reduced their visibility, however slightly, added another layer of difficulty, another level of danger.

"Where are we going, anyway?" Innes asked, looking towards the other two.

"William's plan is to head to where we tracked it." The "it" in question needed no explanation and the "where" didn't either. They were going to the same concealed entrance they had visited three years back.

"And?"

"Well, he reckons that wherever this sinkhole is, it can't be a million miles away, so then we're going to spread out and search."

"What, you mean split up?"

"That's the plan."

"That's a shite plan."

"I told you. There's nothing about this that I like."

"Aye, well—"

"Quiet," Calum hissed.

"What? What is it?"

"Listen." They listened intently. The conversations of those around them continued, but the nearest dog was whimpering. "What's wrong with Molly, Andrew?"

"Och, don't ask me. The stupid bitch just parked her arse and she won't move."

Calum went across to her and knelt down, making a fuss of the collie, but she wasn't interested. "Molly? Molly?" No matter how much he stroked her or how gently he spoke, he could not get the dog's attention. Her whole body was shaking, and her gaze was fixed towards the darkness beyond. He moved the beam of his torch in the direction she was staring, and as he did, she let out a yelp and started walking away at speed.

He turned the torch back towards her to see she was retracing their steps. Her tail was tucked between her legs, and on the periphery of his torch beam, the other dog that had set out on this mission with them was also retreating.

"Molly. MOLLY," Andrew shouted before whistling a command like he had done a thousand times before when he'd been out with her rounding up sheep. The collie had been programmed to take heed of his commands, and a similar whistle went up for the other dog, but they were unreachable. Andrew's brow furrowed. "What the fuck?"

Calum rejoined his friends. "Obviously, she thinks her owner's an eejit as well," Innes said, chuckling.

"No. Well, yeah, but no. A dog wouldn't just turn tail and run like that."

"MOLLY," Andrew yelled again.

"Keep your fucking voice down," Calum growled.

"What's wrong with you, man?" Andrew asked. "There are more than forty of us out here. Nothing's going to come near."

"Yeah, somehow I don't think Molly agrees."

"Ach, she's spent too much time in the kitchen with Caroline. She's fucking coddled," he replied. "MOLLY."

"What the fuck did I just say?"

"I don't know where you think you get off talking to me like that," Andrew said, marching across to the other man with the small group of friends he'd been walking with by his side.

"I'll tell you where I get off. You and your pals had a fucking skinful before coming out, and I don't know if it's that or if you're just fucking dense, but we're not in a situation where we should be drawing attention to ourselves. Furthermore, that's not fucking normal behaviour for a dog, and if you can't see that something's not right—"

"Ach, you're not fucking right," he said, causing a small ripple of laughter among his friends. "You and your pals have always thought you were something more than you are." He puffed his chest out and raised his head. "Look at us. We're fucking big men. We killed the Deamhan Oidhche. Well, y'din't do a good fucking job, did you?" More laughter erupted around him.

"What's going on here?" William asked, and Andrew immediately shrunk back.

"Err … nothing. We were just…."

"Just what?" he croaked.

"Nothing. Molly just ran off and we were just talking about it, that's all."

"Dogs don't just run off like that," Calum said.

"Aye, well, some dogs are strange, just like people," William replied. "Maybe she sensed the tension in the air tonight and thought better of it." He turned to Andrew. "I dare say she smelt your Caroline baking and decided a nice warm spot in the corner of the kitchen would beat this any day, aye?" He smiled and patted Andrew on the shoulder.

You're all fucking idiots. Calum had always treated his dogs like family instead of sheep herding machines. They always slept in the bedroom rather than in the barn, and when they'd died, he grieved and cried real tears. He knew dogs just about as well as anyone on the island, and he knew that this was strange behaviour.

"Bricks. Bricks," one of the men called out. Bricks' father had been a builder, and his nickname had also been Bricks. Imagination was not in rich supply on Cora, but as Bricks Senior was seventy-six and only had one foot thanks to diabetes, everyone knew which Bricks was in question when the shout came.

The face-off between Andrew and Calum paused for a moment as they, along with their spectators, turned towards the sound of the concerned cry. "He'll be taking a whizz," Andrew said, heralding more laughter from his small fan club.

"BRI—"
"HEL—"
"MALC—"
"YAAGGH!"

All the shouts rang out in the space of a second. They came from the left flank. Torches cartwheeled through the air, lighting the forest in intermittent rays before crashing to the ground or disappearing into bushes.

"What the fuck's going on?" Andrew asked as he and all the rest of the men were thrown into a state of shock.

BOOM. CRACK.

Two shots echoed, and these were quickly followed by two more screams. Then another two.

"Come on," Doug ordered, leading the charge across to where the attack was taking place.

"F-fuck this," Andrew replied, beginning to run in the direction his dog had taken. His six friends all glanced towards William guiltily before following suit. Then another group turned and ran too.

"No," William called after them. "We need to stick together." But they were already on their way and no amount of pleading would change that.

*

The muddy pool was icy cold and coated the pair in a silky film of filth, but it wasn't deep, and by the time Seb had reached the edge, they were both being helped out onto the ridge by Thomas.

When the distant sound of gunfire thundered through the forest, their discomfort was forgotten.

"Oh shit," Summer hissed.

"Murdo, come on," Seb shouted up as the older man remained at the top of the embankment with his back to them. He was still diligently scouring the area, but the shots told him that the horror was unfolding elsewhere, for the time being at least.

He turned and gradually started to make his way down.

"Be careful, Murdo," Summer called as she took hold of Thomas's hand and found a firm footing on the ridge.

Seb stayed in front of the pool, guarding the spot where Summer and Luna had fallen in, like a keeper defending a goal mouth. If the old man slipped, he would save him from the same fate. Seb was worried about his wife and daughter being in freezing clothes, but if the same thing happened to Murdo, it could easily be the death of him.

He descended slowly, side-stepping all the way down, giving his boots as much purchase as possible. Finally, he made it to Seb, and the pair edged around the perimeter of the pool together. When they reached the ledge, Seb grabbed his wife and daughter. He didn't care about getting wet; he just wanted to hold them for a moment. Luna's torch had stopped working, but Summer's still shone brightly, and while he embraced her, she shone it into the mouth of the cave.

"I don't wish to sound uncaring," Thomas said, "but we need to carry on. There might be more of those things waiting for us here, but we know for a fact there are some elsewhere at the moment." He gestured towards the sound of the shots they had heard.

"Aye. He's right," Murdo replied. "The sooner we get this done the sooner we can get you two back home and into warm clothes."

"I don't care about me," Luna said, doing her best not to allow her teeth to start chattering. "I just want to find my brother."

Thomas nodded. "Come on then."

*

"Jesus fucking Christ," Calum cried as he and the others reached the site of the attack. The two shots had been the only ones fired before the owners of the guns had vanished from view as well.

When they'd set off from MacDougal's, there had been more than forty of them. Andrew and the others fleeing had taken that number down to twenty-five. Now, as they panned the torches around the bodies lying on the ground, they realised they were at least another six down.

"Shit," Doug hissed with his shotgun still raised but his eyes firmly on the mangled corpses. Further horrified cries went up as others saw what had happened to their fellow hunters.

"Steven? No. No." Doug broke his stare for a moment to look across at Steven's brother, Jason, as he dropped to his knees. The attack had been swift and brutal. Doug followed the beams of some of the other torches as they danced from body to body. It was like something out of a horror film.

The throats of two of his friends had been ripped from their necks, leaving gaping bloody holes. The head of another was almost at a right angle to its frame. The thick coat that he'd been wearing had four bloody lines trailing across the stomach where a claw had gouged the flesh.

Another figure lay on the ground decapitated, the one next to him was missing half his face and his entrails spilled out onto the forest floor, while the sixth lay face down in a massive crimson pool. No good would come of seeing how he'd died, but dead he was.

"K-Keep your eyes peeled," Doug said. It was all he could think of for the moment. Somebody threw up to his left, and he heard more crying to his right.

"Everybody form a circle," Innes ordered. "Come on now. Back to back. Form a circle. We need to make sure these things don't get a chance to attack again." Some of the men didn't move. They were frozen in horror and grief for their friends and loved ones who would not be returning home with them. But a few still possessed enough of a survival instinct to do as Innes said. Even William and the other elders, who normally would take orders from no man, did as suggested.

"What the hell is this?" Calum asked as he took position next to Doug and Innes. Every man in the circle had their weapons raised, shining their torches out into the forest, knowing the same thing could happen again at any moment.

"It's pretty obvious, isn't it?" Doug replied.

"We've never seen anything like this before. There have never been bodies left behind. There've never been fucking mangled corpses."

"I don't know. Maybe they sensed us as a threat and attacked."

"Aye. Somehow, I don't think we're the threat."

"Steven. Ste-v-en." It was heart-breaking for all present to hear the younger man's voice stutter and crack as he called out the name of his dead brother.

"It was seconds," Innes said, still peering into the woods, scanning the darkness for movement. "It was seconds before the first shout and ... this."

"Aye," Doug replied, shaking his head a little. "I've never heard of anything that could attack like that."

"M-Maybe this is what they say."

"What do you mean?"

"Maybe they are demons."

"Give over, man. Demons are about as real as unicorns."

"Oh aye? Then maybe it was fucking unicorns that did this then."

*

The only sounds were those of breathing and their own footsteps as they headed further into the tunnel. Murdo and Thomas took the lead, each with their weapons raised, while the others aimed their torches as far into the distance as possible. The smell was even stronger here, and it took all of them time to get used to it before carrying on.

They listened, they watched, they sniffed the air searching for any clues. Summer wanted to scream Charlie's name in the hope her son would hear her and shout back. She felt lost. Even though Luna walked by her side, it was like she was alone in this world without one of her children. They were parts of her and all of her. A quivering breath left her mouth and Seb wrapped his arm around her shoulder. He had given Luna his jacket and Summer his sweater leaving himself in just a T-shirt. But for the time being, at least, he could barely feel the cold.

A combination of fear-fuelled adrenaline and fury surged through his body to keep him warm. His comfort meant nothing right now. All he wanted was to find Charlie and get them all to safety. He pulled his mobile phone from his pocket. He had long since lost the signal, but there were dozens of missed messages and texts. If nothing else, it told him help would be coming, if not right now then when the storm on the mainland had cleared. Granted, by then, it might be too late, but it was a small source of hope at least.

"Okay. Looks like we've got a bit of a squeeze," Thomas announced. Their torches shone towards what first appeared to be a dead end, but as they followed the blockage up to the ceiling, they all saw a narrow gap.

"How do you want to play this?" Seb asked.

"It's wide enough to get two through, so how about you and I go first?"

Seb nodded. "You shout if you see anything," he said to Summer, pointing his torch back down the way they had just come from. He handed Luna his phone. "Here. This'll give you some light at least."

She flicked on the torch function. "Th-thanks, Dad." Despite the jacket, she was shivering, and Seb rubbed her arms and back vigorously.

"Stamp about a bit. Get your circulation going." She nodded and immediately did as he suggested. They could all hear the squelching sound rising from her boots, but it wasn't as if they could do anything about it.

"Be careful," Summer said.

"You too." He leaned in, kissing her on the lips. He kissed Luna on her head then joined Thomas as they hoisted themselves up and into the gap. It was tall enough for them to crawl through, and the pair did so slowly, not sure what awaited them on the other side.

"I love you." Summer's call seemed sad and desperate as if she might never see her husband again. All he wanted to do was go back and hold her, tell her it was all going to be okay, but he knew that was a promise he wouldn't be able to keep.

"Thank you for doing this," Seb whispered.

"I'm not just doing it for you. This has to end. If Tara chooses to stay on this island, and it's a big if, I don't want this hanging over her like it hung over me all my life." Seb let out a small sharp laugh. "Have I said something funny?"

"No. It's just ... we moved here because we thought it was a safe place to bring up our kids. We thought we could give them a better life."

"If we do this; if we can end this thing tonight, then you can."

"Yeah. Luna used to suffer from night terrors. It took a lot of therapy for her to get over them. Somehow, I think this might start them again."

"Aye. Well, there's not much I can do about that."

The pair reached the other side and Thomas lay flat on his stomach with his shotgun aiming ahead while Seb panned his torch around. "It looks clear."

"Aye. Looks it."

"I'll climb down first," Seb said, shuffling through the opening and lowering himself over the smooth rock to the ground. When Thomas joined him and brought up his shotgun, he let out a breath of relief. "Do we check it out first or do we get the others through?"

"I don't like the idea of us splitting up."

"Fair point," Seb replied before calling out. "Summer. We're through."

"Okay. We're coming."

"Stay together and let Murdo take the rear," Thomas ordered. His voice continued to echo in the darkness long after his last word was spoken. He glanced towards Seb in the dim arc of torchlight and then the pair resumed their vigil while the others made their way to join them.

*

"I heard Duncan killed one," Calum said.

"And?" Innes replied.

"Well ... maybe before it was about something else ... food. But now...."

The tension and fear in the air were palpable as the loose circle kept its formation. "You're talking about revenge, Calum," Doug said. "That's a human thing. Animals don't seek revenge."

Calum turned towards Doug. The moonlight and torchlight allowed him to see his friend's face, and he could tell he was trying his hardest to make him feel better, to make them all feel better. "Then tell me what this is. Because in my life, I've never seen anything like it."

Doug turned his head towards Jason, who had dropped his torch and gun and was just kneeling by his brother's side with his head bowed. Tears glistened as they fell from his cheeks onto the still-warm body of his sibling. "I ... I don't know."

"Exactly."

"Maybe now you'll hear my words a little clearer," William said, and their hearts sank. They thought they had been talking quietly enough not to be heard, but a man like William heard everything, and as he raised his voice, he made sure others heard him too. "These are no animals we're dealing with. Our fathers and our grandfathers and their grandfathers knew what this thing was, what these things were." He paused, still finding it hard to believe that there was more than one of them. Just one had been enough to force an entire way of existence, a fear-filled regimen that had lasted through the generations. But a legion? "We are being tested."

"This isn't helping, William," Doug replied.

The old man lowered his rifle, reached into his coat and pulled out a dog-eared Bible. "He's testing us now. But He will protect us." Mutters of agreement came from some of the others.

"This is nothing to do with Him," Doug snapped back.

"This is everything to do with—"

"Listen to me. All of you," Doug cried out, lowering his shotgun and stepping into the circle. Some turned to look at the man who dared interrupt William, but most kept their eyes towards the forest. "Whatever these things are, they're flesh and blood. They bleed and they die. They're no more demonic or hellish than any of us."

"Acts Twenty: Thirty-One," William shouted, holding his Bible higher and gaining the attention of even more of the men. "Be on the alert, remembering that night and day for a period of three years." He waved the Bible once more. "Three years. Do you think it's a coincidence that it's been three years since we thought we'd put an end to this?"

Some of the other men now looked more concerned than ever. "Is that what it really says?" one of them asked.

"It's here in black and white for all to see, boy," William replied before descending into a coughing fit.

"Are you for real?" Doug asked, looking at the other men. "Three years gets mentioned in the Bible and you think it's a prophecy? Every fucking thing under the sun gets mentioned in there. Ach, it's coincidence, y'stupid bastards."

"You call this a coincidence?" Jason cried angrily, climbing to his feet and gesturing to the shredded corpse of his brother.

"I call it a tragedy. But it's nothing to do with God or the devil or demons or the Bible or—"

"Everything is to do with the Bible. Everything is to do with God," William proclaimed loudly.

"Listen to me. All of you. In case you haven't figured it out, we're in harm's way out here. These things are in the forest. They could be watching us right now for all we know. They could be planning their next attack. We need to keep our wits about us and treat them the same as we would if it was a rabid animal."

"They vanished," William said. "Did anyone see them? Did anyone see a sign of them? They killed these men then vanished into thin air."

"They didn't vanish into thin air. They're around somewhere, just waiting to strike again."

"Josh, Peter. Come back," a voice shouted, and they all turned to see two figures tearing into the woods in the direction of home.

"Y'see? Y'see what your mad ramblings are doing?" Doug cried.

BOOM! A deafening crack erupted and all their heads turned to its source. Another echoed, then another. The circle formation splintered, and now all but Doug's, Calum's and Innes's weapons were firing in the same direction.

Branches fell, bark chipped, and the ground exploded in the glow of the torch beams, but no one had a clue as to what they were firing at. They just hoped by following the others they would hit something. That, somehow, they could bring this night to an end.

21

Andrew and his companions had converged with the other group. They had all been running in roughly the same direction, but when they spotted each other's dancing torch beams, they met up. They had continued to sprint, risking sprains and falls, to get back to the cars and safety as quickly as they could.

When the booming shots began to echo behind them, they all slowed to a stop to catch their breath. If the creatures were back there, then they couldn't be following them.

"We're going to be called cowards," said one of the men.

"They can call us what they like," Andrew replied. "At least we'll be alive for them to call us something."

"We'll be living in shame."

"Aye. But we'll be living."

"Your Molly knew," Andrew's cousin, Kenny, said.

"Aye." Distant shots continued, but the relief this gave was only temporary as the darkness of the forest and the mist continued to surround them. "Come on. I don't want to be in these woods all night."

"Wait," Kenny replied. "This isn't the way we came. We've gone off course somewhere."

"What do you mean, man? We were running in a straight line, more or less," one of the others replied.

"Aye, but a straight line in the wrong direction."

"Nae. You're all turned around out here. This is the way I'm telling you."

The group began to move again, but now their torches and lanterns scoured the woodland, not looking for threats but for traces of the path they'd originally taken. The longer they walked the more they realised Kenny was right.

The sound of gunfire had finally died out, and silence hung in the air. "I told you. We never saw anything like this on the way here."

All their torches pointed to the lake of fog that spread in the dip in front of them. It glowed white, reflecting the moon's solemn gaze. There wasn't a man among them who hadn't seen a mist like this. Often it hung over the moors and crofts, but not one of them had ever been in the forest after dark, so this was the first time they'd seen one in woodland.

"The sooner we get through this the sooner we'll be home," Andrew said.

"Jesus. We don't even know which fucking way we're going."

"This isn't the Cairngorms. We keep walking in a straight line and we'll get out of it eventually."

"I just want to go on record as saying this is a really shitty plan," Kenny replied.

Andrew looked at him for a moment then descended into the dip. The dense cloud reached above his belly button, but as he continued through it and angled his torch up, he could see that it was not too far to the other side. He threw a quick glance over his shoulder and, one by one, the others were following him now. It's *true. We're going to be pariahs. We turned like cowards and ran.* "Careful where you're walking. There are some serious puddles in here."

The rain from a few nights before would be slow to seep away in places, and in a dip like this there was no natural drainage.

"Whoa," cried Kenny, stumbling forward. Andrew spun around quickly, as did all the others. They watched as he disappeared into the low-lying fog. Panic seized each of them for a moment, but still they could not pull their eyes away from the spot where he had vanished. "Fucking tree stump," he growled, reappearing and causing all those present to start laughing.

It felt good. They had all shared the same horror, all fearing the worst when Kenny had disappeared. "You clumsy walloper," Andrew said. "I told you to watch what you were doing."

"It's not my fucking fault. I can't see a thing in this soup. It's like walking through paint."

"Aye, well, just watch where you're going. There's only so much more my heart can take."

The others laughed at this too. They all felt the same way. "Och. Come on, man. Let's get out of here."

They carried on, each more careful now, feeling out their way a little with the tips of their boots to make sure the same thing didn't happen to them.

"Waagh!" came another cry, and they turned to see Gary had gone down too.

All the men laughed once more. "What did I just say to all of you?" Andrew asked. "C'mon, y'clumsy bastard. It's going to take us all night to get out of the forest at this rate." The seconds dragged on. "Gary? Gary?"

"Arrgghh!" Out of the corner of his eye, Andrew saw another of his friends vanish. It was followed by a far louder scream and a ripping noise that sounded like a thick piece of leather was being torn down the middle.

"AN—" A third figure, then a fourth disappeared, and the tormented cries became even louder. "A-N-D-REW." The agonised howl could barely be heard over the furious, unfamiliar growls. The tortured plea lasted only a matter of seconds before it fell silent.

The other men looked towards one another, desperately wanting to flee, but their feet felt glued to the ground. They would be next. It was inevitable.

"RUN," Andrew cried, finally breaking the spell and putting one boot in front of the other.

"NOOO." Another agonised shriek sounded as a fifth man went down.

"ANDY!" Then a sixth vanished, but Andrew only caught a fleeting glimpse of it as he sprinted flat out. *That was Kenny.* They had grown up together like brothers. They were best friends.

BOOM! BOOM! BOOM! The remaining men began to fire indiscriminately and blindly.

Andrew could hear more cries beneath the thunder. *I should help. I should help and fight.* Tears streamed from his eyes as he continued. He looked back once more, and now he saw an arm raised out of the mist. It wasn't human. It was … something else, something chilling … horrifying, something he would never see in a thousand wildlife documentaries. A shiver ran through his entire body as if liquid nitrogen had just been injected into his bloodstream.

He could not even imagine the fear of being dragged down into the dense mist only to be torn apart by some devilish beast.

"AGGHH!" BOOM! BOOM!

"HELP… ME!"

He looked back again, shining his powerful torch, to see Kenny emerging from the fog. He paused. Part of him wanted to go back and help, but as Kenny turned towards him, he saw a gaping hole where his throat had been. His left eye was missing, and clawed, bloody welts ran down his face.

There was another deafening crack, and Kenny flew two metres as the shotgun blast inadvertently struck him rather than its intended target. Andrew looked to see Chips, a lifelong friend, with a look of pure panic on his face. He had been the one to pull the trigger. His mouth fell open as he watched his victim disappear into the lake of haze.

Instinctively, Chips turned as though, somehow, he knew he had an audience. The torch attached to his jacket illuminated his own face perfectly, but he could only see an outline of Andrew. It was enough for him to know that the other man had witnessed the whole tragic event take place. "I...." he began, but he didn't get the chance to finish the thought as he vanished into the ghostly cloud in a hail of short-lived screams.

It had only been seconds, but most of the band he had set off with was already gone. Andrew turned again and started to run as the last howls, pleas, and shots rang out. His foot thudded against something, causing him to stumble. He went flailing to the ground, and his shotgun cartwheeled as his torch cracked against something solid. It immediately began to flash as if it was about to go out.

No. No. No. He swept the ground with his hand for a moment, hoping he would make contact with the cold metal of the gun as the chorus of his friends' wails began to die down further.

I need to get out of here. He sprang back to his feet, casting a swift glimpse back to the scene behind him, only to find that not one of his compatriots remained vertical. A small handful of cries and gurgles told him they were still alive ... just, however.

Andrew started to run once more, hoping the beasts, the demons, whatever they may be, were too preoccupied with the others to think about him. He realised what a selfish and cowardly thought that was as soon as it entered his head, but fear trumped all other cards at that moment.

He charged faster and faster, finally reaching the rise on the other side. He headed up the shallow embankment with virtually no loss of pace and, step by step, broke free of the haunting fog. He glanced back again, and in the glow of moonlight, he could see four figures rise from its depths. He couldn't make out details, only outlines.

They were tall, thin, unnatural looking, and as they turned in his direction, their eyes glowed white momentarily as they caught in the broken fans of torchlight rising from the ground. The hellish quartet just stood there staring towards him perfectly still as he continued to make his getaway. Something shiny and wet painted their mouths and the lower part of their faces. It took a couple of seconds for Andrew to understand, but then he realised it was the blood of the creatures' victims. It had taken on a morbid hue in the light of the moon, and his whole body shuddered again.

The four beasts suddenly erupted in a chorus of unearthly sound. High-pitched grating howls travelled towards him in a moving wall of noise sending fresh vibrations of terror through every fibre of his body.

He returned his gaze to his direction of travel. The torch was still flashing on and off in his hand, but it was providing him with enough illumination to find his way through the trees, which were now much thicker out of the dip. He zigged and zagged hoping he could put enough distance between himself and the beasts to somehow lose them.

Don't look back. Don't look back. Don't look back.

The icy air made his entire chest burn as he inhaled, but it was a pain he could endure. He would endure any pain to escape the fate that had befallen the others. He had heard no more strange noises. The only sounds were those of his feet and his rasping breaths. He carried on, upholding his vow not to look back as the intermittent flash of the torch guided him through the woods. Then, suddenly, he skidded to a stop. For a second, he thought it had just been an optical illusion, his mind playing tricks, or some visual anomaly caused by the winking light, but then he saw it again.

Movement. It was ahead of him. *No way could those things have overtaken me. I was running flat out.* He held the torch up and gasped as a single figure began to walk towards him. *No, no, no.*

He turned right, ready to sprint in a different direction, but instead remained glued to the spot. Another monster advanced from this direction. He made an about-face only to see a third. Finally, he turned to the direction he had run from to see a fourth, seemingly taller than the rest, slowly advancing towards him. *No. No.* "Mam," he screamed. His mother had always been there to mop up his problems. She'd always been there to chase away his nightmares and doubts, and now he reverted to childhood once more. Maybe she could swoop in one last time and save him from this. "Mam," he called again as more tears than ever poured down his cheeks, and he dropped to his knees, letting the failing torch spill out of his hand.

It continued to flash as the monsters made their silent approach and as he continued to sob and plead for his mother. "Mam."

The four beasts all converged before coming to a stop and looking down at the hopeless creature in front of them as he wept and pleaded for help that wouldn't come. Finally, the tallest of the beasts stepped forward and reached down, clamping its giant hand around Andrew's throat, who began to wail in pain and panic as he rose from the ground.

He could feel blood trickling down the sides of his neck as the razor claws pierced his skin. He held his eyes shut tight, not wanting to see the face of the horror that had torn his friends to pieces, that was about to do the same to him. But when his feet finally left the ground, and he was still rising, he couldn't help it. His eyes shot open. He tried to gasp for breath but none would come. The hand around his throat was like a vice, clamped in place by the claws, which somehow he knew were not extended to their full capacity.

His feet kicked desperately, searching for the ground, but there was no hope of finding a firm footing and as he stared into the black, soulless mirrors that devoured him he felt something warm trickle down his leg and realised he had lost control of his bladder. *Flash. Flash. Flash.* It was as if he had become a human camera, and each time the torch flickered, the shutter in his mind closed, recording a hellish imprint that he knew would be one of the images he would take to his death.

There was a swift jolt as the beast whipped its other clawed hand across Andrew's belly. For a few seconds, he didn't understand what was happening, but then there was a sound beyond that of his own breathing and crying. It was a slopping sound. The kind of sound that came from emptying a bucket of blood and offal. Only, this wasn't a bucket.

The accompanying pain finally kicked in as if it was on some kind of delay timer. It was unparalleled to anything he had previously experienced, a devilish brew of physical and mental torment all mixed together in fiery torture. Andrew screamed, but it merely came out as a muffled grunt as the beast clamped its claws a little tighter around his neck.

The light continued to strobe, burning more hellish snapshots into Andrew's brain. The creature's lips peeled back, revealing blood-stained, blade-shaped teeth. Then, with a lighting-fast jerk, it clenched its fist, taking Andrew's throat with it.

He was still alive when he dropped to the ground. He could hear the splosh as he landed on his own entrails. He could feel a warm wet bed of them between him and the ground. The torch continued to wink but the pain was fading fast. A gurgling sound emanated from the area where his throat once was. It carried on as he watched the beasts that had done this to him disappear back into the forest one by one. He'd have given anything for one last breath. It was like being underwater, knowing he would never reach the surface in time.

His mind flashed back to leaving Doug, Calum and the others. It flashed to seeing Kenny's face as he watched him die. As well as the pain, there was disbelief that he could turn his back on his cousin in such a way. Then he saw an image of his mother. When this all came out, he would be remembered as a coward. A coward who ran to save his own life but couldn't even do that. A final tear bled from his eye as he pictured his mother's face crying with sadness but shame too.

I'm sorry, Mam.

*

The far-off rumble of gunshots had travelled through the tunnel to join them, but the further they ventured into the underground cave system the less they heard until the only sounds became those around them. The smell had not diminished, it had got stronger, but gradually, their noses had acclimatised to it, and now their attention was set firmly towards finding the cavern, rescuing the others and making their escape.

"Shit. It's going to be easy to get turned around down here if we're in a hurry," Summer said as they reached a junction of sorts. Only one passage lay in front of them, and this was the one they'd take, but there was a fork running almost parallel to the way they had just taken and two more that veered off in another direction.

"Wait a minute. Stay here," Luna said, walking to the other side of the junction and turning back around with her father's phone raised. She took a picture.

"What are you doing?" Thomas asked.

"When we come back this way, if we're confused about which tunnel to take, we can just check the photo."

"That's ... pretty smart, actually."

"He said in a not at all condescending way."

Thomas laughed. "I'm sorry. I didn't mean it to sound like that."

"Come on," Seb said, moving forward and shining his torch into the long passageway ahead. Thomas joined him while Summer and Luna stayed with Murdo.

"Are you alright, sweetheart?" Summer asked, placing her arm around her daughter as they walked.

"Cold, but I'll live."

Summer vigorously rubbed Luna's arm in the hope it would help warm her up a little. "Thanks, Mum, but I don't think that's going to work, somehow."

"No. Sorry." Summer removed her hand, but the pair continued to walk side by side.

"I don't really think we should be talking, do you?" Thomas whispered, looking back. Even his whisper echoed a little in the tunnel, so his point was well made.

The quintet continued until, finally, the cave began to widen. Thomas put his hand up to bring the small troop to a halt while simultaneously raising his shotgun with the other.

"How do you want to play this?" Seb whispered.

"We don't really have a lot of options. It's not like we can go in there in the dark, is it?" Thomas looked towards Summer and Luna, then finally nodded towards Murdo, who returned the gesture. This was it.

They all sped up, aiming their beams as far ahead as they could. Thomas and Murdo remained stoic in their approach while Seb clutched the crowbar tightly in one hand. His heart was beating like a timpani drum, and even though the shotguns were their main and most effective form of defence, he would do whatever it took to protect his wife and daughter and get his son back.

They slowed as they reached the opening to the cavern, and they all stood in disbelief as their beams travelled across the sea of bones in front of them.

"Oh, God," Luna whispered, suddenly becoming rigid with fear. She had swallowed every selfish instinct to head out with her parents and look for her twin, but now all she wanted to do was run back home as fast as she could and hide under her bed, like she used to when she was a child and something terrified her.

"Oh. My. God," Thomas said, forgetting his duties as their protector momentarily as he took in the unfathomable and gruesome sight too.

Murdo lowered his shotgun and began to weep. "Hey. Hey," Summer said, placing an arm around him.

"My Mary. This is where they must have brought her. This is where she is … what's left of her."

Thomas shook his head, remembering why they were there and what he was doing. He straightened his back, and now the awe had dissipated a little, he started to move his torch around searching for threats. "You see anything move, you tell me."

"Oh, don't you worry about that," Seb replied. Unlike the others, he'd been scanning the cavern from the second they'd arrived. The ray from his torch cast out a wider and wider net, fanning from where he was standing across the massive bone yard one section at a time.

It was silent inside, but for an echoing drip, drip, drip from somewhere. "Over there," Summer said, angling her powerful beam to the far end of the cavern. The others all moved theirs across too, and although the light dispersed before it could reflect off the far wall, they could just make out a ridge. "It's Charlie."

"There's no way we can tell that from—" Before Thomas could finish his sentence, there was a crash, and they looked down to see Summer had leapt into the sea of bones. It was only a short drop, but she let out an exclamation of pain as her ankle twisted a little before she found a firm footing and began to trudge through the uneven graveyard, displacing more debris of the dead with each stride she took.

She raised her torch in one hand, lighting her path, and kept the hatchet clenched tightly in the other. She had no idea whether more of those things were skulking in the shadows or not, but she didn't care. She was a mother, and this was instinctive, primal. She heard gentle rattles from behind and glanced over her shoulder to see Luna, Seb and Thomas climbing down while Murdo stood guard on the ridge. He had pulled another small camping lantern from his pocket and set it down by the entrance.

The white LED threw out a surprising amount of light for an object so small, and it provided a beacon for all of them. "You see or hear anything, and you shout. Okay, Murdo?" Thomas said before carrying on.

Murdo's eyes were cast across the sea of bones, but he nodded nonetheless as the others made their way towards the ledge. The four of them kept pausing, panning their torches around, looking for signs of life, scouring the shadows for movement.

Murdo just stood there, occasionally glancing across to the far side of the cavern. *This is where they'll have brought my Mary. I could have rescued her. I could have tracked that thing and found my Mary.*

This was the lowest he'd been since losing his beloved wife. The realisation that she was alive far longer than he'd thought made his heart break again, and as he watched the others continue their journey, there was a selfish part of him that wanted them to find the bodies laid out on the other ledge dead. It was horrible for him to even think it, but if they were alive as Duncan had said, then his Mary would have been alive, and who knows, she might have even woken up like Duncan. *She might have woken up in the dark, calling my name, screaming for help.* More tears rolled down his cheeks. *If I only knew then what I know now.*

*

Nowhere in the forest was safe. That was plain for all to see, and whether in a group of forty or by oneself, the creatures were relentless in their pursuit. Some of the men Doug and the others were with had wasted who knew how much ammunition firing at ghosts in the dark. They were all jumpy, and several had drunk way too much in MacDougal's. It was a dangerous combination, and when the sound of faraway shotgun blasts swept through the forest to greet them, causing even more mayhem and uncertainty, Doug, Calum and Innes took advantage of the fear and confusion that seized the other men to head off on their own.

"We stand just as much chance of being shot by those eejits as we do being attacked by those things," Doug said after they had sunk into the forest without a trace. When they were sure they were far enough away from the others, they switched their torches back on.

The group, led by William and the elders, had been heading in the wrong direction for several minutes before they departed. Calum had almost put them right, but Doug had deliberately foiled his attempt to do so, realising the rest of the group was far more of a liability than a help.

"You realise that if we get through tonight, nothing will be the same again," Calum said.

"Aye, well, that's a big if," Doug replied. There was no humour in his voice as he said the words.

"We'll be outcasts. William will make sure of it."

"Look. If we do get through tonight, we won't have to worry about being outcasts or William or anything else. This island will never be the same again. The police will come here, and there'll be a reckoning for everything that's happened. Cora will be a different place after that, so worrying about being outcasts is the last thing on my list right now. I just want to find Angus, John, Joseph and the others."

"But this is our home."

"Aye. But it's built on a foundation of cowardice, lies and secrets. And tonight, all that comes falling down."

22

Summer was the first to heave herself up onto the ledge. She'd had to skirt around until she found a pile of bones high enough to give her the leg up she needed, but, eventually, she had and the others followed. There was a part of her that felt like Indiana Jones and fully expected a giant stone ball to come tearing towards her from somewhere. She panned her torch around, poking its beam into every nook and cranny before helping her daughter up.

Thomas and Seb climbed onto the parapet themselves, and the four of them stood still for a moment, just looking at the bodies lined up in front of them. On a raised bed was the corpse of a creature they had never laid eyes on before, but judging by the head injuries it had sustained, it could only be the thing Duncan had described killing.

"Jesus," Summer whispered. "What the hell are these things?"

It was a good question. It was human-like in some ways, but it was completely hairless. Its limbs were elongated, and its body was thin, almost stretched. Its skin looked like hard-worn leather; its feet were long and thin with toes that looked like talons. Razor-sharp claws extended from its hands, and its mouth was frozen open in a final scream revealing dagger-like teeth.

"Jesus," Seb echoed as they continued to stare for a moment. A flash pulled them all from their contemplation, and they turned to see Luna taking photos.

"What the hell are you doing, Luna?" Summer demanded.

"Nobody's going to believe this," she replied, continuing to take more snaps.

"We're here for your brother. I don't care if people believe us or not." They followed the ledge around a bend, and there was Charlie lined up with another eight bodies.

"Oh my God," Thomas said, lowering his weapon.

This time, Summer was not interested in searching the darkness for threats. She ran towards her son and knelt down as torrents flooded from her eyes. "Seb. I think he's…." She couldn't bring herself to say the words. He looked pale, and his body was cold to the touch.

"No," Luna cried, now forgetting about chronicling the strangeness within the giant cavern. Tears began to start running down her face too.

Seb's crowbar clanked on the stone floor as he knelt down on the other side. Just as Duncan had said, there was a strange clear jelly covering his son's mouth and face. Seb placed his hand firmly on Charlie's chest.

"Te-ll me he's al-ive, Seb. Pl-ease," Summer stuttered between her pained sobs.

Du- there was a long pause as the terrified father held his palm in place. Dum. He kept it there, blocking out everything else, blocking out the strangeness of this place, blocking out his wife's and daughter's cries. Du- he waited once more for what seemed like forever. Dum. "No. There's … a beat or something. Something's happening. We need to get that stuff off his face." He reached up and grabbed the gooey substance, pulling it away. It felt like thick egg white in his hand, but it all came off in one piece, and he flung it to the side.

Charlie's mouth and face were red where the substance had been, and Seb was hoping that removing it would make him wake instantly like Sleeping Beauty, but this was clearly no fairy tale, and as they watched, his demeanour didn't change.

"You-you've got to do something, Seb."

The father glanced towards Thomas, who was staring down at the other bodies. Up until this point, he had been stronger than any of them, but now there was childlike fear in his eyes. Seb opened Charlie's mouth and shone his torch inside. *No obstructions.* He angled his son's head back a little then shifted down to his chest, planting the heel of his palm in the centre. He placed his other hand over that and laced his fingers together before he started pumping in a rhythmic beat. He remembered years before, there had been a TV ad campaign where CPR had been demonstrated to the beat of *Stayin' Alive* by the Bee Gees. This was the song that played in his head now. In a vast underground cavern, which was the lair of some strange, never before seen creature, he was singing along to a disco song in his head while desperately trying to bring his son around.

The sobs of his wife and daughter fuelled his resolve as he continued. *Come on, Charlie. Come on, Charlie.* "Come on, Charlie. COME ON, CHARLIE!" He stopped pressing and moved up to his son's head, where he pinched his nose and moved his lips down to cover Charlie's. Before he could blow, Charlie spluttered and sucked in a lungful of air.

His eyes sprang open wide, mirroring the terror of all those present. "What's happening? What's happening?" he croaked as if being awoken from a petrifying dream. He felt someone squeeze his left hand. For a few seconds, he couldn't focus on anything but the beams of the torches. *What's happening to me?* Slowly, familiar voices began to soothe his fear. "Mum? Mum is that you?" he asked after a few seconds.

"Yes, sweetheart, I'm here."

"Wh-what's happening? Where am I?"

"It's okay, Charlie. Take it slowly," Seb said.

Another figure appeared in the light, and he grasped his sister. Summer reached across with her other hand to squeeze her husband's arm. She was the strongest woman he knew, but in that brief moment when she had believed her son to be dead, she was broken. He placed his hand firmly over hers then lifted it to his mouth and kissed it before climbing to his feet and walking over to Thomas as words of comfort began to spew from Luna's and Summer's mouths.

"So, they're all alive?" Thomas said, looking down at the other bodies.

"That would be my guess. For the time being, anyway."

"I don't understand. Why keep them alive like this?"

"Fresh meat."

"What?"

"When Murdo told us about this thing, he said the attacks only took place in the winter months and only ever in the dark. Some creatures hibernate in the winter. What if these things hibernate the rest of the year and only wake up in winter?" Both men angled their torches towards the sea of bones.

"But ... there was only a disappearance once in a while. Why so many all at once?"

Seb shrugged. "You said that, three years ago, you sealed these things in. They're animals. Their instinct is to survive. Maybe they wanted to stock up in case it happened again." He moved the beam to skeletons similar to those of the dead creature but far bigger, which had carefully been laid out. "My guess is when they were sealed up down here, they turned on one another like rats to survive."

Thomas shook his head. "Jesus. Decades. Generations we've lived with this legend, and all that time, it's just some animal."

"Well, not just some animal. It's something no one's ever seen before." The sound of coughing made them both turn. "Is he okay?" Seb asked, rushing over to the others.

"I-I'm fine," Charlie said, gathering himself a little more and leaning up on one elbow.

Seb let out a breath of relief. "Okay." He turned back to Thomas. "We need to bring the others around then get the hell out of this place."

"No arguments here."

"Oh, man. This has been some—" Seb didn't have time to finish his thought before the lantern at the far end of the cavern went out.

Thomas and Seb exchanged frightened glances. Beyond the cones of light cast by their torches, everything else was as black as pitch, and neither of them moved from their respective spots for a moment as they continued to stare, hoping the light would turn on again or at least that they'd see Murdo's torch fire up. The seconds ticked by and nothing happened.

"Summer," Seb called across in a hushed voice.

Summer raised her head. She still held her son's hand, and a smile was ingrained on her face until she saw Seb's expression. He nodded towards the entrance, and her eyes followed his. She immediately grabbed the hatchet from the ground next to her and stood, putting herself between the graveyard and her children.

"What is it?" Luna asked, and then she noticed the blackness beyond the bone yard.

"What is it?" Charlie echoed.

"Just stay put and stay quiet, Charlie," Summer replied.

"Murdo?" Thomas called out. "Murdo," he cried a little louder, but still no reply came. He glanced nervously towards Seb and then raised his shotgun.

*

Murdo had heard something. He wasn't sure what, but his impulse, right or wrong, had been to turn the lantern off. He walked a little further into the tunnel, and now he was in total blackness.

He could hear his name being called out from behind him, but only just. He closed his eyes, concentrating as hard as he could. *What did I hear?* He had the lantern clipped to his belt, ready to flick on again in a heartbeat. Hopefully, he'd get a couple of shots off, which would give Thomas and the others more than enough warning. He held his breath. *Listen. Listen. Listen, old man, listen.*

A flash. Just fleeting, but there nonetheless. Then another. The tunnel weaved and waned, but as the seconds passed, he saw more and more light, and now he felt sure he could hear whispered conversation.

"Hello?" he said, quietly at first but then louder. "Hello?"

"Hello?" a call came back.

"Calum, is that you?" Seconds later, Calum, Doug and Innes appeared around the bend. The three of them had all come to pay their respects the night they had tracked the beast back to its lair. They did not head into the village and celebrate like the others. They had sat in solemn contemplation with Murdo, and each raised a glass to mourn Mary.

"Murdo," Calum replied with noticeable relief in his voice. "Where are the others?"

"They're in the cavern. Are you the only ones who came?" he asked, looking behind them.

Doug shook his head. "All hell's breaking, Murdo. The sooner we're out of this place the better."

"What do you mean hell's breaking loose?"

"People are dead, Murdo. Right now, I don't know how many, but I can tell you that, by morning, it will be a lot more, and if we don't look lively, we might be among them."

*

William had not been present that night three years earlier. He was not someone who normally acted but commanded. His position as head of the island council and church elder made him the unofficial King of Cora, and the only reason he was out here now was that there were so many willing participants, and he felt his safety was almost guaranteed.

With each loss they had incurred due to death or desertion, his confidence had waned a little more, and as the news came that no one could find Doug, Calum or Innes, he began to feel fear, real fear. He had never allowed himself to get in harm's way, but this was certainly that and more.

On this occasion, he needed to be involved. He needed to be at ground zero to help mould the story to tell others what they should and would say. This night was too important, and with his own son abandoning him, he needed to wield his influence over the rest of the population, but the population was diminishing fast.

"Which way do we go now?" asked Jamie, a much younger man and one of his second cousins. Fear was thick in the air, and they had lingered aimlessly in a clearing, bathing in the light of the moon for several minutes. There were just fourteen of them left, including the elders. None of them knew the fate of the others.

"They're picking us off, one at a time," another man said, and murmured agreement fluttered around him.

"They're not picking us off," William eventually said, trying to take control of the situation. "There are some cowards who have run out on us, and that's all."

"It's not all," Jamie fired back. "We saw bodies. You did as well as me. You saw what those things did to our friends and our kin. I tell you, they're picking us off."

"Silence," William ordered, coughing a little before regaining his composure. He shone his torch in the younger man's face. "Yes, we lost a few, and that's why our resolve must remain strong. We're doing this for our families. We can't let this evil hang over them for one night longer."

"I say we should go back." More sounds of agreement murmured behind Jamie. "If we know where these things are, then there's no difference being out here tonight than tomorrow morning. At least in daylight, we'll be able to see."

There was every difference. If the weather lifted on the mainland, there was an outside chance the police would arrive on the island the following day, and if that happened, any hope of William being able to control this story would be gone. "We stay. We stay and get the job done," he ordered.

"No."

"What?" He stormed up to the younger man. "You remember who you're talking to."

"We've had enough. We've all had enough. We're heading back." Without waiting for a response, Jamie started walking away, back in the direction they had originally come from. "We should have done this when Andrew suggested it."

"Come back here. Come back," William growled, immediately beginning to splutter and hack.

One by one, the others followed Jamie as he lit the path with his torch. "I'm sorry," one of them muttered as they walked by the older man, who remained planted on the spot.

William's resolve remained for a while until the elders filed past him too. "Where are you going?"

"I'm sorry, William," one of them replied, not able to look him in the face. "He's right." Then, in a more conciliatory manner, he added, "We could come out before first light tomorrow. We could find this place and—"

A loud thud followed by another then a scream erupted. Both men looked towards the line as two more shadowy figures flew from the forest, tackling another pair of islanders to the ground. BOOM! BOOM!

More shots began to ring out, making the whole woodland quake. When they fell quiet, they realised they were four islanders fewer, and no one had an idea where the attackers had vanished.

"Where the fuck have they gone?" Jamie cried. No sooner had the words left his mouth than three more of his companions broke into a run. "Wait. We need to stick together." His warning fell on deaf ears, and he watched them as their lights weaved between the trees.

Thud. Thud. Thud. The shrieks that came next made his blood curdle. He could not imagine what kind of pain was involved for such screams to rise. He turned towards the elders and ran back to rejoin them. "Are you happy now?" William demanded. "Their blood's on your hands."

"No. It's on yours. We should never have come out here tonight."

"Ach, I don't remember you saying that when you were buying rounds in MacDougal's. Sure, you were full of piss and vinegar then. You had a word or two to say about your cousin too."

It was as though the air had been squeezed out of Jamie's lungs. It was true. He had been the first to criticise Thomas for turning his back on the island, on his father, in favour of the incomers. "We need to stick together. We're not going to make it out of here otherwise." It took a moment, but the others all nodded, even William.

They looked back to where the figures had vanished just a minute before and did an about-face. This route would not take them back to their cars, but the priority was staying away from those things and getting out of the forest. They walked as quickly as they could, keeping their weapons ready and scanning their surroundings with their torches.

One hundred metres, two hundred metres, three hundred metres, and no attack came. There were no unnerving sounds. There were no shapes or shadows in the periphery of the torchlight. Four hundred metres, five hundred metres. "I think we've shaken them," William whispered.

"Aye, well, I wouldn't be celebrating just yet," Jamie replied. "These things don't really strike me as the quitting kind."

"Maybe not, but they could be at the other end of the forest for all we know. A lot of people ran out on us. What if they tracked them instead?"

It was true. Jamie had no idea how many men had run, some in groups, some by themselves. "You could be right, but there's no reason for us to let our guard down."

"Aye," Woolly, another of the elders, replied. "We should keep our—" Thump.

They all turned, panning their lights towards Woolly. His face was locked in an expression of agonised horror. His thick three-quarter-length coat swirled open in the breeze, and none of the other men could comprehend why he was frozen like a statue until a claw exploded from his stomach, spraying blood like a garden hose.

His finger squeezed the trigger of his shotgun reflexively, and the reverberating crack made the air rumble. Out of the corner of his eye, William could see one of the other elders fly back, but he could not tear his gaze away from Woolly as he now rose up. His head lolled forward, but still, his body went higher.

The remaining men were rendered senseless by the grisly spectacle. All they could do was watch. The gory claw withdrew, and Woolly's body jerked upwards, lifted like a free weight above the head of his reaper.

"Oh, sweet Lord," William whispered, raising his torch, following the ray as it climbed the beast's body. Pockmarks from the shotgun blast three years prior still patterned the creature's shoulder. Finally, he moved the beam to the elongated monster's face. For the briefest second, its eyes caught in the powerful LED light and reflected a ghoulish white straight back at him before it turned its head, hissing loudly as if somehow pained by the illuminating arc. It flung Woolly's corpse towards them as if it was no heavier than a pillow.

William and Jamie took the brunt of the blow, both falling backwards and smashing against the ground with loud thuds. BOOM! Only one of the remaining elders managed to get a shot off before the attack came from the flanks.

Howls and shrieks soared into the night air as, one by one, they were torn to shreds. Jamie rolled out from underneath Woolly's warm, blood-soaked body. Still on the ground, he brought his shotgun around and fired. The thundering boom was drowned out by the otherworldly screech that rose up through the canopy of the trees.

Before he could fire another shot, he felt razors tear into his flesh and slice his bone. "AAAGGGHHH!" It was a guttural, primal sound that left the back of his throat. The pain was so intense his body spasmed, and he watched as his shotgun fell. His feet left the ground and he remained there for one second, two, three before being launched through the air like a human cannonball.

He heard a loud hollow pop as his skull fractured. Jamie fell into a heap on the ground, everything tinted red as blood ran down the side of his face and over his eyes. *I'm paralysed.* He felt no pain anywhere in his body, which was far more frightening than the alternative.

He tried to move, tried to shuffle away as the creature paced towards him, but he couldn't shift as much as a finger. He couldn't feel it, but now he was being lifted again by the neck and head, this time as if he was no heavier than a freshly rung-out mop.

A tree. Why am I facing a tree? Nothing was making sense. His field of vision seemed to be closing in. Thud.

Jamie's head smashed against the trunk. Thump.

In addition to blood, there was something else running over his eyes now. It was a semi-solid tissue. He let out a silent scream because even his vocal cords were paralysed. He cried empty tears because they were the only kind he had left. It's my brain. It's my—THUD!

*

William was still trapped beneath Woolly's ample frame. After his initial struggle to get out, he had given up. Three of the creatures surrounded him, and he knew there was no chance of escape. Maybe if he lay still, they would think he was dead. He kept his eyes closed, but his facial contortions as he heard Jamie's head being cracked open like a coconut gave him away.

He remained there like a petrified bairn hiding under his bed. A foul smell surrounded him, warm and pungent in the otherwise chilled night air. *Oh, God. I've soiled myself.*

The weight of Woolly's body shifted, and William yowled as he felt claws sink into his chest and pull him up. He was a big man, but even his feet left the ground as the tallest of these monsters dragged him up.

He hung there in abject agony as the black, soulless eyes of his captor stared back at him. Another shudder ran down his spine. He had seen the same eyes reflect white when caught in the direct beam of the LEDs, but as he saw them now in the periphery of the light arcs, they were as black as anything he had ever witnessed.

He felt himself being lowered, and the razor-like talons retracted, causing thick lines of blood to run down his body. The creature raised its arm and this time clamped its elongated hand around his face. William felt the claws reach around ripping into his left cheek and the skin beneath his right ear. He let out another muffled scream, which instantly rose an octave higher as he felt and heard tearing.

A second later, a flap of bloody flesh the size of a small plate was hanging from the beast's claw, and William could feel the air against the side of his tongue.

He reached up to his face and felt his teeth and gums with no cheek there to protect them. He let out another tormented howl, only now it sounded distorted as it escaped into the air too soon, falling out of his mouth like a piece of food.

The creature flung the rag of flesh to the ground and then sunk its left talons into William's shoulder, lifting him a little before drilling its right claw into his stomach. William couldn't scream. The agony was more intense even than having his cheek ripped off. The sensation of a monster digging around in his belly like an overexcited child feeling around in a lucky dip was beyond any torture he could imagine, but the pain was too much to express outwardly.

Tears poured from his eyes, and the little that was left in his bowels emptied, as did his bladder. The pain and fear were more acute than anything written about in his beloved Bible. He managed to angle his head down as what looked like metres of unlinked sausages flopped from the gaping hole the creature's fist had made.

The beast unclenched its other claw, and William fell back, smashing his head against the cold forest floor. Now a scream did leave his lips. It was the loudest noise he had ever made, and it grew in intensity and volume as he managed to skew his neck one last time to see his innards splayed out next to him. With the scream came his last breath, followed by an unending silence.

23

They had all adjusted to the even more potent stench in the cavern. It was one of death and decay, and although they had gotten used to it, the sooner they were all out of there the better. The arrival of Doug, Innes and Calum was a welcome one. They had briefly informed the others of the mayhem that had unfolded above ground and their intention to bring this whole episode to an end once and for all.

Thomas had thanked them before they all got to the task of freeing the other captives from the strange gel-like substance keeping them in a comatose state. In the end, they decided to leave Angus as he was. For the time being, his heart continued to beat, albeit very slowly. With one leg torn from its socket, however, none of them were sure if that would remain the case if he was suddenly brought back around.

The first thing David asked about when he came around was Duncan. The news that his son had walked out of the forest alive aided his recovery, coming around faster than the others. It took several minutes for them to gather enough strength to sit up and several minutes more before they could stand.

"It's going to be a trial getting Angus out of here," Innes said.

"We'll take it in turns to carry him," Seb replied. "When we get into the forest, maybe we can cobble together a couple of boughs and make some kind of stretcher or something."

Innes nodded appreciatively. "Aye. That's not a bad idea. In the meantime, I'll be the first to take him."

"No," Seb said a little too loudly, and everyone looked towards him. "Sorry. I mean it makes a lot more sense for those of us who don't have guns to shoulder the burden, don't you think? I mean, if we were to run into any of those things, I'd feel much better having an extra shotgun than a crowbar, wouldn't you?" He raised the heavy strip of black metal.

"Fair enough," Innes replied, smiling.

"We'll carry him first," John said, guiding his brother across to Angus's body.

"Neeps and I will take him next," David added.

"Okay," Thomas said. "Is everyone feeling up to the walk?" He looked around at the assembled group. The ones who had been catatonic not twenty minutes before all had the nasty-looking rash on their faces in roughly the same place, and although not brimming with life, they were alive and walking, having the appearance of recovering from a really bad hangover.

One by one, they climbed down into the pit. John and Joseph brought up the rear carrying Angus's living but wounded body. David, Neeps and the Ross brothers, more dazed than the others, followed. They all trudged through the sea of bones like they were wading through snow. Sometimes it was ankle-deep. Sometimes, there were drifts where they needed all their strength to fight through.

"I'm not going to be wearing skirts anytime soon," Summer said as she felt the sharp edges dig into her ankles and legs.

"Me neither," Seb replied, but no one smiled.

"Hey, where's Murdo gone?" Luna asked.

They all looked across to see the glow of the lantern had vanished. "Some of the others have probably arrived at last," Thomas said. "It's taken them long enough."

"Let's hope William doesn't seal the entrance knowing you could be in here," Calum said, but he was only half joking. If it came to making a decision as to whether William loved his son or the island more, no one would take the bet.

A cartwheeling black object caught in the light of one of the torch beams causing the others to all angle theirs in its general direction. It could not be clearly identified due to the light dispersal as the cavern was so huge, but it registered with Thomas immediately. "That's a shotgun." It continued, clattering loudly against the opposite wall to the entrance.

The speed and power with which the object travelled suggested it had been fired by some mechanical means. No man could throw it half that distance. They all stopped, moving their beams back to the entrance.

"Is-is it them?" Charlie asked, reaching out and grasping his mother's hand. They were about a third of the way across, and there was no quick route back to the ledge.

Summer couldn't answer. Her eyes were fixed on the mouth of the cavern. They all gasped as the small but powerful lantern flew out like a bullet. They watched as that, too, hit the opposite wall, but rather than clattering to the bone-covered floor, it smashed into a hundred pieces.

The seconds ticked on, but none of them moved. Something else shot out of the darkness, and for a brief moment, they couldn't understand what it was. Only when Summer screamed at the top of her voice and the bloody spray danced and shimmered in the light as Murdo's head somersaulted through the air did they comprehend.

Reflexively, Thomas, Doug, Calum and Innes all brought their shotguns up. "God help us," Thomas whispered.

Seb waded forward a little putting himself between his family and the entrance, holding on to the crowbar tighter than ever, but sure at the same time that if it came to a hand-to-hand fight with these things, in all likelihood, he would end up like Murdo.

The vigil dragged on, but still nothing appeared until, suddenly, four figures burst from the blackness. One, two, three shots fired, but the beasts were too fast, diving into the sea of bones. They did not stumble or cry out. Their thick skin more than protected them from the garden of jagged ribs, antlers, carcasses and who knew what else.

Another shot boomed, and one of the creatures flew back, disappearing into the debris as if it was an actual sea. The other three carried on, staying low, but moving fast.

"Don't waste your shots," Thomas ordered as he heard his friends spread out. Another creature seemingly vanished from view while two more continued towards them. When they were fifteen metres away, a second barrage of gunfire sounded. One of the beasts let out a chilling yawp of pain before falling silent as a further blast removed part of its skull. It collapsed back with a clatter as it took its final resting place.

The other creature leapt, and now the survivors were back in the realms of disbelief as they watched it almost fly through the air. Calum, Innes and Doug reloaded their shotguns while Thomas could only stare, unable to comprehend how anything could jump so high. The monster landed in front of Seb, causing an explosion of bony debris.

Shit. Can't get a shot. Thomas began to wade forward once more, hoping for a better angle. The other men finished reloading and aimed too, realising the same thing. They began to advance but all held the belief it was already too late.

Seb's mouth dropped open as the monstrous thing loomed over him. It was more than a foot taller, and if it hadn't been for his family standing behind him, he would have turned and run. He brought up his torch, and the beast recoiled a little, swiping with one of its hands at the bright light. Seb wielded it like a weapon, moving forward a little more, causing the monster to turn its head further, but then a powerful blind sweep with its right arm connected with Seb's side. He let out a grunt of pain as he heard his ribs crack, and suddenly he was airborne before crashing down three metres away.

The hard calcium tines of an exposed rib cage tore at his face, and he let out another shout of pain as he fell still for a few seconds.

*

"Seb," Summer screamed, torn between running to her husband's side and staying with her children.

BOOM! BOOM! The creature was in the air again before the first shot left the barrel.

*

It was impossible for Calum or Innes to adjust their aim in time, and again they were left dumbstruck as they watched the thing they had known all their lives as the Night Demon jump unnaturally high.

A shot went off from one of the other guns, but the creature moved faster than the torch beams, and it was like skeet shooting in the dark. It crashed down, hammering its clawed hands through the foreheads of the two friends before they could so much as let out a cry.

"J-e-s-u-s," Doug gasped as his lifelong companions crumpled to the ground.

*

Two sudden eruptions made everyone scream again. Heart-pounding terror gripped them all as the beast that had dived into the morbid sea of bones seconds before burst upward, spewing debris in every direction like a living volcano.

Two more shots cracked. One winged the creature that had killed Calum and Innes; the other soared into oblivion.

*

"DAD," Luna cried, breaking free from her mother's grasp and scrambling towards her father.

Summer was still in too much shock to process what was happening in real time. These things were lightning. She had never seen anything in the natural world move the way they did. It took a few beats before she realised her daughter had let go and another few before she started after her, dragging Charlie along too.

*

Doug's weapon boomed again, and the shot dispersed into the blackness. The speed of the creatures was not too great for the guns, but it was for the operators.

Another of the ghoulish figures landed in a crouch in front of him before rising up like a tower of black smoke. Its arm blurred as it reached out, grabbing him by the throat and pulling him free of the detritus.

An eerie, piercing screech echoed through the giant chamber as the banshee-like thing opened its mouth and bared its teeth. Its head tilted a little as it regarded its prey. Doug's mind was awash with thoughts of death, unable to reason for a moment as the monster just stared.

*

The third beast, bleeding from the shot in its stomach that they thought had finished it, crashed down in front of John and Joseph, who instinctively dropped Angus's body. They hadn't meant to, but they couldn't help it. They had no torch of their own, and the thing that loomed in front of them was nothing more than a silhouette in the shadowy light, but that just made it all the more terrifying.

Its clawed hands formed pincers, which shot out, punching through the cartilage of each of its victims' noses, carrying on until it reached the backs of their skulls then stretching its hands out once more, withdrawing them with cannon force and pulling their faces off too. Fragments of bone, skin and sinew cascaded through the air as their bodies fell.

*

David, Neeps and the Ross brothers stood with their mouths agape. The soporific effects of the strange gel-like substance had still not worn off fully, and although they couldn't make out much in the shadows, they heard the sounds and saw glistening red spray spread over the surrounding carpet of debris as the monsters tore their friends to pieces.

They all reached for whatever objects they could to defend themselves, but too late. There was no measure in the ferocity of the attack. The beast lunged, slicing, hacking, and clawing with pure, unbridled malevolence.

Before any of the five figures could so much as put up an arm in defence, they were down, bleeding on the pile of bones, breathing their final breaths.

*

This can't be happening. This can't be happening. The whole scene unfolded in a matter of seconds. Where a human would apply tactics and reason, these monsters went purely on instinct. They were killing machines with an inbuilt sense of threat management.

Thomas took a breath, aimed and fired. The explosion made the whole cavern quake, drowning out the hellish sounds of the beasts for a moment before one of them shrieked with pain as a dark red hole appeared in its side. It dropped Doug, falling back a little.

*

Doug collapsed. He felt something sharp pierce his clothes and stab the small of his back, causing him to let out a scream but nothing to rival that of the howling creature that had dropped him. He jumped back to his feet and angled his torch down as Thomas's weapon cracked again.

He brought up his own shotgun and held the flashlight beneath the barrel, angling it towards the wounded beast. It flinched, already in pain but now sharply turning its head away from the bright light that shone towards it.

Doug paused for only a beat. It had four mounds on the upper half of its body, each one with a dark peak. *They're breasts. This one's female.* Up until this moment, the myth that had surrounded these things still played a part in him seeing them as something not of this world, but this realisation eased some of his fear as he squeezed the trigger.

*

Thomas turned as something flew through the darkness towards him. He had fired another wayward shot at a second beast heading towards Doug, but as he reloaded, he realised his time was up.

He dived forward, avoiding the grasp of the demonic missile by mere centimetres. He felt sharp edges scratch against his face as he landed, and he could taste blood in his mouth, but far worse than any of that, his torch had fallen into the sea of bones, and his movement had buried it further, meaning there was less light than ever for him to see the devilish attackers.

*

"THOM—" Doug's cry fell silent as the largest of the creatures parried his shotgun and flashlight, then tore his throat out along with half his neck. There was no final breath, no agonised scream; he simply fell back, clattering on the ruffled carpet of carcasses.

*

"Oh shit," Seb hissed as the other beast began to make a beeline towards him and his family. There was enough light for him to see that the largest of the creatures had turned almost as quickly as it had released Doug and was heading across to where Thomas was still fumbling desperately, looking for his torch.

Seb shuffled in front of his wife and children, torch in one hand, crowbar in the other. Pain shuddered through him with each movement, but he'd had broken ribs before, and there was no level of agony he would not endure to protect his family.

The beast began to charge, bones and debris flying up with each pace. *Shit. Shit. Shit.*

*

Summer's entire body was shaking as she toiled the few metres to join her husband. She stood with him shoulder to shoulder, and she knew that if the creature had not been just a couple of seconds away, he would have fought her, telling her to go back, but it was too late for that. It was too late for anything.

"I love you." Her voice quivered as she said it, and there was no time to hear a reply as the beast lunged.

*

Luna had seen how the creatures had reacted to light. It was almost as if it burned their eyes. The brighter it was the more violently they reacted. It was a Hail Mary if ever there was one, but she hit the camera app as the creature made its approach. She aimed, hit the shutter button and hoped for the best.

*

Thomas felt himself being hoisted as if some giant crane was winching him. He had been only centimetres away from grabbing his torch, but now any hope of finding it was gone forever.

His arms, shotgun and all, flailed as he rose higher and higher above the creature's head; then, suddenly, he was airborne, flying into the darkest reaches of the cavern as the powerful beast flung him with no more effort than he would throw a football.

He was not normally one for screaming, but now a scream did leave his mouth as he flew through the darkness.

*

Flash. Flash. Flash. Flash. It was on the red-eye setting, and the creature squealed, turning its head at the same time. It crashed into Summer's body, and she let out a shriek as she fell back.

"SEB."

*

It had been a long time since Seb had fought. In the foster care system, it could often be a daily occurrence if you were put with the wrong family, but he'd left all that behind. Summer had civilised him, saved him, but hearing her scream so hopelessly turned him feral.

The creature began to scramble on the ground, quickly recovering from its strobe-induced daze. It climbed to its feet and reached out, grabbing Summer's hair.

Flash. Flash. Flash. Flash. It let it go again just as quickly as it turned its head, shielding its eyes and squealing, and that was the pause that Seb needed.

He threw his torch to Charlie and leapt high, bringing the crowbar up way over his shoulder. He could feel the seething pain in his ribs, but it didn't matter. He growled loudly as he brought the makeshift weapon down with jackhammer force.

The loud crack reverberated around the walls of the cavern and the beast instantly fell. Seb landed awkwardly on top of it but gathered himself quickly and struck again and again and again. Each time, more blood sprayed his face. He could taste it on his lips and tongue as he continued to brutalise the already dead creature.

"Dad." Even Luna's cries could not stop him as he carried on pounding and bashing. "DAD." Finally, he relented, looking towards her. He thought she was asking him to stop because the creature was dead and he should show a little mercy, but he followed the trajectory of her stare and realised it was because the final beast, the alpha male, was staring directly towards him.

It loomed on the perimeter of the light exuding from Charlie's and Summer's torches. It let out a wailing rasp far louder, far more powerful than anything they had heard so far. It angled its head up as if it was screaming towards Heaven before turning back to focus on the man who had bludgeoned the last of its family to death.

It jumped, launching high into the air, heralding screams from Luna, Charlie and Summer as she scrambled to climb back to her feet. Seb stood firm, holding the crowbar in both hands as if he was swinging a baseball bat. The creature crashed down, lunging for Seb at the same time. His swing smashed into its stomach, missing its ribs, and although causing a small squeal of pain, it did little to deter its intention. It swiped outward with its left hand, and Seb jumped back at the same moment. There was a tearing sound as the claws ripped through his T-shirt and flesh.

There was another much louder noise as Seb screamed in pain before charging forward again and swinging the crowbar even harder. This time, he struck the seven-foot beast on the side of its face, and its jaw jutted before it reached out once more.

Flash. Flash. Flash. Flash. The creature held Seb's body up, deflecting most of the painful light. It hissed loudly as thick gel-like saliva dribbled from the sides of its mouth.

Thump. It immediately dropped Seb, letting out a tortured squeal as it stumbled, trying to reach behind. Summer stood there, barely believing what she had done. She looked at the hatchet sticking out of the centre of the creature's back as it desperately tried to remove it.

Seb clambered back to his feet and swung the crowbar with every gram of strength he could muster. It smashed against the monster's head, making it stagger a little. He swung it again. Crack. It wavered a little more.

Flash. Flash. Flash. Flash.

It yowled, pausing in its efforts to reach the small axe buried in its back and doing its best to fend off the blinding light instead.

Seb swung again, but this time, the beast grabbed the crowbar, pulling it out of his attacker's hand and flinging it across the cavern. It bounced off the wall, ringing like a church bell, and the creature swung around using its forearm like a bat and smashing Summer to the ground before spinning and hammering Seb with the other. He went flailing too, and the monster began to reach back once more, desperate to dislodge the hatchet.

Flash. Flash. Flash. Flash.

Another tortured screech left its mouth, and it started forward towards Luna, who tried to retreat but toppled backwards instead. Charlie, still dazed but realising his twin was in trouble, pointed his torch beam at the creature. It wasn't as bright as it once was, and although the beast averted its gaze a little, it did nothing to stop its advance.

"Nooo." He reached down, taking his sister's hand, hoping he could pull her up and they could both escape the relentless monster before it reached them, but, suddenly, a clatter erupted from somewhere, and Seb dived, smashing his shoulder into the beast's side. They both crashed down, and the ghoulish figure let out another scream of pain as the blade of the hatchet juddered.

Seb didn't waste any time. He climbed the creature's body as if it was a toppled stepladder, and before it had the chance to gather itself, he reached around, plucked the kitchen knife from his belt and plunged it into the beast's right eye.

It opened its mouth wide as if it was going to howl, but, instead, a foul rasp of hot air left its throat and it fell still. Seb stayed there, just looking at it for several seconds before he finally scrambled to his feet. He went across to help up Summer; then they both joined their children, clutching them tightly, kissing them as if they were the last kisses they would ever give.

"Was that it? Was that the last of them?" Charlie asked.

"Yes, Son. That was the last one."

A clatter sounded from elsewhere in the cavern and pangs of terror jolted through them all. "Oh shit," Summer cried, stumbling and crawling in the direction of the alpha male to retrieve her hatchet.

Seb had no idea what had happened to his crowbar, but he joined his wife, withdrawing the knife from his victim's eye socket with a slooping squelch. He helped her turn the body over, and she yanked out the hatchet, causing a crimson spray to soak her hand.

They both stood and turned. Summer angled her torch up, looking for the source of the noise. Wherever it was, it was out of the range of the beam. They stayed put, keeping themselves between whatever was making the sound and their children. A shadowy figure on the periphery of the light rose up.

"Thomas?" Seb asked.

Somehow, the shotgun was still in his hand as he limped in their direction, displacing the bones, antlers and carcasses as he trudged. "We thought you were dead," Summer said, staring towards him.

"Actually, I thought I was dead. Are you sure I'm not?"

"Well, if you are, you're not alone. Stay there, we'll come to you. That's the way out anyway."

"The others?" Thomas asked.

"I'm sorry," Seb replied. "They're all gone … apart from the injured one." He reached across and took Summer's torch. "I'll go get him."

"You're injured," Summer replied. "I don't think you're in any shape to be carrying someone, do you?"

"We can't just leave him down here, Summer."

"Well, I'll give you a hand." She turned to the twins. "Head to the entrance. See if Mister Munro needs help."

Summer and Seb scrambled toward the body. Sometimes their feet hit the ground, sometimes they crawled over the top of all the debris. They stared in horror as the torch beam flashed over the others who had been killed. "Jesus," Seb whispered.

Eventually, they reached Angus, and together they lifted him. It took them several minutes to reach the ledge near the entrance and another ten minutes to get to the sinkhole. The adrenaline had kept Summer and Luna going, but out in the cold night air again, their wet jeans coated their legs like icy paint. They shivered and trembled as they began the trek back to their house.

On level ground once more, Charlie helped his father with Angus's body while Summer did her best to support Thomas.

"I've got a bar," Luna cried, a few metres from the edge of the forest. She had been checking the phone constantly, and everyone immediately understood what she meant.

Thomas pulled his own phone out, and he had one too. He scrolled down his contacts and hit speed dial.

"Hello?"

"Isobel. It's me. Get Jane, Annie, yourself and anybody who can walk and has a decent head on their shoulders over to the Richardses' place now. Tell Jane to bring whatever medical supplies she's got."

"Oh, my God. Are you alright?"

"Banged up, but I'll live."

"Did … did you…."

"We found Angus and Charlie Richards, but it was bad. We lost a lot of people, Isobel."

"Your father. Is he with you?"

Thomas turned and looked back into the woods. It was a feeling more than anything else, but, somehow, he knew William hadn't made it.

"No."

"Is he…."

"I need to get patched up then I'll organise a search. There might be people still in the forest needing help."

"Thomas, you can't go back out there tonight."

"These are our people, Isobel. If I don't go back out, then who will?"

By the time they reached the house, two more cars were already parked outside and another pair were pulling into the courtyard. Jane was the first to exit one of the vehicles. She had a rucksack over her shoulder, ready to do whatever was needed, but even she let out a gasp when she saw Angus. After a short discussion with Annie, they decided to leave him in the strange comatose state until they could get an air ambulance to take him to Glasgow. He was placed on a bed in the spare room, and Annie was told she could sleep there too.

Jane patched up Seb and Thomas and gave them painkillers but told them they both needed x-rays and a lot of rest.

Both men thanked her, but neither heeded her last piece of advice. As soon as his ankle was strapped up, Thomas was keen to organise search teams. "Hey, look," Seb said. "I don't want to leave my family right now, but I'm more than happy for you to use this place as your base if you want."

Thomas looked across to Summer and the children, who had all changed into fresh warm clothes and were dishing out hot drinks to the people who had come to join the search. It was mainly women and old men worried about their loved ones who had gone out in the hunting party earlier in the evening.

Some of them were crying. Some of them had impatient expressions adorning their faces as they waited for the expedition to get underway. Thomas turned to Seb and nodded. "All things considered, I think you've done enough tonight."

"One could say the same about you."

Thomas shook his head sadly. "Like I said, these are my people. This is my island, but I will take you up on your offer to use this as a base."

Seb nodded. "I doubt we'll be getting much in the way of sleep anyway."

Thomas let out a short laugh. "Aye. I get that."

"Look," Seb said. "I want to thank you for what you did. I had you all wrong earlier on."

Thomas shook his head. "If I was in your position, I think I'd have been exactly the same. There's a lot wrong with this community. So many secrets, so many lies," he said, looking around at some of the faces. "But hopefully, that changes now. We've got a whole lot of pain waiting for us in that forest. But the healing starts tonight."

Seb extended his hand and Thomas took it. They both shook firmly. "I hope it's not as bad as you fear out there."

"Aye. Me too."

EPILOGUE

Seb stood away from the bathroom cabinet, admiring his handiwork for a moment. He reached for the spirit level and placed it on top, moving back a little further. His face lit with a smile as the bubble finally came to rest dead centre.

This was a far cry from the cabinet Summer had selected all that time ago. This was new, and the wood was shiny and easily wipeable. In fact, he doubted that it was even real wood. It looked good, but it was probably veneer over chipboard. Still, it served its purpose, and it wouldn't fall apart when the mirrored doors closed.

"Dad. It's nearly time," Charlie called out from down the hall.

Seb glanced towards the matching toilet roll holder and towel rail. They would have to wait for the moment. He put down his drill and headed along the hallway. The living room had boxes stacked in small islands all over the floor, but the TV was up on the wall, and the Christmas tree was already half-decorated.

"I made you a coffee," Luna said as she walked in with one for herself too. "There you go, Charlie." She handed him a can of Pepsi.

"Thanks," he replied, smiling gratefully.

The news finished, and the familiar faces of the presenters from the *BBC Breakfast* programme appeared on the screen. "Welcome back," said Lisa, the longstanding female anchor. "Almost a year to the day, our next guest joined us on the sofa to talk about her new book. She's here again today to talk about her latest release, but this one's very different." She turned in her seat. "Welcome back, Summer Richards."

The camera panned to Summer, whose face lit up. "Thank you for having me on again."

"Oh, please. How could we not?" She turned back to the camera. "Summer's new book, *Night of the Demons,* isn't a work of fiction like everything else she's written. Many of you will remember the shocking events that took place on the Hebridean island of Cora just before Christmas last year. Thirty-three people lost their lives that night, and this is the story of what happened." She turned back to Summer. "Tell me, what was it like reliving what happened in the book?"

Summer didn't answer for a moment; the camera just stayed on her face. Eventually, she filled the dead air. "Well … it was traumatic … and cathartic in a way. I think doing the book helped me put that chapter of our life to bed."

"You'd just moved up there when this had happened. Am I right in saying that?"

Summer nodded. "Yes. We were building our dream home," she replied with an ironic laugh.

"*Were* past tense?"

"Yes. We don't live there anymore. In fact, after it all happened, we went to live with my parents until we could get something more permanent sorted out."

"How are your family now? Your children were—" The phone started ringing and Seb reluctantly climbed out of his chair.

He walked out into the hall and picked it up. "Hello?"

"Hi, darling."

"Y'know, Summer, one day, you're going to do an interview on television and I'm going to be able to watch the whole thing live."

"We can both watch it together tonight. Did I look okay? I was worried that I looked tired, but the make-up girl said she had something for my eyes. Did it work?"

"You looked beautiful like you always do."

"Aww. You always know what to say."

"There is only one right answer in that instance."

"So, you did think I looked tired."

"Ugh. No, you looked great. I swear on your mother's life."

"Hey."

"Okay, I swear on Charlie's life."

"Without knowing what he's been like today, I still can't ascertain how much faith to have in your words." They both giggled.

"He's good."

"They both slept okay?"

"Yeah."

"That's a positive. Y'know, I'm pretty certain we've paid for the new extension on Doctor Patel's house."

"I'd rather pay for her whole house than have them the way they were."

"Yeah." After the incident, both of them had suffered with vivid nightmares for several months, and although not completely eradicated, their frequency and severity had lessened considerably. "Is the tree going to be up when I get back?"

"I promise you on Luna's life, it will be up."

"Do you think you could stop offering our children's lives as bargaining chips instead of just giving me your word that something's true?"

"That's a novel concept. I'll have to get back to you on that. Let me think about it."

Summer laughed again. "I should be home at about twelve. What do you say we all go to DeMarco's for lunch?"

"Ooh, I like that idea. I was trying to decide whether to make beans on toast or beans and sausages on toast, so this saves me from that dilemma."

"Thank God for DeMarco's. Oh, by the way. Buddy said the publisher wants to talk to me about doing a series of books."

"What series?"

"They want to call them Scares in Scotland. Each one will look at legends and myths specific to certain islands or certain parts of the country. I did some preliminary research, and there are literally hundreds of these legends. It could be fascinating."

"Uh-huh. Reality check, Mrs Richards. How do you think our children are going to take it if you head north of the border in search of more monsters and demons?"

There was a long pause. "I ... I didn't think."

"You're a fiction writer, Summer. You wrote *Night of the Demons* because you needed to. Your words, not mine. That's behind us now, and that's where we all need to keep it."

There was another long pause. "You're right."

"Listen. I've still got some bits to finish off in the bathroom and I need to beat the children a bit to get them back to work on the tree. I'll see you in a couple of hours."

"Okay. Love you."

"Love you too."

Seb hung up the receiver and went back into the living room to find Charlie and Luna already hanging decorations on the tree. "It's over," Luna said, seeing her dad look at the screen. "Mum looked tired."

"No, she didn't."

"She did. Especially around her eyes."

"I swear, Luna. If you so much as joke about that to your mother, I'm going to post all your primary school pictures on Instagram."

"Okay. Don't have an aneurysm. I was just saying."

"We're going out to DeMarco's for lunch."

"Yes," she said, punching the air. "I definitely won't say anything then."

"Good girl. And remind me, we'll need to put food down for Porridge before we go out." The tabby let out a grumpy meow but remained perfectly still, staring at the baubles as they were placed one by one on the tree. "And under no circumstances is she allowed in here when we're not around."

"That's probably wise," Luna replied. "I'm pretty certain she's already eaten a load of tinsel."

"Well, at least it will be festive when it comes out of the other end."

"I'll be back in a minute," Charlie said, looking at his phone with a badly hidden smile on his face. The redness from where the strange gel had adhered had not vanished completely, and he was self-conscious about it, but Doctor Patel was helping with that too.

"What's that all about?" Seb asked as his son disappeared down the hallway.

"I'm bound by the twin's oath not to say a word."

"Just tell me it's not something I need to worry about."

Luna shook her head. "You don't need to worry about it, Dad. I've got Charlie's back, y'know."

Seb smiled and leaned in, kissing his daughter on the head. "Yeah, I do. And do I need to worry about you?"

"No. I'm good."

"Good?"

"Well, I'm getting there. I'm looking forward to us all being together for a couple of weeks before school starts again."

"Yeah. Me too." Seb reached down and took an ornament out of the box then placed it carefully on the tree. "Y'know your mum and me are always here for you, don't you?"

Luna's mind drifted back to that night in the cavern before she turned towards her father and smiled. "Yeah, Dad. There are lots of things I'm not sure about in life. But that's something I'll never doubt. Neither of us will."

The End

NIGHT OF THE DEMONS

A NOTE FROM THE AUTHOR

I really hope you enjoyed this book and would be very grateful if you took a minute to leave a review on Amazon and Goodreads.

If you would like to stay informed about what I'm doing, including current writing projects, and all the latest news and release information; these are the places to go:

Join the fan club on Facebook
https://www.facebook.com/groups/127693634504226

Like the Christopher Artinian author page
https://www.facebook.com/safehaventrilogy/

Buy exclusive and signed books and merchandise, subscribe to the newsletter and follow the blog:
https://www.christopherartinian.com/

Follow me on Twitter
https://twitter.com/Christo71635959

Follow me on Youtube:
https://www.youtube.com/channel/UCfJymx31VvzttB_Q-x5otYg

Follow me on Amazon
https://amzn.to/2I1llU6

Follow me on Goodreads
https://bit.ly/2P7iDzX

Other books by Christopher Artinian:

Safe Haven: Rise of the RAMs
Safe Haven: Realm of the Raiders
Safe Haven: Reap of the Righteous
Safe Haven: Ice
Safe Haven: Vengeance
Safe Haven: Is This the End of Everything?
Safe Haven: Neverland (Part 1)
Safe Haven: Doomsday
Safe Haven: Neverland (Part 2)
Safe Haven: Hope Street
Before Safe Haven: Lucy
Before Safe Haven: Alex
Before Safe Haven: Mike
Before Safe Haven: Jules

The End of Everything: Book 1
The End of Everything: Book 2
The End of Everything: Book 3
The End of Everything: Book 4
The End of Everything: Book 5
The End of Everything: Book 6
The End of Everything: Book 7
The End of Everything: Book 8
The End of Everything: Book 9
The End of Everything: Book 10
The End of Everything: Book 11
The End of Everything: Book 12
Relentless
Relentless 2
Relentless 3
The Burning Tree: Book 1 – Salvation
The Burning Tree: Book 2 – Rebirth
The Burning Tree: Book 3 – Infinity
The Burning Tree: Book 4 - Anarchy

CHRISTOPHER ARTINIAN

Christopher Artinian was born and raised in Leeds, West Yorkshire. Wanting to escape life in a big city and concentrate more on working to live than living to work, he and his family moved to the Outer Hebrides in the north-west of Scotland in 2004, where he now works as a full-time author.

Chris is a huge music fan, a cinephile, an avid reader and a supporter of Yorkshire County Cricket Club. When he's not sitting in front of his laptop living out his next post-apocalyptic/dystopian/horror adventure, he will be passionately immersed in one of his other interests.

Printed in Great Britain
by Amazon